WEB of JUSTICE

Rayven T. Hill

Ray of Joy Publishing
Toronto

Books by Rayven T. Hill

Blood and Justice
Cold Justice
Justice for Hire
Captive Justice
Justice Overdue
Justice Returns
Personal Justice
Silent Justice
Web of Justice
Fugitive Justice

Visit rayventhill.com for more information
on these and future releases.

Published by Ray of Joy Publishing
Toronto

ISBN-13: 978-0-9947781-7-8

WEB of JUSTICE

CHAPTER 1

DAY 1 - Monday, 9:06 p.m.

OLIVIA BRAGG SLIPPED off her apron, dropped it onto a hook near the back door, and retrieved her small handbag from another hook below. It'd been a busy day, and she was glad it was over.

Phil had been after her to extend her hours until midnight—again. According to her boss, someone with her looks brought in paying customers and kept them spending. And making money was what it was all about.

For Phil. But not for her.

She'd worked that shift before, and though the losers started coming in by eight o'clock or so, by nine the booze had turned them into slobbering drunks. According to Phil, they loved her long black hair and dark brown eyes, and in their inebriated condition, they never seemed to notice the extra thirty pounds she carried around.

Sure, she could always use the money, but a few extra

dollars in tips wasn't worth the nonstop hassle of sidestepping their crude and rude sexual advances. And at thirty-five years old, she was more than tired of it.

Besides, she needed a little time with Edgar. She got home late enough as it was, and the couple of hours she spent with her hard-working husband were always the highlight of her day.

She brushed past Phil, who stood at the sizzling red-hot grill, slapping together a pair of greasy burgers for a hungry customer. "Good night, boss," she said in a singsong voice, then pushed open the door and stepped into the warm evening air without waiting for an answer.

She always enjoyed the walk home. The apartment she shared with her husband was two blocks from Phil's, and though they lived in an older neighborhood, the area was pleasant and quiet.

The stillness of the evening broke when a car cruised past and came to a quick stop twenty feet away. The backup lights of the vehicle lit up the asphalt as the car reversed and eased to a stop beside her.

Olivia turned to face the vehicle as the driver rolled down his window and poked his head out. An amiable smile lit up his face.

"I'm looking for Hackett Street," he said.

She frowned and shook her head. "I've never heard of it."

He produced a sheet of paper and waved it out the window.

Olivia moved toward the vehicle, took the paper, and scanned the single handwritten page. She didn't see any address on it, and she looked up in bewilderment, then took a cautious step backward as the man swung open the driver door and stepped out.

"I'm sure it's around here somewhere," he said with a shrug, reaching for the paper.

She handed it to him, then frowned and took another step back. "Sorry, I can't help you."

The man folded the paper and tucked it into his shirt pocket. He glanced up and down the quiet street, then took a long stride forward and gripped her by the arm.

Her eyes widened and she gasped. She tried to break loose, but with a quick motion, he spun her around, wrapping one arm around her chest, his other hand across her mouth. Her bag slipped from her hand and dropped to the pavement.

She struggled and tried to scream, producing a stifled whimper. She kicked in desperation at his ankles with one foot and he laughed, then hissed in her ear, "Relax. I'm not gonna hurt you."

Olivia wrenched one arm free, swung it over her head, and grabbed a fistful of his hair. She pulled and he cursed. He removed his hand from her mouth and worked at her fingers, trying to peel them loose.

She gave one last desperate tug to distract him, then let go of his hair and let her body collapse. Slipping free of his hold, she fell to the pavement, then scrambled away on all fours, bruising her bare knees on the rough asphalt.

She rolled and stumbled to her feet. "Help," she screamed, staggering away. Then a hand covered her mouth and muffled her voice, cutting off her air.

He spoke through gritted teeth. "Do as you're told or I'll break your neck."

This time he held her tighter, and she resisted in vain as he pushed her toward the rear of his waiting vehicle.

"If you scream, I'll kill you," he said. "You understand?"

She nodded.

He removed his hand from her mouth and popped the trunk. "Inside. Watch your head." He gave her a shove, and she lost her balance, tumbling headfirst into the trunk. She rolled over and attempted to climb out, but he brought the lid down, whacking her head and stunning her. She drew her hands back to keep her fingers from getting broken as the lid slammed shut.

Then, except for the faint glow of the taillights, her prison was dark. She lay on her back, screamed for help, and kicked at the solid lid. The driver door slammed and the engine hummed, and the vehicle sped away.

Before long, she tired and lay still, her mind whirling as the car bounced over potholes and rough pavement.

Why had he abducted her? Was he going to rape her? And then what? She'd seen his face and could identify him, and she feared he'd never let her go alive.

She thought about Edgar. Her husband would be heartbroken if anything happened to her. And he'd be lost without her. She had to survive for his sake.

The vehicle made several turns before gathering speed. The tires hummed. They were heading out of town. Where was he taking her?

After a few minutes, the car slowed, and she felt it turn,

then it bumped and rattled over uneven ground before coming to a sudden stop.

She cowered deep into the trunk as the engine died. The driver door opened and closed. Footsteps sounded on gravel, then the trunk swung open. By the light of the half-moon she looked into his grinning face.

"We're here," he said, then laughed. His laughter came to an abrupt end and his mouth twisted into a sneer. He stood above her with his arms folded, glaring down at her. "Get out."

She remained still, trembling and unable to move.

"You can scream all you want now," he said. "No one'll hear you."

Her throat felt constricted, and she couldn't breathe. "Where … where are we?" she managed to ask.

"We're home," he said, reaching out a hand toward her. "Here, let me help you out of there."

Olivia shook her head, folded her arms, and shrank back.

Her abductor sighed and leaned forward, grasping her by the leg. He dragged her from the trunk, and she fell prone onto the gravel at his feet. She turned her head and looked into his face as he crouched beside her, his hand heavy on her back.

"Why are you doing this?" Her voice came out as a hoarse whisper. "What do you want?"

He grabbed her by the hair and twisted her head, forcing her face into the gravel. The sharp stones bit into her skin. "Don't look at me," he said.

He kneeled on her back, tightened his grasp on her hair,

and pulled her head back until her neck felt ready to snap. She winced in pain as he slammed her face into the ground.

"Look at me again and I'll take out your eyes." He removed his hand. "You understand?"

She had no choice but to force out a whispered answer. "Yes."

"Never look at my face again," he said.

"I ... I won't."

He slammed the trunk. "Get up."

She struggled to her hands and knees, then staggered to her feet and picked away the slivers of sharp stones that still clung to her skin. Her long hair hung around her bruised and bleeding face as she turned toward him, keeping her eyes on the ground.

"Turn around."

She turned her back and kept her head down, then raised her eyes. A shed the size of a garage stood ten feet in front of the vehicle. The rough wooden exterior was unpainted and weather-beaten, but it appeared solid. Was it to be her prison?

To her right, maybe a hundred feet away, an old two-story house was visible through the gloom. A pale light glowed in the front window. The rest of the house was dark.

He gripped her long hair and prodded her toward the shed. Then, holding her with one hand, he removed a key from his pocket with the other and unlocked the door. It creaked open and slammed against the inner wall. He pushed her through the doorway and into the darkness, stepping in behind her.

CHAPTER 2

DAY 2 - Tuesday, 9:15 a.m.

ANNIE LINCOLN TURNED her gaze from the computer monitor toward the ringing telephone on her desk. She swung her swivel chair around, picked up the receiver, and leaned back.

"Lincoln Investigations. Annie speaking."

A man's worried voice spoke. "My name's Edgar Bragg. I ... I'm calling about my wife. She didn't come home last night, and I know something is wrong. It's not like her at all." He paused a moment before continuing in a pleading voice. "Can you help me, please?"

Annie sighed to herself. She'd been hoping to get a little free time today. She wanted to relax and take it easy for a while, maybe curl up with a good book in the backyard, or waste a little time at the mall.

She pushed aside a file folder, grabbed a pen and a blank sheet of paper, and scribbled down the man's name. "We'll do what we can, Mr. Bragg," she said, her plan of relaxation dissipating. "Have you contacted the police?"

"Yes. Yes, I did, but they won't do anything until my wife's been missing at least twenty-four hours. I can't wait that long. Something is terribly wrong."

Annie looked at her watch. Jake had left an hour or so ago to serve some legal papers. She could go and interview the distraught man without Jake, but he should be back any minute.

"Mr. Bragg, my husband and I will pay you a visit right away. Are you home now?"

"Yes. I … I couldn't go to work today. Not with my wife missing. I'm at 155 Walker Lane, apartment 202. That's in east Richmond Hill."

"I know the street," Annie said, writing down the address. "We'll be there within the hour."

"Please hurry."

That was it, then. Her mini-vacation would have to wait until tomorrow.

She got the man's phone number, then terminated the call and dialed Jake's cell. He'd served the papers without incident, and he expected to be home in less than ten minutes.

She reached for her handbag and peeked inside to be sure she had her notepad, a pen, and her digital recorder. She tucked the paper with Mr. Bragg's address into the bag, put fresh batteries into the recorder, and dropped it back into the handbag. She'd be ready to go as soon as Jake arrived.

Annie turned back to the computer. She finished detailing

a research report she'd been working on, then shut down the monitor and pushed back her chair. The rest of the research could wait. She had some background checks to do for Cranston's, but that could wait as well.

Not so long ago, research and background checks for corporate clients had been her sole business. When Jake had been laid off from his job as a construction engineer at one of Canada's largest land developers, he'd gotten the wild idea to expand Annie's business into investigative work. She had balked at first, but he'd persisted, and after a few weeks of intense study and attending classes at Richmond Community College, they'd each gotten their license along with an official certificate.

Jake had dug a little deeper into the books and taken another course, adding a security license to his repertoire. "You never know when it might come in handy," he had said. At six feet four inches tall, with an impressive physique, he was well suited as a bodyguard or for security service should the occasion demand it.

Since then, they'd never looked back. When Jake's former employers had begged him to return, offering him a sizable salary increase, he'd politely declined. Thanks to recent successes in tracking down bad guys, their once fledgling enterprise now prospered.

Annie wasn't sure what they could do for Edgar Bragg. A missing person often returned with a valid reason for their absence, but that wasn't always the case, and Annie treated every client with the urgency they demanded.

With any luck, they could get this sorted out in no time.

She carried her handbag to the kitchen, set it on the table, and poured the last cup of coffee. As she pulled back a chair and sat down, she heard the unmistakable sound of Jake's Firebird roaring into the driveway.

A moment later, the front door opened and Jake appeared in the kitchen. He dropped into a chair across the table from Annie and grinned.

"Got the papers served. The guy was pretty upset when he realized what they were. I hightailed it out of there before he took his anger out on me." He chuckled. "People are never happy about being sued."

Annie gave an understanding nod, then finished her coffee and pushed back her chair and stood. She glanced out the window toward the sunlit backyard, her comfortable chair on the deck, and thought of the cold pitcher of lemonade in the fridge. She took a deep breath and turned to face Jake. "Are you ready to go?"

"All ready," Jake said, pushing back his chair. "We'll take my car."

~*~

DETECTIVE HANK CORNING raised his head and looked at the officer approaching his desk. It was Officer Spiegle, and the young cop looked like he had something urgent on his mind.

"Diego wants to see you in his office right away," the officer said. "Apparently, it can't wait."

"Thanks, Yappy," Hank said. He yawned, tossed his pen

onto the desk, and pushed back his chair. There hadn't been much doing the last few days, so he'd taken the time to catch up on some mundane paperwork. And though the day was still young, he was ready for a break.

He stood and crossed the precinct floor and tapped on Diego's open door. "What's up, Captain?"

Diego waved him in and motioned toward a man clad in a postal uniform, sitting in the guest chair across the desk from Diego. "This is Luke Rushton." The captain leaned back and pointed toward a small, flat box on his desk. "He brought us an interesting package this morning."

"It's rather early for mail delivery, isn't it?" Hank asked.

"This was a special circumstance," Diego said.

Hank moved in closer and gazed at the package. It had no stamps or special delivery stickers on it. Instead, a handwritten message was taped to the top of the box, scrawled in red ink on a scrap of paper: "Deliver to RHPD ASAP. Urgent."

Hank looked up. "What's in it, Captain? What's so special about it?"

"Take a look," Diego said, leaning forward. "I had the bomb guys go over it before we opened it, and it's been checked for fingerprints. Now I want to know what you make of it."

Hank slid the box closer, folded back the lid, and looked inside. "It's hair," he said, frowning at the captain.

"Human hair," Diego said.

Hank took another look inside the box. It certainly appeared to be human hair—a thick, black lock about twelve inches long, maybe more, nestled in white tissue paper.

Diego nodded toward the postman. "Luke, this is Detective Corning. Tell him how you came across this package."

Luke Rushton straightened his tie, then turned in his chair to face Hank. He cleared his throat. "I got this from a corner mailbox north of here. Normally, I'd dump everything in a bag and take it to the sorting station along with the rest of the mail. But this one caught my attention."

"How so?" Hank asked.

Rushton pointed to the box. "If you look at the outside of the package, you'll see the same note on the top and bottom, and it's written in red ink. Like the sender didn't want me to miss his message." He shrugged. "There's never much in that mailbox for the morning pickup, so it stuck out like a sore thumb."

"And so Luke brought it straight to us," Diego said.

"Thought it might be important," Rushton added.

Hank leaned against the filing cabinet and ran a hand through his short, bristling hair. He had no idea what the package was all about, but people don't mail packages of hair to the police every day.

"What do you make of it?" Diego asked.

Hank pursed his lips. "Dunno. It's strange." He looked at Rushton. "I need to know exactly what mailbox you found it in and the approximate time, as near as possible."

Diego waved a sheet of paper. "It's all here."

"Not sure if this is my department," Hank said. "It might be a prank."

Diego shrugged. "Maybe. Maybe not. You're the best detective I have, so I wanted to run it past you."

Hank grinned. "It doesn't seem like I've been much help, Captain. I'm as lost as you are." He paused and glanced at the package again. "But I'll get a fingerprinter to check out the mailbox right away to see if they can find something."

"Do you need anything else from Luke?"

Hank looked at the postman. "I don't think so. Leave a phone number where I can contact you if necessary."

"Got it here," Diego said, waving the paper again. He stood and offered his hand to Rushton. "Thanks for your help."

Rushton stood and shook Diego's hand, then nodded at Hank and slipped from the office.

Diego dropped back into his chair, brushed at his bristling black mustache, and looked at Hank.

Hank shrugged. "I'll let you know if I find anything, Captain. But don't hold your breath."

Diego dismissed him with a wave. "It might be nothing," he said. He closed the box, handed it to Hank, and pulled over a file folder.

Hank went back to his desk, cleared a corner, and put the box down. He'd have to give it a little thought, but right now, he wanted to finish up the overdue reports.

CHAPTER 3

Tuesday, 10:13 a.m.

JAKE TOUCHED THE BRAKES and swung into the circle driveway of the building Annie was pointing at. He found a vacant slot in the guest parking area and shut down the engine, and they stepped out and surveyed their surroundings.

Number 155 Walker Lane sat half a block down a winding street that led in and around a thirty-year-old subdivision. The three-story apartment building was one of a pair facing each other across the narrow street.

The stingy lawn bordering its concrete-and-asphalt surroundings looked like it hadn't seen a lawnmower in a couple of weeks, and the grass could use a good watering. The building itself had known better days, its white enamel brick starting to chip and fall away. Rusty iron balconies jutted out, some now occupied by residents having a smoke or relaxing in the morning sun.

Jake led the way up the concrete path to the front door. Inside the lobby, Annie scanned the panel for apartment 202 and poked the button. Mr. Bragg must've been waiting. "Come in," came immediately over the speaker, and the inner door buzzed. They entered the main lobby. Much like the outside of the building, the inside could have used a little loving care as well.

They took the stairs to the second floor and Jake knocked on 202. The man who answered the door looked agitated, beaten down, and stressed out.

"Edgar Bragg?" Jake asked.

The man nodded.

Jake introduced them, and Mr. Bragg stepped back and motioned them in. He pointed toward the living room and followed behind as they made their way into the room. The distraught man breathed out a weary sigh and dropped onto a stiff-backed chair. He leaned forward and waited while the Lincolns were seated on a flowery, outdated couch.

Bragg appeared to be in his early thirties and sported a massive shock of uncombed blond hair. He looked at them through tired brown eyes and worked his hands nervously. "I ... I hope you can help me. I didn't know where else to turn."

Annie dug out her digital recorder and switched it on. She moved aside a drooping plant on the coffee table and set the recorder down. "We'll do whatever we can, Mr. Bragg. Do you mind if I record the interview?"

"Not at all. And please, call me Edgar."

Annie found her notepad and pen and sat back. "Edgar, when did you see your wife last?"

"Yesterday morning," Edgar answered. "I went to work as usual. I left about eight and got home around five. Olivia wasn't here. She works from noon until nine, and I expected to see her shortly after."

"Where does she work?" Jake asked.

Edgar motioned vaguely toward the window. "A couple blocks away at a place called Phil's Burgers & Booze."

"She's a waitress?"

"Yes. She's worked there for a couple of years or so." He paused and looked down at his clenched hands a moment, then back up. "I called there at nine thirty when I started to get worried. Phil said she left as usual just after nine, and he hadn't heard from her since."

Annie jotted in her notepad, then looked up. "How long have you been married, Edgar?"

"Almost twelve years," Edgar answered without hesitation. "It'll be twelve years next month."

"In the past twelve years, has she ever stayed out all night without telling you where she was?"

Edgar shook his head adamantly. "No. Never. In fact, there's never been a night we haven't spent together since we got married."

"Does she have a cell phone?" Jake asked.

"No. Neither one of us does." He motioned toward a telephone hanging by the entranceway to the kitchen. "We have a landline, but cell phones are an additional expense we can't afford right now." He forced a weak smile. "We're not much for talking on the phone, anyway."

"What about her friends?" Annie asked. "Does she have any close friends?"

Edgar reached into his shirt pocket and removed a folded piece of paper. He unfolded it and leaned forward, handing it to Annie. "I made a list. She knows two of the girls at work quite well. Other than them, she has a close friend, Jasmine Hyde. But with Olivia's hours, she doesn't socialize a whole lot. We spend most of our spare time together."

Jake glanced over at the paper. Edgar had written down Jasmine's name and phone number, along with the address for Phil's and the names of the two other girls who worked there. Annie tucked the paper into her notepad.

"Do you know if this building has any security cameras?" Jake asked.

"Not a chance. This place isn't maintained all that well. We're lucky to have enough heat in the winter. Spending money isn't a top priority around here."

"Maybe Phil's has some cameras," Annie said, making a note in her pad.

"Do you think it's possible Olivia might've gone on an errand before she came home?" Jake asked.

"I doubt it. She called me from work at six and didn't mention it. Besides, she always comes straight home at nine."

Jake sat back and squared an ankle over one knee, stroking his chin in thought. Phil's was a couple of blocks away, and if Olivia had been abducted, it must've happened somewhere between Phil's and here. There was one obvious route she would've taken home.

"Do you know what Olivia was wearing?" Annie asked.

"All the waitresses at Phil's wear the same uniform. A white blouse with a short red skirt."

Annie jotted something in her notepad. "Does she wear it home, or change there?"

"She puts it on before she leaves here, then wears it back home after work."

"Do you have a recent picture of your wife?" Annie asked.

Edgar rose to his feet, crossed the room, and rifled through a drawer in a small cabinet near the kitchen doorway. He returned a moment later with a photograph. Jake leaned forward, took the photo, and studied the close-up shot of Edgar and Olivia sporting wide smiles, their arms around each other as they faced the camera. Olivia's long black hair hung below her shoulders, framing a pretty face.

Edgar's worried expression grew more intense and a deep frown crossed his brow. "You don't think she's been … kidnapped, do you?"

Annie took the photo, tucked it into her notepad, and glanced at Jake before answering. "We hope not, Edgar, but there don't seem to be any other possibilities. If you're sure Olivia didn't go anywhere without telling you, then she might've been taken by force."

That seemed to worry Edgar more, and he took a sharp breath. In a moment, he breathed normally, but the worry remained in his eyes as he asked, "But who? Why?"

"That's what we need to find out," Jake said. "Can you think of anything else that might help?"

Edgar shook his head. "I've been running it through my mind all night, and I can't come up with any logical conclusion. It doesn't make sense."

Jake slipped a business card from his shirt pocket, stood, and handed it to the overwrought man. "Call me if you think of anything. In the meantime, we'll look into every lead we can find."

Annie picked up the recorder, switched it off, and dropped it into her handbag. "I hate to discuss money at a time like this, but we'll need a small retainer."

"Of course," Edgar said. "I understand." He left the room and returned a few moments later with a check, handing it to Annie. Jake glanced over. The check was for two thousand dollars, enough to make a good start.

Annie tucked the check into her handbag along with her notepad and pen, then stood and followed Jake to the front door.

"Will you let me know if you find anything?" Edgar asked. He wrung his hands, his slumped shoulders showing the strain he was under.

"Of course," Annie said. "We'll get on it right away. And if we don't find anything solid by this evening, we'll talk to the police about getting involved."

Jake added, "If we come across any evidence your wife might've been taken against her will, the police'll get involved immediately."

"We'll keep in touch," Annie said.

"Thank you," Edgar said in an uncertain voice. "I'll be home all day." He opened the door and let them out, and the door clicked shut behind them.

Though Jake felt for Edgar Bragg, he was always ready for a new challenge, and he was raring to get started. He looked at Annie. "I guess the obvious place to start is Phil's. That might be our best lead."

"That might be our only lead," Annie said.

CHAPTER 4

Tuesday, 11:06 a.m.

TERESA HANSON SLIPPED out the rear door of the Commerce Bank, balancing a cup of coffee in one hand and a pack of smokes in the other. Slipping a cigarette from the pack with her teeth, she poked it into her mouth and crossed the narrow lane at the rear of the building.

She was determined to give up the habit one of these days; she just couldn't afford it on a bank teller's salary. With the ever-increasing price of cigarettes, it was getting harder to maintain her one and only vice. Maybe tomorrow. Or next week.

Navigating down the alley, she passed a row of employee vehicles, dumpsters, and chained-up bicycles, and stepped onto the sidewalk. She paused and flicked her lighter, taking a deep drag of the soothing smoke before crossing the street to the small neighborhood park where she could relax for a whole fifteen minutes.

She headed to her usual spot, pleased the bench was unoccupied. Dropping onto the wooden seat, she kicked off her shoes and relished the cool, luxurious grass under her feet. She sipped her coffee, enjoying her smoke and the occasional sounds of nature in the secluded little place in the middle of the city.

Above her, an overhanging tree kept off the heat of the sun. A faint breeze circulated the warm air in and around the towering trees and rows of evergreens. She caught the sound of a squirrel's claws biting into bark as it skittered up a tree, and somewhere behind her, a dog whined.

Light sounds of traffic came from the main street as cars dashed to and fro going who knows where. A girl on a bicycle breezed down the side street fifty feet away, and still, the dog whined.

Then the whimpering sounds of the animal ceased, and she heard the padding of canine feet behind her, coming closer. She turned in her seat. A small dog raced toward her, its collar tags jangling as it tore across the grass.

Teresa didn't know much about dogs, but it looked like a terrier to her. It skidded to a stop, its almond-shaped eyes sparkling with life and intelligence as it watched her, its stubby tail between its legs. The whining began again.

Teresa stretched out a hand. "Hi, pup. What're you doing wandering around here all by yourself?"

The dog moved in with caution and sniffed her hand, then

backed off. It paced and whined, then circled to the front of the bench.

"What's the matter, pup?" Teresa said, turning to face the animal. She leaned forward. "What's bothering you?" She glanced across the lawn expecting to see the dog's owner, but no one was there.

The anxious animal tore away, then stopped short and whined again, then returned. It panted, paced, and circled, stopping now and then to let out a short, urgent bark, its eyes never wavering from hers.

Teresa glanced behind her toward the direction the dog had come from. No one was in sight, but the animal seemed eager to get her attention. Maybe it'd chased a cat up a tree and wanted to get at it, hoping she would help.

But the urgent whine seemed much more than that. Perhaps the animal's owner was in some kind of trouble.

She slipped her shoes on, butted out her smoke, and dropped her empty coffee cup in a garbage bin at the end of the bench.

She paused a moment and looked at her watch, unsure if she should follow the animal, or get back to work so she wouldn't be reprimanded for being late returning from her break.

There was no doubt the dog was trying to get her attention. It crouched down ten feet away, its chin on its front paws, watching her, waiting for her. She took one step toward the animal and it leaped up, bounding away. Then it stopped again, its eyes on hers, still waiting, watching, and whining.

Teresa followed the animal, curious to see what it wanted. The dog trotted ahead, stopping often to make sure Teresa was still following. And she did, across the expansive lawn, around a row of well-trimmed cedars, and behind a lofty oak.

The dog stopped and so did she. Her hands flew to her mouth, and she caught her breath. She stifled a scream and stood frozen, taking short, quick breaths as she stood beside the whining dog, staring at the horrific sight in front of them.

A woman lay flat on her back, her arms folded across her chest, her fingers intertwined.

Her short red skirt and comfortable shoes, along with the snow-white blouse, neatly arranged as though great care had been taken, were all in contrast to the horrendous sight of the woman's tortured face, the leather strap digging into her neck, and her completely shaved head.

She looked like she was resting, but the unseeing eyes and the pale white skin told Teresa otherwise.

The woman was dead.

Teresa took an uneasy step backwards, transfixed by the sight, unable to look away. Then she closed her eyes, took a deep breath, then opened her eyes and moved forward, crouching by the body. Just to be sure, she would check for a heartbeat. But it was no use. The moment she touched the cold skin, she realized no one could help the poor woman now.

Teresa stood and gazed in horror a few seconds before turning away from the unnerving sight that would be burned forever in her mind.

"Come on, pup," she said, her voice quivering as she

spoke. She lit another smoke to calm her jumping nerves, then reached a shaky hand toward the dog. "Let's get out of here."

The animal followed dutifully at her heels as she left the gruesome sight behind, made her way back to her favorite bench, and called 9-1-1.

CHAPTER 5

Tuesday, 11:37 a.m.

HANK WAS IN THE BREAK room when a message came in to dispatch. According to the officer who poked his head into the room and handed Hank a sheet of paper, there'd been a homicide. Hank was needed on the scene.

The detective crumpled up his coffee cup, pushed back his chair, and called Detective Simon King.

"There's been a murder," Hank said into the phone when the cop answered.

King emitted a loud yawn. "Just finishing up an interview. I'll meet you there."

Hank gave him the location and hung up. In the past, Hank had worked alone, but his increasing workload had forced him to depend on King more often than he liked. Not that the younger cop was useless—he had his good points—

but he lacked finesse. Diego had teamed them up for reasons of his own, and King grudgingly surrendered to Hank's lead with a minimal amount of nudging.

Hank stood, tossed his cup into the waste bin, grabbed his briefcase from his desk, and made his way back to the parking lot behind the precinct.

He glanced at the address as he drove from the lot. The scene of the incident was located in a small park on the east side of town. Having been a beat cop for three years, then a detective for fifteen, he knew the city inside out. And he knew exactly where the park was.

Five cruisers were parked along the street when Hank arrived. First responders had secured the scene, and three or four uniforms kept back the curious public. Hank pulled his Chevy in beside the coroner's van and got out.

The Channel 7 Action News van had parked just past the row of police vehicles. Lisa Krunk was the last person Hank wanted to see. The annoying reporter strained at the police barrier, waving her mike around, attempting to get the attention of one of the officers. Her cameraman, Don, had his equipment out, capturing images of the scene.

Lisa spied Hank, waved, and started a purposeful stride his way. The detective avoided eye contact and kept moving. He didn't want to get roped into giving an interview at the moment, especially since he didn't know any more about what'd happened here than she did. He wasn't about to discuss hypotheticals with the nosy newswoman.

Maybe he'd spare her a few minutes before he left. Maybe.

"Detective Corning," she called, still beating a path toward him, her mike shoved out in front of her.

He ignored her, ducked under the yellow tape, and was directed to an area a hundred feet further in.

CSI was documenting the scene with painstaking care. Evidence markers were scattered in a variety of places. A photographer knelt down, snapping shots. Other investigators milled about, taking notes, bagging evidence, and discussing what it all meant.

Hank approached a tall, gaunt man holding a clipboard. Even at six feet tall, Hank had to raise his chin an inch or two to look lead investigator Rod Jameson in the eye. "Morning, Rod," he said.

Jameson gave a one-sided grin and spoke in a deep, hollow voice. "Afternoon, Hank. We're just about done here." He turned and pointed toward a row of evergreens. "You'll find the vic behind those trees."

"Thanks, Rod."

Hank turned when he saw a familiar figure out of the corner of his eye. King strode toward them, then stopped and nodded hello, finger-combing his long, greasy hair back.

"Hey, King," Hank said, giving the cop a quick glance. With his three-day-old beard, his worn-out jeans, and his faded black t-shirt, he looked more like a drug dealer than a cop. In the past, King had been a narc, working undercover as much as possible, busting druggies and drug lords. In that vocation, his daily attire had been an asset, and Hank had long ago given up demanding King invest in some new clothes.

Hank turned and went behind the row of cedars, King following, and they approached the grisly sight. The victim lay on her back, her body arranged as though placed there by an undertaker. Except that her eyes were open, staring blankly at the foliage above, and the leather strap around her neck made it clear what the cause of death had been.

But the most curious thing was that the victim's head had been shaved. Short wisps of hair stuck out at awkward angles. It was obvious the woman's haircut hadn't been done by a professional, and it was unlikely the victim had done it herself.

That left one possibility. The killer had shaved her head, and there was no doubt in Hank's mind the hair the postman had delivered that morning had come from this victim.

A tiny dark-haired woman was crouched down beside the body, examining the victim's throat with a gloved hand. It was Chief Medical Examiner Nancy Pietek. She turned her round, cheerful face toward Hank, her bright eyes shining, and offered a short smile as the detective crouched beside her. "Nice to see you again, Hank."

Hank murmured a hello. "Victim was strangled, Nancy?"

"Almost certainly the cause of death is asphyxiation by strangulation," Nancy replied, pointing to the leather strap around the victim's neck.

The open mouth of the dead woman made the sight even more gruesome. She'd have been gasping for precious air up until her final moments of life.

Hank had seen a lot of horrifying sights in the past fifteen years, many of them still invading his dreams, and he knew this one would stay with him for a long time. He shook it off, forced himself to concentrate on his job, and turned to Nancy.

"Any idea on the time of death?" he asked.

"Three to four hours ago," she said, moving the victim's head from side to side. "Rigor mortis has just started to set in at the neck and jaw." She gently raised one of the victim's arms a couple of inches and let it fall. "Hasn't reached the rest of the muscles yet."

Hank looked at the victim's left hand. She wore a wedding band with an engagement ring that held a tiny diamond. The jewelry wasn't all that valuable, but if the motive had been robbery, the killer would certainly have taken the rings.

And the hasty haircut the woman had received didn't point to robbery, either.

"Any signs of sexual abuse?" Hank asked.

"Not that I can see. Nothing obvious, anyway. I'll give her a thorough examination back at the lab and let you know."

A deep voice sounded from behind. "No ID on the victim, Hank. We're hoping facial recognition or her fingerprints will give us something. That is, if there's any record of her in the system."

Hank stood and faced Jameson. "Nothing on the body?"

"Nope. No purse. There's a small pocket in her skirt, but it was empty."

"Who found her?" King asked.

Jameson consulted his clipboard. "A woman named Teresa Hanson. Came here on her break. An officer took her statement." He waved an arm toward the street. "She a teller at Commerce Bank if you want to speak to her." He jotted the name down on a clean page, ripped it loose, and held it out.

Hank took the paper, tucked it into an inner pocket of his jacket, and turned back to Nancy, who had stood. "Was the woman killed here?"

"Hard to tell, Hank. The beginnings of livor mortis on the front and side would indicate no. I'll have a better idea after the autopsy, but it appears she was killed elsewhere and perhaps lay face down for some time, then deposited here."

"What's the deal with her hair?" King asked.

"That's a good question," Hank said. He told King about the unusual package delivered to the precinct that morning.

King frowned. "The killer's making a statement of some kind. Or sending a message."

"If the hair belongs to this victim, then yes," Hank said, glancing at the body. "But first, we have to find out who this is."

Hank scanned the ground around the body, then turned to Jameson. "Any signs the victim was dragged here?"

"Nothing. It appears she was carried."

"How much do you think she weighs?" Hank asked Nancy.

"A hundred and thirty, maybe forty, pounds."

"Not an easy task to carry that much weight from the street to here," Hank said. "The killer would have to be fairly strong."

"Why bother carrying her here at all?" King said, glancing around. "Why here in the park?"

"That's another good question, King," Hank said. "And we're going to find answers to all of them." He turned to Jameson. "Anything else you can tell me, Rod?"

"Nothing that sticks out. I'll get a complete report to you ASAP, but if anything interesting pops up in the meantime, I'll give you a call."

"I'm especially interested to see if the hair we got in the mail matches up with our Jane Doe."

"I'll let you know," Jameson said.

"Then I guess we're done here," Hank said, turning to King. "Let's go catch us a killer."

CHAPTER 6

Tuesday, 11:56 a.m.

AFTER THE INTERVIEW with Edgar Bragg, the Lincolns had stopped for a quick lunch before heading to Phil's Burgers & Booze. Jake had wanted to grab a burger from Phil's, but Annie had insisted otherwise, stating that an establishment with that name wouldn't even be on a list of places she'd consider eating.

Jake had given in with a shrug, and they'd stopped at a small deli a block from their destination.

After lunch, Annie called Olivia Bragg's best friend, Jasmine Hyde, while Jake steered the Firebird toward Phil's. Following a short conversation, Annie hung up, dropped her cell phone into her handbag, and turned to Jake.

"Jasmine was rather upset, but she said she hasn't seen Olivia in a couple of weeks."

"Did she have any idea whether or not Olivia might've run off somewhere?" Jake asked.

"No. She said the same as Edgar, that it wasn't like Olivia to disappear without a word. She has no idea what might've happened."

Jake pulled into a small parking lot at the side of Phil's and shut down the engine, and they stepped out. Annie glanced at the faded sign, the greasy windows, and the litter blowing about the property, and was glad she'd made the decision not to eat there.

Jake pulled open one of the double doors and Annie stepped inside. Old oil mixed with the odor of something stale permeated the close air inside the restaurant. A faint pungent smell of sizzling onions could be detected.

Three or four of the handful of tables were in use, patrons taking careful bites of sloppy burgers as they enjoyed their fast-food banquet. They were probably the usual crowd, the ones who'd grown so accustomed to the bad aroma they'd stopped noticing. According to Edgar, the place employed two or three full time waitresses in the evening when the booze flowed, proving to Annie that when sufficiently inebriated, smell and taste are of no importance.

A fifty-something stout man sporting a once-white apron stood behind the counter, eyeing them as they approached. A wide smile lit up his blubbery face.

"Good day, folks. What can I do for you?" the man asked with a faint Greek accent.

Annie stepped to the counter. "We're looking for Phil."

"I'm Phil," the man said. He wiped his right hand on his

apron and held it out. "Phil Giannopoulos. I own this place."

Annie shook his hand and introduced herself, motioning toward Jake. "And this is my husband, Jake. We're from Lincoln Investigations, and we'd like to ask you about Olivia Bragg."

Phil turned and glanced at a clock on the wall by the door, a light frown on his brow. "She should've been here by now." He shrugged. "Sometimes she's a few minutes late." His frown deepened. "What're you investigating?"

Annie glanced around the room. No one seemed in urgent need of Phil's services. "Can we sit down a moment?"

Phil pursed his lips, then motioned toward a nearby booth. Jake and Annie sat on one side of the table, while Phil wedged his rounded belly in on the other side, pushed up his sleeves, and dropped his hairy arms on the table.

"What's this all about?" the big man asked.

Annie brushed aside some crumbs, pushed a ketchup bottle back into place, and laid her arms on the table, leaning forward slightly. "Olivia didn't come home last night, and her husband is understandably concerned."

"Didn't go home?" Phil said, tilting his head to one side. "She left here at nine, same as always, and that's the last I heard of her." He frowned and sat back. "I told her husband that last night. You mean to tell me she still never made it home?"

Annie shook her head. "We fear she might've been abducted. Somewhere between here and her home, two blocks away."

Phil leaned forward, his eyes widening. "Abducted?"

"We don't know for sure," Jake said. "There's no evidence of a kidnapping, but Olivia's missing."

Deep concern showed in Phil's eyes. "I'm happy to help you, but I have no idea what might've happened to her."

"If you think back to last night before Olivia left," Jake said, "did you by any chance notice anything or anyone unusual?"

Phil's eyes narrowed and he looked up a moment. "Not that I can think of."

"What about any customers you had, let's say, between eight and nine? Were any of them alone?" Annie asked.

"Lots of people come here alone. Especially in the evening. I got a good price on draft, and they like to sit and fill up."

"Do you know most of the usual customers?" Jake asked.

Phil shrugged. "Just about all of them." He grinned. "Sometimes people come here to eat, too. People drive by and drop in."

"Was there anyone here last night you didn't recognize?"

"Always is. People come and go, you know. Sure, we have regulars, but there're always new customers."

A man approached the cash register, one hand digging in his back pocket for his wallet. He glanced toward the booth, and Phil excused himself. "Just let me take this guy's money and I'll be back," he said, squeezing out of his seat.

Annie scanned the restaurant. There didn't appear to be any cameras in the place.

The cash register dinged open, then slammed, and in a

moment, Phil returned and wedged his way back into the booth.

"I don't see any cameras here," Annie said to Phil.

Phil pointed to the exit door. "Got one outside. Aimed at the front of the building, but there're none inside the place."

Jake turned and looked toward the door. "Does the camera see everyone who comes and goes?"

"Sure does."

"And you record it?" Annie asked.

"Yup."

Annie smiled. "Is it possible to get a copy of the recording? I'd like to see anything from eight o'clock till after nine."

Phil sat back and folded his arms, observing them. Then he scratched his head, leaned forward, and spoke. "Guess it'd be okay." He shrugged. "If it'll help you track down Olivia, then why not?"

He eased back out of the booth. "Give me a minute or two. I'll see if I can figure out how the thing works. Never had to do this before." He glanced around the restaurant, then, satisfied he wasn't needed, he stepped behind the counter and disappeared through an open doorway beside a smoking grill.

"I hope it's not on VHS," Jake said. "I don't wanna have to dig that old player out again."

"I hope it tells us something," Annie said. "It's about all we have to go on right now."

"You don't think Phil's involved, do you?" Jake asked. "He seems like an okay type of guy."

"I don't think so," Annie said, shrugging. "But everyone's a suspect until we rule them out."

Jake grinned. "You're starting to sound like a cop. That's what Hank always says."

"Maybe that's where I picked it up," Annie said with a smile, motioning across the room. "Here comes Phil. Looks like he has something for us."

The restaurateur stepped up to the table and slid a flash drive toward Annie. "Got it figured out. Don't know how long the video is, but it covers the time period you're looking for."

Annie picked up the drive and slipped it into her handbag. "Thanks," she said. "Do you want this back when we're done with it?"

"If you're in the neighborhood you can drop it in," Phil said, waving a hand. "But it doesn't matter that much. They left a whole bunch of them when they set up the system."

Jake slid out of the booth, pulled out a business card, and handed it to Phil. "Give us a shout if you think of anything you think might be important."

Phil took the card and tucked it into his apron pocket. "Can I get you folks anything before you go? I make a nice burger."

Annie stood and smiled. "Thank you, but we ate not long ago. Maybe another time."

Jake and Annie shook hands with Phil, said goodbye, and left the restaurant. Annie turned and glanced at the camera above the door and hoped the video would prove to be of some use.

"What now?" Jake asked as they got into the car.

"I guess we go home and wade our way through this video," Annie said. She turned to face Jake. "Unless you have a better idea."

Jake shrugged and started the car. "Nothing I can think of."

CHAPTER 7

Tuesday, 12:18 p.m.

HANK HAD SENT DETECTIVE King to conduct an interview with the woman who'd discovered the body in the park. He didn't expect the visit would reveal anything useful. He'd already gone over Teresa Hanson's detailed statement, but nothing of immediate use had been gleaned from it.

Forensics had conducted a facial recognition search but hadn't found a match to anyone in the computer records. A fingerprint analysis had also netted nothing. At least Hank knew the unknown woman had no criminal record.

Forensics was also doing a hair examination to ascertain if the lock of hair received in the mail was that of the victim. An expert would carry out a microscopic comparison, and Hank expected to hear it was a positive match.

The body of Jane Doe was now in the morgue. Nancy Pietek would be in the process of examining it in detail, but her complete report would take some time.

Hank's first concern was to find out the identity of the victim.

He twirled in his chair, pulled in to his desk, and faced his computer monitor. He tapped a few keys and was presented with a short list of the missing persons reports from the last seventy-two hours.

At the top of the list of three was an elderly man who'd wandered off. Hank was glad to see an updated report stating the man had been safely found.

The second report was of a man as well, gone for two days and still missing.

The third missing person was a woman named Olivia Bragg. The report had been taken less than twenty-four hours ago, filed by her husband, the call received just after midnight that morning. Unless there was evidence harm had come to the missing person, it was too early for the police to get involved.

Hank leaned in for a closer look. There was no photo attached to the report, but the given information stated Mrs. Bragg had black hair and dark brown eyes—just like the victim. She'd been dressed in a short red skirt and white blouse—just like the victim. And she lived on the east side of Richmond Hill—just like the victim.

Hank was convinced he had a match.

A quick search of the driver's license database brought up a familiar headshot; it was the face of the woman found in the park.

There was no doubt. The victim's name was Olivia Bragg.

Hank sat back. Putting a name to the face suddenly made

it all more real, more personal. He gave a long sigh. The death of one supposed innocent victim would now affect the lives of so many, and the pain of those closest to her would never go away.

He glanced up as Rod Jameson approached his desk and dropped into the chair opposite him. In his usual deep voice, the investigator announced, "The hair from the package matches the victim, Hank. There's no doubt."

Hank shook his head slowly, his eyes on Rod. He had expected a positive ID, and he was determined to find out why this woman was murdered and who'd done the killing.

"I found the victim's name," Hank said. "It's Olivia Bragg."

"I don't envy you your next task, Hank," Rod said. "Any family?"

"A husband."

Rod stood. "I'll get the forensic report from the scene to you as soon as I can. There's nothing right now that sticks out as being of earth-shaking importance, but I'll let you know if we find anything."

"Thanks, Rod," Hank said as the investigator left.

Hank jotted down the address and phone number of Edgar Bragg in his notepad. He picked up the phone, hesitated a moment, then dialed the number.

"Mr. Bragg," Hank began when a man answered the phone. "This is Detective Corning. I'd like to drop by to see you, if that's possible."

The man's voice showed a hint of excitement. "Is this about my wife? About Olivia?"

Hank paused before answering. "Yes, it is."

"Did you find her?"

Hank took a long breath. "May I drop by now? Are you at home?"

"Yes. Yes, I'm home." The voice had changed to one of apprehension.

"I'll be there in fifteen minutes," Hank said. He confirmed the address and hung up. He wasn't about to give Mr. Bragg the news over the phone. Besides, no matter how innocent Bragg seemed, he'd naturally be a chief suspect in his wife's murder. Hank needed to talk to the man face to face, eye to eye.

He glanced at the address again. From what he knew of the area, the park where Mrs. Bragg's body had been found was at least a couple of miles north of the Bragg residence. Had Mrs. Bragg been in that area and then been killed and left in the park? Or had she been abducted closer to home, then killed and transported to the park later? These were questions he was eager to find answers for.

He grabbed his briefcase, left the precinct, and a few minutes later, pulled his car into the driveway of 155 Walker Lane. Once inside the building, Mr. Bragg buzzed him in and Hank took the stairs up. A man stood in the doorway of 202, anxiously watching Hank walk down the hallway toward him.

"Mr. Bragg?" Hank asked.

"Yes."

Hank introduced himself and was invited into the apartment. He sat on the edge of the couch, set his briefcase on the floor, and watched as Bragg sat opposite him.

"Did you find my wife?" the man asked, a deep frown on his worried face. "What's going on? Why won't you tell me?"

"Mr. Bragg," Hank began and took a deep breath, letting it out slowly. There wasn't any easy way to say this. "Mr. Bragg, I'm afraid your wife has been killed."

Bragg's eyes narrowed and he stared at Hank, confusion and unbelief on his face. Then he leaned forward and his eyes widened, his mouth gaping open. "Are … are you sure?" was all he could manage.

Hank leaned back. "I'm sure, Mr. Bragg."

Bragg jumped to his feet and paced the floor furiously. Then he stopped suddenly and spun to face Hank. "What … what happened? How did it happen? Where is she?"

Now for the hardest part. Hank took another breath. "I'm afraid it was homicide, Mr. Bragg."

The distraught man glared. "Homicide? Are you telling me someone … killed her?"

Hank shook his head and answered in a low voice. "Yes."

Bragg dropped into the chair, threw his head back, and closed his eyes. He breathed rapidly awhile, then opened his eyes and looked back at Hank, his face twisted in anger. "Who did it? Who killed my … my wife?"

"We don't know yet, Mr. Bragg. Her body was discovered not long ago, and the investigation has just begun."

"How did it happen?"

"She was strangled."

Bragg closed his eyes and whispered, "Strangled." He took another deep breath and opened his eyes, now alive with fury.

He jumped to his feet, gritted his teeth, and peered at Hank. "She never hurt anyone. Never. She was a good person. Who would do this to her?"

"We're going to do everything in our power to find out, Mr. Bragg." Hank cleared his throat. "The park where your wife was found is two miles north of here. Would she have been in that area last night?"

Bragg shook his head adamantly. "No. She works two blocks away, and she always comes straight home after work at nine o'clock."

"Where does she work?"

"At a dump called Phil's Burgers & Booze." He pointed. "Two blocks from here. She always walks to work and back."

Hank had his notepad out, and he jotted the name of the restaurant down, then took a deep breath. Now for the uncomfortable question. "Where were you last night, Mr. Bragg?"

"I was here. I got home at six. I had a little snack and waited for my wife."

Hank made another notation, then asked, "Did you see anyone during that time?"

Bragg frowned. "Are you suggesting I had something to do with this?"

Hank shook his head. "I have to fill in the pieces. It helps me get a complete picture."

Bragg seemed satisfied and sat back, fidgeting with his hands. He took a deep breath and let out a lot of long sighs. Suddenly, he asked, "Where is she? Where's my wife?"

"The medical examiner's taking care of her," Hank said. "We'll need you to identify her for the record."

Bragg nodded. "I guess I should let you know," he said. "When the police wouldn't do anything this morning to find my wife, I hired some private investigators to see if they could find her."

Hank's eyes widened. "If you want to give me their names, I'll contact them to see if they came up with anything."

"Lincoln Investigations," Bragg said. "I'll call them now. I'd better let them know about my wife, and that you're here."

A faint smile touched Hank's lips. That was good news. There were a few so-called private investigators in the area, and Hank was pleased Bragg had chosen the best. And of course, the fact he and the Lincolns were good friends was a bonus.

CHAPTER 8

Tuesday, 1:11 p.m.

JAKE SAT IN THE OFFICE, leaning forward in the guest chair, his eyes glued to the monitor as Annie fast-forwarded through the video they'd gotten from Phil's. She paused it each time a face appeared on the screen, took a screenshot, and continued on.

A couple of dozen people had visited the restaurant during the time period they were interested in. Some of them came alone, or in pairs, and though Jake suspected they were looking for a single man, Annie painstakingly captured a close-up of them all. She would print them out later, and he suspected, as she did, that one of them could be the person they were looking for.

Jake turned his eyes away from the monitor, sat back in his chair, and answered his ringing cell phone. It was Edgar Bragg, and his voice sounded breathless.

"It's Bragg," Jake whispered to Annie, covering the phone.

Annie paused the video and turned in her chair to face Jake as he put the phone on speaker. Her eyes were wide, her mouth open, as the distraught man explained about the murder of his wife and how the body had been found.

Jake was at a loss for words, taken aback by the unexpected news. He expressed his sympathy to the grieving man, adding, "Annie and I will be right over. Ask Detective Corning to wait. We have something that might be of interest to him."

After hanging up, he slouched back in his chair, let out a long breath, and looked at Annie. They stared speechless at one another for a moment, until finally, Annie sighed and spoke in a soft voice. "I wasn't expecting that."

"Nor I," Jake said. "And now we're looking for a murderer, not just a kidnapper." He pointed to the computer. "Maybe you should make a copy of the video for Hank. He'll wanna take a look."

Annie nodded and turned back to the computer. She duplicated the video onto a second flash drive and handed it to Jake. He dropped it into his shirt pocket and stood.

Annie grabbed her handbag from the kitchen and met Jake outside, and a few minutes later, Jake wheeled the Firebird into the parking lot of Edgar Bragg's apartment building. He pulled in beside Hank's Chevy and they stepped out.

Bragg buzzed them in, and when they reached the second floor, Hank met them in the hallway outside the stairwell. He greeted them with a grim nod and filled them in on the details of the horrific murder, outlining what he knew so far. Annie was visibly shaken, and Jake knew she'd be determined to find the person responsible.

"I haven't given Mr. Bragg all the details yet," Hank said, heading down the hallway toward the apartment. "He appears on the edge of a breakdown now, and I'm afraid the gruesome details might be too much for him."

When they stepped inside the apartment, Bragg was waiting for them, a somber look on his face. His eyes drooped more than before, and his shoulders hunched forward, his whole body showing the heartbreak he felt. He motioned them into the living room.

Jake leaned against the door frame while Hank and Annie sat on the couch. Bragg dropped wearily into a chair and leaned forward, his hands working nervously.

Hank cleared his throat and broke the mournful silence, turning to Jake. "You said you have something for me?"

Jake dug out the drive and tossed it to Hank. "I'm not sure how helpful it might be, but it's a video of everyone who visited Phil's around the time period in question."

"You think he might've been stalking her?" Bragg asked, his brow taking on a deep frown.

"It's possible," Jake said. "Right now we have to look at all possibilities."

"Without a motive, it's hard to tell," Hank added. "She might've been picked at random, or she might've been targeted. That's what I intend to find out."

Annie turned to Bragg. "We'll need to print out a close-up shot of everyone on the video, then you can take a look and see if you recognize anyone."

Hank spoke. "Until then, do you have any idea who might've wanted to harm your wife?"

Bragg shook his head slowly, back and forth, his eyes showing his mind at work. Finally, he answered, "I can't think of anyone at all."

"Anyone suspicious you might've seen hanging around recently?" Hank asked.

Bragg shook his head again. "No. No one I can think of."

Hank turned to Annie. "Have you gone over this video?"

"Yes, but they're all random faces to me. And nothing appears out of the ordinary."

Hank nodded, snapped open his briefcase, and put the drive inside. "I'll have to visit Phil's. Circumstances have … changed drastically since you were there."

"There's one thing we know for sure," Jake said. "The killer would've had a vehicle. Mrs. Bragg was abducted near Phil's and taken to the park."

"Yes, but not until the next morning," Hank said. "So the question is, where was she in the meantime?"

Jake glanced over at Bragg. The man had a renewed look of anguish on his face, probably due to the realization of what his wife might've endured before her death. The thought filled Jake with dread as well, and he vowed to himself to do whatever it took to find out who was responsible for such a heinous murder.

"I talked to Olivia's friend, Jasmine Hyde," Annie said to Bragg. "She hasn't seen your wife for some time."

"We've been keeping rather busy," Bragg said. "We haven't had much time for a social life. We're saving to buy a house." He dropped his head and remained silent awhile. When he raised his head, his eyes were moist, and he glanced around the apartment. Jake knew the man was envisioning a life without his wife.

Hank picked up his briefcase and stood. "I want you to know, Mr. Bragg, finding out who's responsible is my priority."

As Jake and Annie turned to leave, Bragg shook Jake's hand and asked, "I hope you two will continue helping out?"

"We will," Jake said.

"If you need more money—"

"We have enough for now."

Bragg nodded and followed them to the door, turning to Hank as they stepped into the hallway. "Please let me know what you find, Detective Corning."

"I will," Hank said and the door closed behind them.

They made their way in silence out to the parking lot, where Jake leaned against Hank's car and turned to the cop. "Do you have any leads to follow?"

"Just the video," Hank said. "With Phil's help, I intend to identify whoever I can from the recording, then between King and me, we'll make some visits and see what turns up."

"We'll take another look at the video as well," Annie said. "Things have changed, and it's about all we have right now."

Hank nodded, got into his car, and started the engine. He rolled down the window. "I'll let you guys know if I find out anything useful." He waved a hand and pulled from the lot.

CHAPTER 9

Tuesday, 2:28 p.m.

WHEN HANK ARRIVED BACK at the precinct, he set his briefcase beside his chair and went directly to Callaway's desk. The young cop was the go-to guy for any computer-related issues, the absolute whiz everyone turned to when they needed something technical done, and done fast.

Hank took a seat, dropped the flash drive onto Callaway's desk, and slid it over. "Got a minute to take a look at this?"

Callaway reached for the drive and picked it up. "Sure, Hank. What is it?"

"It's a video of everyone visiting a restaurant called Phil's Burgers & Booze. I need you to isolate facial shots of everyone leaving the building and print them out."

"No problem, Hank," Callaway said. He leaned down, pushed the drive into a slot on the computer tower, and leaned forward at his monitor. "Shouldn't take too long. I'll let you know when I'm done."

"Thanks, Callaway," Hank said. He went back to his desk, dropped into his chair, and leaned back. A vague feeling had been niggling at him for the last couple of hours. There was something about the facts of this case that rang a faint bell somewhere in the back of his head, and he couldn't put his finger on it.

Was it because the dead woman had been found in a park? That wasn't so unusual. He leaned forward at his keyboard and did a database search for any crimes that had taken place in and around a park in the city. There were lots of them, and several were homicide related.

But he felt he was on the wrong track. He did another search using the keyword "hair." There were pages of results, so he narrowed the search down to "shaved hair" and the results were more manageable. He waded through the references, then somewhere on the second screenful of listings, his eyes widened and he leaned in. He might've found what had been bugging him all day.

He clicked through to the electronic report and squinted at the screen. It detailed an unsolved case from several years ago—nine, to be exact. He had a fuzzy recollection of the events, and that was what had been bothering him. He ran his eyes down the screen and refreshed his memory of what had taken place.

A woman named Debra Wilde had been discovered early one morning, murdered in her bed by an unknown assailant, choked to death by a belt fastened securely around her throat. But the real kicker was, the hair on her head had been completely shaved off.

The killer had never been identified. The woman's son, Isaiah Wilde, had been the prime suspect, but a solid case against him couldn't be made. Isaiah, who went by the name of Izzy, had been fifteen years old at the time.

Izzy had an older brother named Carter, who had been eighteen when the murder was committed. However, he had been dismissed as a suspect early on. He hadn't been home at the time of the murder, confirmed to have been staying at a friend's house overnight.

Hank tapped a key and separate photos of the victim and the brothers appeared on his screen, taken at the time of the occurrence.

He dug a little deeper into the known facts of the case. According to the police report, Izzy had heard a disturbance in the night, gone to his mother's room, and discovered her body. Her head had been shaved, and though hairs from the woman had been found on Izzy's clothing, he claimed they'd gotten there when he had tried to revive her.

Izzy's parents had been separated, and her former husband was not a suspect. He had remarried and moved to Alberta, and he'd been proven to be home at the time of the murder.

There were many other smaller details, the investigation having taken place over a period of months. But the case had never been solved, and no other viable suspects had been found.

Hank sat back again, rubbed his chin, and stared at the monitor. Though not entirely unheard of, shaving the victim's head was not a common occurrence in murder cases. That was why it had stuck in the back of his mind.

The physical evidence for this case would've been stored away long ago, and he'd wanted to see what it consisted of. And he might need to talk with the detective who'd been in charge of the original investigation.

He glanced up as Detective King came through the precinct doors, crossed the floor, and headed down a hallway at the back of the room. King was likely headed for the break room, one of his favorite spots.

A voice sounded behind him. "Hank." It was Callaway calling.

Hank spun around. The young cop was waving a stack of papers. Hank rolled his chair over and took the printouts.

"I got some pretty clear shots," Callaway said, motioning toward the stack. "Some are a little fuzzy, but I think you can get a pretty good idea."

"Thanks, Callaway," Hank said. He wheeled back, dropped the papers onto his desk, and thumbed through them.

Most of the images were of men. There was an occasional woman, generally in the company of a male companion. Others had exited the establishment in groups of two or three.

Hank stopped, leaned in, and smiled grimly. He'd be several years older now, but the face in front of Hank's eyes sure looked like the same attractive face, with high cheekbones and dark, deep-set eyes, that stared at him from his monitor.

The face of Izzy Wilde.

And the timestamp on the printout showed him leaving

Phil's just before nine o'clock the previous evening—a few minutes before Olivia Bragg had left.

Hank continued to leaf through the papers. At timestamp 9:07 p.m., an image of Olivia's face had been captured as she'd exited the building.

Was it a coincidence? Hank didn't think so. In fact, he knew a judge wouldn't think so either, and it would be enough to get a search warrant for Izzy Wilde's place of residence.

Hank turned back to the computer and found Wilde's address. According to his driver's license, he still resided in the same house on the northern outskirts of the city where he'd lived all his life—the house where his mother had been found murdered.

King approached Hank's desk, slouched back in the guest chair, and dropped a sneakered shoe on the corner of the desk. He sipped at a coffee and looked at Hank.

Hank frowned at the foot and then looked at King. "We might have our killer," he said.

King's eyes widened. "Already?"

Hank swiveled the monitor so King could see the photos, held up the printout, and explained what he had discovered. "It's too much of a coincidence that Wilde would be at the same restaurant at that time, especially given the circumstances of his mother's murder."

King whistled. "It's the shaved head that tells the real story. If we can get him for this killing, it might lead to getting him for the murder of his mother."

"That's what I'm hoping," Hank said. "It's always nice to clean up a cold case."

"Should we pick him up and see what he has to say?"

"We don't have enough for an arrest. It's all circumstantial evidence. But it's enough to bring this guy in for an interview. And I'm sure we can get a search warrant for the house and property."

King grinned, slipped his foot off the desk, and stood, heading away. "Let me know when you get the warrant, Hank. I'll be in the break room."

Hank rolled his eyes and slipped open a drawer, then turned his head and called, "King."

King turned back.

"Did you talk to the woman who found the body?"

King shrugged. "Talked to her. Didn't get anything other than what was already in her statement."

"What about the dog? Did you find the owner?"

"No. She said the dog ran off right after she called 9-1-1."

Hank nodded and turned back to his desk. He filled out the paperwork for the warrant, slipped it into his briefcase, and headed off to find a judge.

CHAPTER 10

Tuesday, 3:17 p.m.

HANK FOLLOWED CLOSE behind as half a dozen cruisers streamed up Whistler Road, their lights flashing, their sirens off.

It was uncertain whether or not Izzy Wilde would be home. The front office of Richmond Printing, where Wilde worked as a warehouse assistant, confirmed he hadn't clocked in that morning. Apparently, it was nothing unusual, and the talkative receptionist had informed Hank that Wilde was on the short list to be replaced.

Hank considered the evidence against Izzy Wilde. It was all circumstantial, but his gut told him it was more than that. He didn't want to take any chances and allow the suspect to get away.

The vehicles drove silently up the long gravel lane leading to the century-old house. A rusty pickup sat on the grass in front of the building, a couple of other cars nearby, one up on blocks. Grass had grown up around the tires. Hank would leave them until last; they hadn't been moved recently.

He pulled his car up by the side of the house and he and King stepped out. Officers poured from their vehicles and surrounded the building, their weapons drawn. They would guard against any attempt Wilde might make to escape should he be inside.

Hank glanced around the property. The lane came to a stop at an old garage, fifty feet past the house. Once covered with light blue paint, the exterior was now chipped and faded. He motioned toward the building and a pair of cops sprang into action. They would check for a vehicle inside and secure the garage.

A hundred feet off to the left, an ancient shed stood alone, nestled in among a group of young trees. Tire tracks had worn a rutted path across the lawn in the direction of the building. Hank motioned toward the shed, directing a pair of officers to secure it. He'd give it a thorough search later.

He and King approached the door of the house and Hank knocked. "RHPD. Open the door." He stood back and waited a moment.

A second knock went unanswered, and King touched Hank's shoulder. "Stand back, Hank. I'll break it down."

Hank chuckled. "Good luck with that, King. That door's stronger than you are." He beckoned to an officer. The cop removed a battering ram from the trunk of his cruiser, and in a moment, the frame shattered, the latch snapped loose, and the door swung inward.

Hank led the way into the building, King directly behind

him, four officers following. A few minutes later, the officers had cleared the house and returned to the foyer.

"No one here, Hank."

Hank nodded grimly, then turned to King and pointed toward a wooden staircase leading to the second floor. "We need to look for any evidence Olivia Bragg might've been held here. Check the bedrooms."

As King headed upstairs, Hank found the doorway to the basement leading off from the kitchen. He opened the door, fumbled inside for a light switch, and flicked it on. A faint glow at the bottom of the steps lit up the aged wooden stairs.

Hank drew his weapon and proceeded with caution down the steps. The basement was divided into two rooms, and after glancing around the dusty space, he crossed the pitted floor and pushed open a door that led to another area.

He flicked on his Maglite and stepped inside the dark room. The space appeared to be used for storage—junk, really. Sagging lamps, broken chairs, and piles of castoffs lay on makeshift shelving or heaped on the floor.

He went back to the main room and peeked, prodded, and poked into boxes and cupboards, soon coming to the conclusion that if Izzy Wilde was the killer, he wasn't using the basement for his deadly activities.

He returned to the main floor, where King was digging through the kitchen cupboards.

"Find anything, King?"

King slammed a cupboard door and turned around. He shook his head, leaned against the counter, and tucked his hands into his pockets. "Nothing. There're four bedrooms upstairs, and one of them appears to be in use. Looks like Wilde's. The rest are half-empty and filled with dust. Couldn't find anything in Wilde's drawers or closet that ties him to the murder."

"Nothing in the basement, either," Hank said. "We'll check the rest of the buildings."

They stepped outside and crossed the driveway, and Hank motioned toward the shed. A cop stood near the front door of the windowless building. The other one was undoubtedly at the back making sure it was secure.

"We'll search there first," Hank said. He crouched down and pointed at tire tracks that had furrowed their way through the grass. "There's been a vehicle through here. Recently."

A gunshot sounded and Hank jerked his head up. The officer at the front of the shed hit the ground, and the door of the building burst open. A masked figure ran out, heading across an open field toward a forested area some ways off.

King leaped into action, drawing his weapon as he raced toward the shooter. The other cop appeared from behind the building and joined the chase, his weapon out and ready.

Running to the fallen cop, Hank came to a stop and crouched down. The officer had been hit point blank in the chest. His vest had saved his life, but he was going to be in a lot of pain for some time.

The cop opened his eyes, groaned, and blinked a few times. "I'm okay."

"Can you breathe?" Hank asked.

The cop gave a weak nod.

Hank slipped out his phone and made a call. "Ambulance

is on its way," he said. "Don't try to move. You're gonna be all right."

The officer turned his eyes toward the building. "He shot me right through a hole."

Hank looked at the swinging door. The bullet had chipped away fresh splinters as it made its way through a knothole, chest high. The cop had never seen it coming.

He glanced toward the chase. King was gaining some ground, but it wouldn't be enough. The shooter had a long head start, and it appeared he was going to make it to the trees in safety.

Then the fugitive stopped and spun around, aimed his weapon toward his pursuers, and took a shot. King hit the ground, rolled, and was up a moment later. The shooter had missed, and King continued on, the other cop lagging behind. Hank knew his partner would persevere until he was convinced the chase was futile.

Later, Hank would organize a manhunt, but he didn't expect it to be productive. If they had a helicopter, they would stand a better chance, but he didn't see that in the near future. The department was always strapped for cash, and by the time they could scrounge one up from Toronto, it would be nothing more than a waste of time.

He stood and turned his attention to the shed. He stepped inside and flashed his light around, spying a switch inside the door. He flicked it on, flooded the building with light, and Hank's mouth dropped open.

They had the right man. Hank had no doubt.

An area on the far wall was covered with long locks of

black hair secured to the unpainted drywall with packing tape. Hank approached a homemade workbench along the right wall. An electric razor sat on top, still plugged into an extension cord winding its way to an outlet on the wall.

A woman's handbag hung from a hook above the bench. Hank had no doubt it belonged to Olivia Bragg. A coil of rope hung beside it.

In the middle of the floor, with wisps of hair surrounding it, stood a sturdy wooden chair. Bits of rope clung to the arms and legs. Wilde's victim had no doubt sat in that chair, been shaved and probably strangled to death in the same spot before being transported to the park and dumped.

Hank turned his attention to a cot against the left wall. It was covered by a plain white sheet, a pillow at one end. The bed appeared to have been slept in. Hank frowned, attempting to understand its significance. Would Wilde be sleeping here, surrounded by his trophies, or was it meant for someone else?

Had he tied his victim to the bed and spent the night guarding her, finally killing her the next day?

Hank snapped a few pictures with his cell phone, being careful not to touch anything. CSI would soon be called in to document the contents of the building in detail.

A cop poked his head into the doorway. "There's a car in the garage, Hank."

"Be right there," Hank said. He took a last glance around and left the building. He'd seen enough.

He went to the garage and peered through a dusty side window. A midsized car sat in the darkened building. He couldn't tell what make it was, but it would soon be towed in and gone over thoroughly.

Hank returned to the house and glanced across the lawn. King strode toward him and stepped onto the driveway, shaking his head, a grim look on his face.

"Lost him, Hank."

"We'll get him," Hank said. He filled his partner in on what he'd discovered in the shed.

King's eyes narrowed. "I should've shot him in the back when I had the chance."

"Maybe he deserves it," Hank said. "But he's not worth getting an early retirement over." Hank crossed his arms, frowned toward the trees, and repeated, "We'll get him."

CHAPTER 11

Tuesday, 5:54 p.m.

JAKE HUNG UP HIS CELL phone and tucked it into his shirt pocket. He'd just talked to Hank, and the cop had filled him in on the events of the afternoon. Jake was concerned that, although they'd almost nabbed the suspect, he was still on the loose and possibly more dangerous than ever.

Hank had issued a BOLO for the fugitive as well as organizing a manhunt in the neighborhood of Izzy Wilde's residence and the forest beyond. But there were a lot of places to hide.

Jake went into the office where Annie sat at her desk, going over her scant notes of the case. She leaned forward, her brow furrowed, as Jake filled her in on Hank's phone call.

"We have to talk to Carter Wilde," Annie said when Jake had finished. "If he's the only family left, Izzy might turn to him."

"Hank already talked to him," Jake said. "Carter claims to

have no knowledge of his brother's whereabouts. Says he hasn't been in contact with him for several months."

Annie leaned back and frowned. "There's no use in us going to Izzy's house. The cops aren't going to let us poke around the shed. It's a crime scene. And I'm sure the house'll be off-limits as well." She paused. "We need to come up with something else."

"He could be anywhere," Jake said.

"He has to be somewhere."

"Between Hank and King, they'll either talk to, or visit, everyone Izzy knew," Jake said. "There's not much point in us covering the same ground."

"I don't know enough about Izzy to know how intelligent he is, but if he murdered his mother and got away with it, he must have something going for him."

"What's your point?" Jake asked.

"I'm sure Izzy knows the police would be visiting his brother right away. He might stay away until then, but I think he'll contact him as soon as he feels safe."

"If he does," Jake said, "it's because he knows his brother won't turn him in."

"Maybe. Maybe not."

"Perhaps I should stake out Carter Wilde's place," Jake said.

"That's my point," Annie said with a smile. "I know you don't like stakeouts much, but do you have a better idea?"

Jake shook his head. "Nothing I can think of right now."

"I'd go with you," Annie said, "but I have no one to watch

Matty tonight. Chrissy's not home and I don't wanna call my mother."

Jake sighed and stood. "Get me a picture of the two of them as well as Carter Wilde's address. I'll round up what I need."

He picked a shoulder bag off a shelf in the office and dropped in a pair of binoculars along with a Nikon digital camera. He went to the kitchen, grabbed some bottles of water from the fridge, put them in the bag, and went back to the office.

Annie handed him a folder and he flipped it open. It contained black-and-white photos of the brothers along with their addresses. "That was fast," he said.

"Not when you know the right people. I gave Callaway a call and he emailed them to me."

Jake tucked the folder into the duffel bag, zipped it up, and slung it over his shoulder. "Don't know when I'll be back," he said, strolling from the office.

He poked his head back in a moment later. "And I'm taking your car."

He grabbed Annie's keys from a wicker basket on the kitchen counter, and two minutes later, he pulled her Ford Escort from the driveway. The Firebird would draw too much attention, especially during daylight hours, and it was important to remain as nondescript as possible.

As he drove, Jake kept one eye on the road while he studied the information Annie had obtained. Carter Wilde lived in an apartment at 1166 Red Ridge Street where he'd been the superintendent for some time. The apartment building was in a growing part of the city, about a mile from the outskirts and the old house where Izzy Wilde lived.

When Jake arrived, he pulled into the visitors' parking area and backed into a spot. He had a good view of the front door and would be able to see anyone coming and going.

The building, stretching up eight stories, appeared to be a recent addition to the city, possibly built within the past five years or so. The lawns and greenery were well maintained, with a large grassy area set aside for the residents' use. A handful of people sat at a picnic table nearby, enjoying their surroundings as they consumed their evening meal.

He pushed the driver seat back to its limit, removed the binoculars from the shoulder bag, and settled in for a long wait.

Residents came and went, cars pulled in and out of the underground parking lot, and Jake zoomed in on everything that moved. If Izzy Wilde came to see his brother, Jake was determined to nab him.

But Wilde never showed up, and two hours later, Jake yawned, finished off another bottle of water, and got out of the car to stretch his cramping legs.

That's when he saw Izzy Wilde's face for the first time.

A car turned off the street, drove into the circle driveway, and rattled toward Jake. The driver glanced his way, then leaned into the steering wheel and stepped hard on the gas. Jake dove for the Escort, grabbed the binoculars, and zoomed in on the driver's face as the vehicle circled the driveway, heading back to the street.

There was no doubt. Jake had studied the printout, and

the driver of the car was definitely the fugitive. But where had he gotten the vehicle? It was an old Honda—probably a dozen years old—and by the sound of the engine, it was ready to be recycled.

Jake started the Escort and spun from the lot. He steered with one hand, grabbed the camera with the other, and zoomed in on the license plate of the fleeing vehicle. He memorized the plate number, snapped a picture, and dropped the camera onto the passenger seat.

He shoved the gas pedal to the floor, and though the Escort breezed along at a brisk pace, Izzy was pushing the Honda to the limit, and Jake wasn't gaining any ground. Now he wished he'd brought the Firebird.

He took out his cell phone and dialed Hank. A direct call to the detective would be faster than going through 9-1-1 and waiting for dispatch to get the message.

"Detective Hank Corning."

"Hank, it's Jake. I'm following Izzy Wilde. He's driving a beat-up Honda, but I might lose him. Ontario plates 719 SDX. It's ten or so years old. Navy blue. He just left his brother's apartment building, heading south."

"Hold on."

Jake put his cell on speaker and propped it up against the dashboard as the Honda made a right turn a block ahead of him. Jake slowed for a jaywalker, then hit the gas and pulled a right turn. He peered through the windshield and slapped the steering wheel. Wilde was gone. Jake continued on, checking both directions at the next intersection, but the Honda was nowhere to be seen.

He drove another block, took a left, and glanced around.

Hank came back on the phone. "Dispatch has sent all available units to the area and issued a BOLO for the vehicle."

"I don't see him anywhere," Jake said. "But he can't be far away."

"Stay on the phone."

Jake peered in all directions, hoping to see the elusive vehicle. At the next street, he took a wide left and there it was, stopped halfway onto the curb, the driver door hanging open. Jake ground to a stop beside it, grabbed his phone, and jumped from the Escort.

Izzy Wilde was tearing across the front lawn of the adjacent house. He scrambled over a high wooden fence and disappeared from view.

"He's on foot," Jake said into the phone, racing across the grass. "He dumped the car."

Jake vaulted over the fence as Wilde hit the next street, crossed over and ran to his left, out of view.

Jake followed, stepped onto the sidewalk, and scanned the area. He squinted at a figure ambling toward him. It wasn't Wilde.

The fugitive was gone.

"I'm on Silverpine," Jake said into the phone. "I've lost him."

Dozens of houses lined the street, and Izzy could be hidden from view behind any of them. The suspect seemed to know he was being chased, and he'd be determined to get out of the area as soon as possible.

"Cruisers will be there shortly," Hank said.

Jake sprinted up the street, hoping to see the wanted man, but it was futile. He jogged back to the Escort, gave Hank the location of the abandoned vehicle, and drove around a few minutes longer. Cruisers had now arrived and were patrolling the streets.

Half an hour later, Jake was convinced the slippery fugitive had eluded capture once again.

CHAPTER 12

Tuesday, 8:35 p.m.

LISA KRUNK WAS FUMING. She hadn't been able to get any comment from Detective Corning that morning regarding the murdered woman in the park. She had planned to corner him when he left the scene, but he'd somehow managed to slip away and leave her hanging.

Though he'd circled the entire area, Don had been unable to get any actual shots of the victim. The real action had taken place behind a group of trees, and she'd had to settle for some almost useless footage of cops milling about behind the taped-off park. And though Don had captured the sheet-covered gurney as it had been taken to the coroner's van, it would be insufficient to satisfy her multitude of waiting fans.

A trip to Izzy Wilde's place of residence had netted her nothing useful. She'd been denied access to the property, and from the road there was little to see, even with Don's powerful zoom lens.

As the best reporter in the city, probably in the country, she felt slighted that someone of her stature should be pushed aside. Her unequalled investigative skills had aided the police many times in the past, and though she'd always demanded something in return for her efforts, she'd often been indispensable to their investigations.

There was no doubt her stories often appeared to cast the police department in a bad light, but surely Hank understood she was just doing her job. There was nothing personal about it.

The worst part of this case was, if it weren't for her contact in the police department, she wouldn't even have the victim's and suspect's names.

But the names were a start. And though the murder would be old news before long, she was determined to breathe new life into it, so to speak.

She'd found out the suspect had a brother living close by, and it didn't take her long to track him down. An interview with him would be better than nothing, and she might be able to piece together a juicy story to lead off the eleven o'clock news.

She had to pay Carter Wilde a visit. There wasn't much else she could do.

Don swung the Channel 7 Action News van into the parking lot of 1166 Red Ridge Street and hopped out. Lisa waited while he grabbed his equipment from the back of the vehicle and dropped the camera onto his shoulder. She slammed the passenger door and strode to the entranceway of the apartment building, Don struggling to keep up.

She evaded the security lock by slipping into the main lobby of the building behind a little old lady who was kind enough to hold the door open for them.

The building superintendent usually had an apartment on the main floor, and this building was no exception. She went to apartment 101, took a deep breath, and rapped on the door. She raised her head, looked down her thin, sharp nose and waited.

The door swung open and a man appeared, his brow raised in question. "Yes?"

Lisa gave her best smile, her generous mouth revealing a row of perfect teeth. "Carter Wilde?" she asked.

"Yes."

She studied his face. A well-trimmed beard decorated his square jaw. He had a receding hairline, with a widow's peak pointing toward his strong nose.

"I'm Lisa Krunk from Channel 7 Action News. May I talk to you about your brother?"

She steeled herself for an immediate refusal, the usual first response. On occasions like this, the trick was to get her target to open up—not always an easy task. Oddly enough, the ones who were familiar with her were usually the hardest to crack.

But not this time.

His reaction caught her off guard. He stroked his beard and smiled. "Come in." He took a step back and motioned for them to enter.

Lisa stepped inside, Don behind her. Wilde held a cane in his right hand and walked with a visible limp as he led the way into a large modern living room.

He pointed toward a couch, dropped his sturdily built body into a comfortable chair, and set his cane beside him, his right leg stretched out in a straight line. He brushed back his short hair, rested his arms on the armrests, and smiled at his guests. "Please call me Carter."

Lisa avoided the couch and pulled up a wooden chair sitting against the wall. She pushed it in front of Wilde, sat down, and switched on her cordless mike. The camera hummed beside her and its red light glowed.

"Carter," she began, shoving the mike at him. "As I'm sure you're aware, your brother's a suspect in the murder of Olivia Bragg."

Carter's smile faded and he nodded. "A detective came to see me earlier. It's a sad situation. Unfortunately, I wasn't able to help him with anything useful."

"When was the last time you saw your brother?"

The man shook his head and frowned in thought. "It's been several months." He let out a light sigh. "He might be my brother, but we've never been close. He's always been odd."

Lisa leaned forward. "Odd? In what way?"

Carter pursed his lips. "I don't want to reveal too much of our family history. Let's just say he has a lot of quirks. He's three years younger than me, and though boys often try to emulate an older brother, with him it was too much. After my mother … died, I had to break all ties with him and move out of the house."

Lisa was getting to the meat of the story at last. "You were eighteen when your mother was murdered, is that right?"

Carter nodded. "That's when I moved out. I couldn't stay there any longer after that."

"Your brother Izzy was suspected to have been the killer. What's your take on that?"

Carter leaned forward, massaged his game leg, then sat back again. "I don't think it was him. He was sincerely heartbroken. Clung to me even more after that."

"Even after the murder of Olivia Bragg, you still believe someone else killed your mother?"

Carter took a deep breath. "I don't know what to believe anymore."

"The police think he did it."

"The police don't know Izzy the way I do."

Lisa narrowed her eyes and spoke into the mike. "Carter, did your brother murder Olivia Bragg?"

Carter hesitated, glared down at the mike now held under his nose, and spoke in a soft voice. "I don't know."

Lisa studied his face. His look told her the whole story. Carter was convinced his brother was guilty.

"Do you know where he might be hiding out?" she asked.

"No idea. He has very few friends as far as I know. Maybe none. And if he can't go back to the house, then he could be anywhere."

"Has he tried to contact you?"

"No. I don't see any reason for him to be in touch with me." He shrugged. "I'll let the police figure it out."

The interview was interesting, but Lisa hadn't gotten anything sensational. She needed something more. It was time for a whopper of a lie.

"Carter, certain stories claim you and your brother were both involved in the murder of your mother. Is there any truth to that?"

The man frowned deeply. "Where did you hear that? It's ridiculous."

"Just rumors," Lisa said. She was finding it hard to get this guy upset, and so far she hadn't even secured a sound bite she could take out of context and build a story around.

She sat back, flicked off the mike, and looked at Don. She drew a finger across her throat and the camera blinked off. She leaned forward, smiled at Carter, and spoke in a low voice. "What I want is to interview your brother. If you can put me in contact with him, I'd be grateful. Any information you can give me will be completely off the record."

Carter's spoke in a steady voice. "I'm sorry, Ms. Krunk. I don't know where he is." He picked up his cane and struggled to his feet. "And now, if there're no more questions, I have things to take care of." He smiled down at her. "But perhaps when this is all over, we could discuss it further over a drink."

Lisa stood slowly and faked another smile. "Thank you, Carter." She thought fast. "Perhaps we might," she said, knowing it was out of the question. As handsome as Carter Wilde was, she wasn't about to get involved with someone who had such a seriously dysfunctional family history. She decided to leave it open-ended. She might have further use for him. "I'll let you know."

She turned and snapped her fingers at Don. The cameraman produced a business card from his pocket and held it out. She took the card and set it on a small table by

Carter's chair. "If you change your mind about setting me up with an interview, please give me a call."

Carter limped to the door and saw them out, closing the door behind them.

Lisa led the way out of the building to the van. She climbed inside, more frustrated now than before. The interview had been a flop, and she seriously doubted if she could put a story together that would be the least bit compelling.

Her dedicated fans would have to wait another day, but she was determined not to let them down. She'd make something of this story yet, one way or another.

CHAPTER 13

Tuesday, 11:44 p.m.

LINDY METZ SMILED, her dark brown eyes sparkling as she smiled and waved goodbye. She walked down the path to the sidewalk, hugging her handbag, and thought about the thirty dollars she'd earned babysitting that evening.

In the whole scheme of things, it wasn't a lot of money, but after adding it to the growing amount in her bank account, she'd be that much closer to her goal. College tuition was costly, but every penny she could save would reduce the size of the student loan she'd require.

Her parents weren't well off, but they'd promised to kick in as much as they could scrape up, fully supporting her dream to be a personal care aide. She loved the thought of helping to take care of those who needed a little extra love and encouragement to live a full and happy life.

She stepped off the sidewalk, crossed the parking lot of a strip plaza, and went into a 7-Eleven. She treated herself to a

French vanilla iced coffee—her favorite. Suppressing the impulse to buy a slice of pizza, she left the shop, sipping at her drink.

She turned down the next street. The house where she lived with her parents was three blocks away, and after the heat of the day, she enjoyed the cool evening walk.

Lindy turned her head as a car drove by. It pulled over half a block ahead and the lights died. A man got out and stepped onto the sidewalk, carrying a plastic grocery bag in one hand. It slipped from his grasp and fell to the sidewalk.

He crouched down to gather up his belongings as she drew closer. Now only a few feet away, he stood, the bag in his hand.

"Good evening," he said, a wide smile crossing his face.

She smiled back as he stepped aside to let her pass. But she didn't get past. He took a step toward her and slipped the bag over her head, his strong hands tightening it around her neck.

Her attempts to scream were stifled by the lack of air in the bag and the viselike grip around her throat. Her drink hit the sidewalk, the cool liquid splashing her legs as she grabbed frantically at his wrists and struggled to free herself.

She grew weak, her head faint from lack of oxygen. He spun her around, and she fought to hold her footing as he wrapped an arm about her neck and dragged her off the sidewalk. She stumbled over the curb, twisted her right leg, and felt a sharp pain in her ankle.

He hissed in her ear. "Stay still or I'll kill you."

A ring of keys jingled, the trunk of his vehicle popped

open, and he pushed her inside. Her head struck the lid, stunning her, and she fell to her back. She clawed at the suffocating bag, ripped it loose, and took a deep gasp of air as the trunk lid slammed.

She screamed, "Help!" Her muffled voice echoed in the confined area. "Help!"

A car door closed, the muffler rumbled beneath her, and the vehicle pulled away. Tires whined as the car gathered speed.

Panic engulfed her, and her heart raced, thumping uncontrollably in her chest. She lay on her back and took deep breaths to clear her mind. What would her father tell her to do? He had taught her to remain calm in any emergency, to try to relax and think her way through.

A weapon. She needed something to protect herself with. Anything she could use against him when he opened the trunk. If he ever did.

Lindy scrambled to her knees and searched in the darkness, but found nothing she could use. The trunk was absolutely empty.

All attempts to find an interior latch went unrewarded. Until he opened the lid, there was no way out of the trunk.

She was at his mercy, overwhelmed by a sense of total helplessness, and she fought back a sudden surge of hysteria.

Why had he chosen her? She'd walked down that street in her quiet neighborhood many times, often late at night, and never sensed any danger. Nothing like this had ever happened to anyone she knew.

She rummaged through the pocket of her jeans and pulled

out her key ring. It was all she had to protect herself. She held the keys in her right hand, one key protruding between her fingers, her fist tightened around the rest.

Then an idea struck her. She'd heard on a TV show that if you were kidnapped and held in the trunk of a car, the best thing was to break out the taillight. She'd never expected to be in such a situation, and though it seemed like a long shot, it was worth a try.

She twisted around and lay on her back, facing the rear of the vehicle. From her awkward position, she managed to work one foot forward and back, forward and back, kicking like a piston at the faint glow of the taillight. It wasn't as easy as they'd made it sound on TV, and she only managed to make a lot of noise. Nothing gave way.

A muffled voice sounded through the backseat. Her kidnapper had heard her banging, and by the tone of his voice, he was angry. Good.

She had another idea. She spun around and, using her keys, she ripped at the lining covering the backseat of the vehicle. Maybe she could work her way through. He was still cursing as she tugged at the small hole she'd made and tore the fabric away. It wasn't much, but it was a start.

Lindy braced her back and kicked at the seat. She had no idea what she'd do if she managed to break through, but anything that played havoc with his plans was a good thing. A moment later she felt something give. The seat rattled as she kicked, but it held, and he was getting angrier.

She screamed as she worked at the seat, adding to the noise, and adding to his rage. His anger made her calmer. She was disrupting his plans, and the racket wouldn't go unheard if anyone happened to be close by.

His cursing stopped as the vehicle took a sudden turn, throwing Lindy to one side. Then tires screeched and the car came to a quick stop. A door opened and slammed, and her kidnapper muttered something as his footsteps sounded by the side of the vehicle.

He might be angry enough to kill her on the spot, just to shut her up. Lindy had but one shot. Only one chance.

She twisted to face the rear of the vehicle and crouched down with her head against the lid, the keys gripped in her fist. She waited.

The trunk lid opened. She sprang upright and swung her arm with all her strength. Her aim was accurate, and the protruding key raked her abductor's face. His eyes widened, his breath shot out, and he stumbled backwards.

Lindy jumped from the trunk, clenched her teeth, and swung again. He ducked to avoid her onslaught and lost his balance, went down, and hit the asphalt with one shoulder.

Now was her chance.

The dark side street stretched out in front of her. To her right were rows of houses. Dead ahead was nothing but a long expanse of asphalt.

She turned to run, but a shooting pain in her ankle made her leg buckle, and she fell heavily to one knee. She heard him scramble to his feet behind her, and she managed to rise, wincing at each careful step. Then renewed pain caused her to stumble, and she sagged to the sidewalk.

A hand covered her mouth and she tasted his sweat. She

shook her head and worked her jaw, struggling to open her mouth enough to clamp her teeth into his fingers.

He howled as she bit down and held on, the taste of his warm blood now in her mouth. A sudden blow to the side of her head stunned her, and he pulled his hand from the grip of her teeth, grasped her long black ponytail, and dragged her to her feet.

Lindy fought back another surge of panic. She was terrified, but if she let her fear overcome her, she'd have no chance of escape. She was determined to give it all she had.

She screamed, and her abductor repeated his mistake. This time she was ready for him, and as he clamped his hand over her mouth, she sank her teeth into his flesh, this time to the bone.

He howled and worked his hand free. Lindy spun around. Her abductor stood with his mouth gaping, his eyes wide, gazing at the blood dripping from his injured hand and pooling on the pavement at his feet.

She disregarded the pain in her ankle and stumbled toward the sidewalk. Then a car door slammed and an engine roared. As she succumbed to exhaustion and crumpled to the ground, through her dimming eyes she saw her abductor drive out of sight.

She had won.

CHAPTER 14

DAY 3 - Wednesday, 7:35 a.m.

THE MURDER OF OLIVIA Bragg had weighed heavily on Annie's mind most of the night, and she'd been up with the sun. With the police manhunt underway, it was a matter of time before Izzy Wilde was apprehended, but she feared what could happen in the meantime. The almost ritual murder, the way the body had been posed in the park, and the trophies found in the shed, were all hallmarks of a serial killer.

That meant Wilde could very well strike again, and she had tasked herself with finding out who and why. But with little to go on, she was getting nowhere.

It appeared she wasn't going to get the much-needed rest she yearned for anytime soon.

She closed the file folder, pushed it aside, and leaned back in her chair when Jake stepped into the office. Clad in a towel around his waist, his rippling muscles glistened with sweat from his intensive daily workout. He polished off a bottle of water, let out a loud satisfied breath, and grinned at her.

"You were up early," he said.

"Couldn't sleep," Annie said. "Too much on my mind."

Jake nodded with understanding. "We'll find him," he said as he turned to leave the office. "I'll take a shower and we'll get back at it as soon as Matty's off to school."

Annie heard her son already rustling around in the kitchen. She'd have to put her thoughts aside until after breakfast and tend to her boys. Though they were capable of taking care of themselves, and often did, she loved to pamper them.

She rose from her chair and went into the kitchen. Matty sat at the table, beeps, chimes, and ringing sounds coming from an iPad gripped in one hand, his eyes glued to the screen.

Annie pulled back a chair, sat sideways, and watched the expression on his face change with each triumph. Then his shoulders slumped as the universal sound of "Game Over" came from the iPad.

"What's up, Mom?" he said, setting the tablet down and turning toward his mother.

She smiled. "Nothing."

"Why're you staring at me like that?"

"Because I love you."

He frowned. "That doesn't even make sense."

Annie laughed and stood. "Someday it will."

Matty wandered from the room and Annie turned to making breakfast. As the bacon sizzled in the pan, she thought about Izzy Wilde and his brother Carter. It was clear that Izzy had attempted to visit the apartment building where

Carter lived. Whether or not the two brothers had met in the last couple of days was unknown, but with no one else to turn to, and with his home under police control, Izzy might've been looking to his brother for some refuge.

Annie laid the finished bacon on paper towels and broke some eggs into the pan. Jake wandered into the room, Matty trudging behind. The boy dropped his backpack beside the fridge and sat opposite his father.

"I've been thinking about Izzy," Annie said as she flipped the eggs. "And I don't think he'll return to his brother's."

"Maybe not," Jake said. "I don't know how bright he is, but it should be obvious the police'll be watching Carter closely."

Matty leaned forward and picked up his fork when his mother set a plate in front of him. "Is this another bad guy you're trying to catch?"

Annie brought two more plates, sat at the end of the table, and pulled in her chair. "There's no shortage of bad guys."

"Is he a killer?"

Annie sighed. "Unfortunately, yes."

"You and Uncle Hank'll get him," Matty said matter-of-factly. "You guys are good at that."

"I hope so," Annie said. She prayed Matty was right, and that Izzy would be caught sooner rather than later.

When they finished their breakfast, a tapping sounded on the back door.

"It's Kyle," Matty said. Kyle was Matty's best friend, the eight-year-old son of Annie's friend Chrissy, who lived next door to the Lincolns.

Matty pushed back from the table, ran to the door, and pulled it open. "Hey, Kyle."

Kyle stepped inside and sported a wide grin, his backpack over his shoulder. "Hi, Mrs. Lincoln. Hi, Mr. Lincoln," he said and followed Matty from the kitchen without waiting for an answer. The boys would be leaving for school in a few minutes, and they would walk the two blocks.

Jake stood and gathered up the dishes, setting them in the sink. He sat back down and leaned forward, resting his arms on the table. "What's on the agenda for today?"

"I'd like to drop by and see Hank later this morning," Annie said. "Between the three of us, we might be able to come up with something."

~*~

HANK PUSHED his plate aside, leaned forward at the table, and looked at Amelia. He hadn't seen much of her lately, and this early-morning breakfast at a nearby cafe might be all the time he could manage to spend with his uncomplaining girlfriend for a few days. His hectic schedule was crazy enough, but with a killer on the loose, his free hours were going to be at a minimum for an unknown period of time.

Amelia dabbed at her lips with a napkin, folded it with care, and laid it on her plate. "Thank you for breakfast, Hank."

Hank grinned, reached across the table, and smothered her small hand with his. "My pleasure. I only wish we had more time."

"More time would be nice," she said in her usual sweet, soft voice. "But the first time I met you, I knew you were dedicated to your job." She placed her other hand on his and gave him an understanding smile. "I knew what I was getting into." She laughed a quiet, wonderful little laugh. "If I was a teenager, I might be jealous of your work."

Hank sat back and sighed lightly. He was nuts over this woman. Though he'd only known her a short time, he could see himself spending the rest of his life with her. He was pretty sure she felt the same, and one of these days, he was going to pop the question. Just when, he wasn't sure, but he knew that coming home to her, even though their time together might be sketchy, would be a lot better than going home to an empty apartment.

Hank glanced at his watch and wondered where all the time had gone. He had to be at work soon. "We'd better go," he said with regret, signaling the waitress for the bill.

A bubbly young girl approached the table, a wide smile on her pretty face. "There you go, Detective," she said, setting the bill down. She smiled at Amelia and said, "Nice to see you again," and went to take care of another customer.

Hank dropped some bills on the table, leaving a nice tip, and followed Amelia to his vehicle. He creaked open the passenger door for her, closed it with care, then got in the driver side.

He drove the few blocks to Amelia's near-mansion, pulled into the driveway behind her Mercedes, and was reminded how much he loved her even more for not noticing the wreck he drove.

After walking her to the door and giving her an extended goodbye kiss, he drove for work, forcing himself to turn his mind to the job at hand. He had to catch a killer.

When he arrived at the precinct, he was surprised to see Detective King's car parked in the lot. That was unusual. His partner usually wandered in sometime after nine.

Hank went into the precinct and headed for his desk. Callaway eyed him as he approached, and the young whiz came over, waving a sheet of paper. "Got a hit on Wilde's car. Turns out it was bought for cash yesterday through an online ad site."

Hank sat, pulled in his chair, and took the paper from Callaway. He gave it a brief glance. "The ownership papers weren't even changed over."

"Guess he didn't have time."

"Or didn't bother, knowing he was a wanted man." Hank set the printout down on the side of his desk. "Thanks, Callaway."

Callaway grunted and left.

Hank would get King to pay a visit to the prior owner of the car, though he didn't expect it would help much. They already knew who was in possession of the vehicle. Not that Hank doubted Jake had correctly identified Izzy Wilde as the driver, but Hank liked to be thorough. Sometimes valuable leads came from the most improbable sources.

Detective King wandered over, tossed a file folder onto Hank's desk, and dropped into the guest chair.

Hank flipped the folder open. "What's this?"

King cocked a foot on the corner of Hank's desk, tilted his

head back, and drained his coffee cup. He belched once, set the cup down, and squinted at Hank.

"Pretty sure it's related. An attempted kidnapping late last night."

Hank scanned the police report taken by an officer in the wee hours of the morning. Seventeen-year-old Lindy Metz had been found lying unconscious on the sidewalk of a poorly lit side street. The passerby had called 9-1-1, and an ambulance had taken Lindy to the hospital. An officer had interviewed her shortly thereafter, then she had been released, and the young woman's parents had taken her home.

King motioned toward the folder. "Take a look at the photo. She looks a lot like Olivia Bragg. I think it's the same guy."

"Then why'd he let her go?"

"There's another report there," King said, pointing. "The guy who found her said he saw a car taking off in an almighty hurry. I think our Good Samaritan came along just in time to scare off the perp."

Hank leafed through the papers. "Give me a few minutes to study this, then we'll pay them both a visit."

CHAPTER 15

Wednesday, 10:49 a.m.

ANNIE HAD GIVEN HANK a call on his cell phone a little earlier. The cop was in the middle of an interview, but he fully expected to be back at his desk by 10:30.

She'd also taken a call from her mother, and for once she'd been happy to say she would be extremely busy all day and would have no time for a visit. Annie would sooner put in long hours, even a day of drudgery, than spend more than a few minutes with her overbearing mother.

Jake was ready to go, and they took the Firebird, arriving at the precinct in near record time. Jake parked the car in a guest spot, and he and Annie got out and went inside. Captain Diego spied them from his office and beckoned them over.

Jake poked his head inside the doorway. "Morning, Captain."

Diego sat back and crossed his arms above his rounded belly. "You two find out anything?"

Annie stood in the doorway. "Not yet, but we're working on it."

Diego gave her a quizzical look. "And you plan to share anything you find with us, is that right?"

Annie laughed. "Don't we always?"

"That's not an answer," Diego said with a hint of a frown.

"Don't worry, Captain, we want this guy as bad as you do," Jake said.

"That's still not an answer."

Jake laughed, loud and long. "Of course we'll share. And one of these days you're gonna have to put us on your payroll."

Diego narrowed his eyes and stared at Jake. Annie couldn't tell if he was giving Jake's comment some serious thought or trying to ascertain whether or not Jake was serious. Finally, the captain cleared his throat and said, "If I didn't like you two so much, you wouldn't even be here now." He picked up his pen and dismissed them with a wave. "Be careful."

"Always," Annie said as she and Jake turned away. She glanced toward Hank's desk. The cop was watching them, and she was sure that even from twenty feet away, she saw a twinkle in his eye.

"Diego giving you a hard time?" he asked as they approached his desk.

Annie sat in the only vacant chair across from Hank. Jake pulled up another one from a nearby desk and eased into it.

"He's reminding us how lucky we are to be here," Annie said.

Hank looked toward the captain's office. "He's okay. Talks tougher than he sounds. He knows we're short-staffed here most of the time, and he's more concerned with results than with who gets those results."

Annie got down to business. "Hank, what's this you were telling me about another kidnapping?"

Hank flipped a folder around and slid it across the desk toward Annie. "The victim's name is Lindy Metz. And she IDed the photo of Izzy Wilde as her would-be abductor. He nearly got away with it, too."

Annie picked up the folder and flipped it open, filled with a sudden surge of anger as she peered at a photo of a young girl. She was relieved the girl was safe, though no doubt she had undergone a traumatic experience.

"It sure looks like he has a type," she said, studying the picture. "Both victims have long black hair."

"And dark brown eyes," Hank added. He slipped a photo from a folder, turned it around, and held it up. "Just like Izzy Wilde's mother."

Jake whistled. "He must've really hated her. He's trying to kill his mother over and over again."

"Any other connection between the victims?" Annie asked.

Hank shook his head. "Not that I could find. Both seem to have been targeted because of their appearance, but other than that, I think they happened to be in the wrong place at the wrong time."

"And they have no obvious connection to Wilde?" Annie asked.

"Nope. King and I talked to Lindy and her parents. They claim they don't know him."

"What about the witness?" Jake asked. "Did he have anything useful for you?"

"Not that I can see," Hank said. "I'll go over his statement again, but he didn't get a close look at the vehicle."

"I expect Wilde will ditch the car anyway," Jake said. "Like he did with the last one. He's not gonna take any chances."

"Probably," Hank said. "But on the other hand, he doesn't seem to be planning his actions all that carefully. And that's good. It means he's gonna slip up sooner or later."

"Like visiting his brother's place," Annie said. "Any thinking person should've known his brother would be under surveillance."

Hank looked at Jake. "He must've been familiar with you. Known who you are. Otherwise, why else would he run when he saw you?"

"We *have* made a few headlines lately," Annie said. "We're not exactly as anonymous as we used to be."

"The main question is, why would he be visiting his brother?" Hank said. "It didn't seem prearranged. Carter Wilde wasn't home at the time. Hadn't been there all afternoon, and he didn't get home till later in the evening. I checked his story to be sure. He was attending some meetings related to his position as superintendent. It's solid."

"Izzy probably expected his brother was home," Jake said with a shrug. "Maybe dropped by in case. Likely had nowhere else to go. His house was overrun with cops."

"That means he's either desperate," Annie said, "or

clueless about what to do next." She set the folder on the desk and leaned back. "Or both."

Jake pursed his lips in thought. "He must've had someplace lined up. He tried to kidnap another girl. He had to take her somewhere."

"He could be living out of his car," Hank said. "Needless to say, we have all available officers scouring the city. I checked with the sergeant who supervised the canvassing where Wilde got away from you, Jake, but it didn't turn anything up. No one in the area noticed anything unusual."

"He might've left the city by now," Jake said. He picked up the folder and thumbed through the pages.

"We have a nationwide BOLO out on him in case he does."

"I think he's still around somewhere," Annie said. "He has ties here. Besides, though he doesn't seem too bright, he must know he can't get far without money."

"According to his financial records, he doesn't have much of that," Hank said. "His bank account's almost dry. We're monitoring his credit card, but it's near its limit. He must be living on whatever cash he might've had on hand."

"Or he's getting assistance from someone," Annie said.

"Perhaps. But I don't think it's his brother." Hank paused, twiddled with his pen a moment, then narrowed his eyes. "If Izzy gets desperate enough, he might try to contact Carter again. I've arranged to have a talk with Carter Wilde. My intentions are to convince the man to support us in our hunt for his brother."

"He might not be too eager to help," Annie said.

Hank shrugged. "If he knows something and keeps it from us, it's accessory after the fact. A serious offense. And aiding and abetting a fugitive is just as serious. I've got all kinds of things I can throw at him. Obstruction of justice and so on," Hank said and paused. "But I'd sooner have his willing cooperation."

Jake pulled a photo from the folder and held it up. "Hank, what's the significance of this cot in Izzy Wilde's shed?"

Hank shook his head. "Can't figure that one out. There's no evidence Olivia Bragg had been raped, and it's doubtful Izzy was sleeping there."

"Maybe someplace for his victims to sleep," Annie suggested.

"Perhaps," Hank said. "CSI found evidence Olivia had been on the bed as well as in the chair." He sat back and crossed his arms. "We also know the car we found in Izzy's garage was the one he used to kidnap her."

Jake closed the folder and dropped it onto the desk. "Anything in the house that might show where Wilde is hiding out?"

Hank shook his head. "Not that I could find."

Annie looked around the precinct. "Where's Detective King?"

"Got him tracing Lindy Metz's route from last night. From the time she left her babysitting job until she was abducted." He paused and frowned. "I'd like to find out what kind of car Wilde was driving. All we know is Lindy IDed it as a midsized gray sedan. There must be a million of them around."

97

"He can't be far," Annie said.

Hank looked at his watch. "I have to run. I have an appointment with Carter Wilde at noon." He picked up his briefcase, stuffed some files inside, and stood.

Jake and Annie accompanied Hank to the parking lot. The cop got into his Chevy and rolled down the window. "Be careful," he said with a wave and pulled away.

Annie stood still and watched him leave, a faint frown on her face.

"What's on your mind?" Jake asked. "I know that look."

"I have an idea that might lead somewhere." She strode toward the Firebird. "Come on. Let's get home."

CHAPTER 16

Wednesday, 12:25 p.m.

JAKE FOLLOWED ANNIE into the house and stopped in the kitchen for a drink before going to the office. Annie was booting up the iMac, tapping her fingers impatiently on the desk while she waited for the warm glow of the monitor to appear.

Jake settled into a chair. "So, what's your big idea?"

"Something you said got me thinking," Annie answered.

"I said a lot of things."

"What you said about Izzy needing a place to take his victims."

Jake cocked his head. "And you think you know where that is?"

"No, but he obviously has another car," Annie said. "If you include the one he left in his garage, this is his third vehicle."

"But he probably dumped it already."

Annie smiled. "Exactly. And that means he needs another one."

Jake chuckled. "Now you're making some sense. You know where he's gonna get it, don't you?"

"Yup." Annie spun her chair and faced the computer. "The same place he got the last one."

Jake leaned forward and rested his arms on the desk, watching as Annie navigated to the online site where, according to Callaway, Izzy had purchased his prior vehicle.

After a few clicks of the mouse, Annie brought up a long list of vehicles advertised as private sales.

"You can probably eliminate any recent models," Jake said. "He'll be looking for the cheapest car he can find."

Annie filtered the search results for anything under a thousand dollars, but they were still faced with a dozen vehicles.

Jake stood and leaned in a little closer, his eyes glued to the screen. He pointed. "You can get rid of those three. They're being sold as is, and likely not even in running condition." He ran his finger down the screen. "And those two are a bit too flashy for him. He's gonna want something nondescript." He peered a little closer. "And those two are out of town."

"That still leaves us with five possibilities," Annie said.

"Four," Jake said. "You can eliminate that hatchback. He likes his vehicles with a trunk."

"I'll make some phone calls," Annie said. She spun her chair, picked up the desk phone, and referred to the phone number on the monitor while she dialed.

A few minutes and four short conversations later, she hung up the phone and turned to Jake with a triumphant smile. "For one of them, I got an answering machine saying to call back this evening after six. One of the others is sold, and the buyer in no way matches Izzy's description. The third doesn't run. Needs some work first." She paused and sat back.

Jake sighed lightly and took his cue. "And the last one?"

"Could be him. It's a 2004 Hyundai Sonata for eight hundred dollars. The seller is expecting a prospective buyer in less than an hour. I asked him not to sell it until we've had a chance to look at it. Says he can't do it. It's first come, first served."

Jake stood. "Then we'd better be on our way."

Annie printed out the address and phone number of the seller, grabbed her handbag, and followed Jake to the Firebird.

"It shouldn't take us more than fifteen minutes to get there," Annie said as she fastened her seat belt.

"Bet I could do it in ten," Jake said, starting the engine.

"I already factored your usual excessive speed into the equation."

Jake grinned and pulled from the driveway. "In that case, we'll be there in fifteen minutes. Just guide me."

Fourteen minutes later, Jake eased the vehicle down a middle-class street. Annie peered at the house numbers and, a moment later, motioned toward the curb. "We'd better pull over here. We're looking for number twenty-five." She pointed up the street on the other side. "It's right there. Past that big tree."

Jake pulled over and stopped the vehicle. He reached into the backseat, retrieved a pair of binoculars, and trained them on the house.

"See anything?" Annie asked.

"I see a Hyundai Sonata backed into the driveway. It looks pretty rough. No wonder it's so cheap."

"The owner said it's roadworthy."

Jake lowered the glasses and looked at Annie. "Think we should call Hank?"

"Not yet. But if we see Izzy, we will."

Jake handed the binoculars to Annie. "You watch the house while I take a closer look." He reached into the backseat, found a smaller pair, and hung them around his neck.

He climbed from the car, crossed the street, and approached the house with caution. If Annie was right, and she usually was, then he'd better be careful not to be seen. If Wilde had abandoned his car, he might be on foot, possibly taking the bus or a cab. Of course, there was an off chance he was still driving the gray sedan Lindy had described.

There was no one to be seen, so Jake crossed back over the street and selected a spot beside an overgrown hedge. From his vantage point across from the house, he'd be hidden, but he had a clear view of the house and the driveway. He sat down and waited.

A few minutes later, Jake squinted down the street. Someone was coming. He focused the binoculars. Whoever it was, he wore a baseball cap pulled down over his eyes. The man's head was lowered, and his face couldn't be seen.

Jake pulled out his cell phone and called Annie. "I think Wilde's here." He waited and watched. The man's head was turned away now, perhaps looking at the house numbers as he walked. He stopped in front of number 25 and glanced up and down the street. Jake got a clear view of the visitor's face before he turned and strode up the driveway.

"It's him," Jake said into the phone. "Call Hank."

Jake slipped his phone back into his pocket, worked himself further back into the bush, and watched the house.

Izzy knocked on the side door, and a few moments later, it swung open. A burly man stepped out and had a brief exchange of words with the prospective buyer, then they moved toward the Hyundai. The owner opened the car door and climbed inside, and the headlights came on as the car came to life.

Izzy's hand went to his pocket and he removed a roll of bills, awkwardly counting through them with a bandaged hand. He wasn't wasting any time. At this rate, the car would have a new owner, and Izzy would be long gone before the police got here.

Jake had to do something.

He slipped from his hiding spot, jogged down the sidewalk twenty feet, then crossed the street. He wanted to get as close as possible before being seen by either of the two men.

He approached a short hedge at the side of the driveway, ducked low, and took a quick look through the greenery. Izzy was facing the street, and Jake decided to wait until the man's back was turned before he approached.

He glanced at his watch and then looked up and down the

street. It'd been several minutes since he'd asked Annie to call Hank, and there were no police cars in sight.

A car door slammed, an engine roared, and the waiting was over. Jake stepped out from behind the hedge and tore up the driveway toward the Hyundai.

The vehicle was thirty feet away, but before Jake could make it, the driver-side door opened and Izzy tumbled out. The fugitive made it to his feet, dashed toward the rear of the vehicle, and looked around frantically.

There were high fences at the rear and one side of the property, with the house on the other side. Izzy spun back around. Jake stood near the front of the vehicle between him and Wilde's path to freedom.

The seller stood with his mouth open, his head moving back and forth between Wilde and Jake.

"You might as well give up," Jake said. "The police are on their way."

Wilde's face reddened and his lips curled back. He glanced from side to side and then back at Jake. A moment later he dashed toward the house, pushed open the door, and disappeared inside.

Jake took three long leaps and stopped the closing door with one hand. He stepped inside. Wilde had dashed up a short flight of stairs, taken a left, and vanished out of sight. Jake took the steps two at a time and followed. The route led him into the living room in time to see Wilde disappear out the front door of the house.

Wilde had escaped once before, and Jake was determined not to let him get away this time. But the man was fast. Faster than Jake had expected.

By the time Jake was able to get through the door, Wilde had made it across the front lawn, had leaped over the hedge, and was running up the street toward freedom. He'd soon be running right past a startled Annie, Jake hard on his heels.

A familiar engine roared and tires squealed. The Firebird swung into the middle of the street, directly into the path of the fugitive. Wilde had no time to react. He threw up his arms to protect himself as he plowed into the front fender of the vehicle. He bounced backwards, landed on the asphalt, and lay still.

Annie stepped from the vehicle as Jake came to a stop beside the defeated fugitive. "I thought you could use a hand," she said with a smile.

CHAPTER 17

Wednesday, 1:38 p.m.

HANK SAT ON THE CORNER of his desk, his arms folded, grinning with pleasure as a pair of officers escorted Izzy Wilde across the precinct floor. The suspect held his head high in defiance, anger clouding his face.

Jake and Annie came through the front doors and stopped in front of Diego's office, where the captain was leaning against the door frame. Diego looked pleased as he offered a handshake of appreciation to the investigators.

Hank went over to where the three stood. "Nice job, guys."

"Annie was the genius on this one," Jake said, glancing at his wife.

"We're a team," Annie said.

Hank turned as Wilde was prodded down a hallway at the back of the precinct. He was being taken to an interview room, and Hank was looking forward to the interrogation.

Detective King left his spot by the watercooler and wandered over with one hand shoved deep into a pocket, the other holding a cup of coffee. He slugged Jake on the shoulder, tipped his hat to Annie, and turned to Hank.

"Can't wait to see what this clown has to say." King drained his coffee and crinkled up the cup, making an expert toss into a nearby wastebasket.

Hank nodded. "All set? Let's do it." He beckoned for the Lincolns to follow him and then led them down the hallway and into a small room. One wall held a large two-way mirror with another door beside it. Jake and Annie sat on a pair of semi-comfortable chairs. From there they could watch and listen to the interview.

Hank and King went through the door into an adjoining room, closing the door behind them.

Izzy Wilde sat on the far side of a metal table, his hands cuffed and chained securely to a metal ring embedded into the tabletop. He scowled up at the detectives, then turned his face away, glancing around the sparse room, finally bringing his eyes to rest on the two-way mirror.

No doubt he knew he was being watched, and his scowl turned into a sneer. Then the chains rattled as he yanked wildly at them.

Hank spoke calmly to the enraged man as he slid a chair over and sat, resting his arms on the table. "Relax, Wilde." Hank pointed to the cuffs. "And get used to those bracelets. You're gonna be wearing them for a long time."

Wilde emitted a low growl, gave one final ferocious tug, and then sat still, grinding his bared teeth in anger.

King leaned against the wall and pointed at the suspect's bandaged hand. "What happened to your hand?"

Wilde looked up for a brief moment and shot King a black look.

"I heard a girl got the best of you," King said and laughed.

The prisoner turned his head away and didn't answer.

King leaned over the desk. "That's nothing compared to what you have coming," he said, then glared at Wilde a few moments before leaning back again and crossing his arms.

Hank allowed a brief silence to pass before speaking. "Wilde, we have you for one count of murder, one of attempted murder, and kidnapping as well." Hank tapped his fingers on the table. "What I want to know is, why?"

Wilde looked up and narrowed his eyes at Hank. "I didn't kill no one."

Hank leaned in. "You killed Olivia Bragg. We found all the evidence we need at your property. You shot a police officer. That's serious stuff. And then you kidnapped Lindy Metz. We have two witnesses."

"If you cooperate and give us the details," King said, "this'll go a lot easier for you."

Wilde scowled again. "Maybe I kidnapped a girl, but I didn't kill no one. You couldn't have seen me 'cause I weren't there."

"Your prints were all over the shed," Hank said.

"Course they were. I own the place. I haven't used it for a while is all." He shrugged. "Somebody else was using it."

King laughed. "You think a jury is gonna believe that?"

"It's true." Wilde paused. "All I did was try to kidnap a girl. No harm done. I let her go again."

King leaned in and raised his voice. "We know you killed your mother as well."

Wilde looked confused. "My mother? I was the one who found her. Why would I kill her?" His voice softened and shook as he spoke. "She was all I had. I ... I loved her."

Hank sighed, then spoke in a gentle voice. "Tell me why you kidnapped Lindy Metz."

"Never said I did."

Hank chuckled. "I'm pretty sure you did. About two minutes ago."

Wilde narrowed his eyes, then dropped his head and remained still a moment. Then he said quietly, "I ... I dunno why."

"I know why," Hank said.

The suspect's head shot up and he frowned.

"Because she looks like your mother," Hank continued. "And so did Olivia Bragg. You killed Mrs. Bragg, and you tried to kill Lindy Metz because you hated your mother so much."

Wilde shook his head, pain showing in his eyes. "No," he said. "It ain't true."

"Who else did you murder?" King asked. "Were there others?"

"No. No others."

"Are you trying to tell me you only killed two women?"

Wilde stared at King and blinked rapidly, then looked at Hank. "I ... uh ..."

The suspect was getting confused. That was good. Hank tried a different tactic. "We have a video of you at Phil's restaurant. You stalked Olivia Bragg, then followed her and kidnapped her. We have witnesses, and your DNA was on her body."

The prisoner shook his head.

"You're not helping yourself," King said. "You're going away for the rest of your life if you don't confess. Do you know what they do to guys like you in prison?" He laughed. "You're gonna be somebody's lover and you're gonna like it."

Wilde began to shake, almost imperceptibly at first, then his breath became erratic, and the chains rattled as his body quivered uncontrollably. He looked at Hank, pleading in his eyes.

"It's true," Hank said with a shrug. "But if you confess, it might not happen. You're still going to prison, but I can ensure things are a little easier for you in there."

The suspect swallowed hard, then closed his eyes and breathed slowly in an attempt to calm himself down. A curious look of peace filled his face, and finally he opened his eyes and spoke in a calm voice. "Call my brother. I want a lawyer."

"A lawyer won't help you," King said.

"My brother'll know what to do."

Hank sighed, glared at Wilde a moment, then stood and followed King from the room, closing the door behind them.

Jake stood and spoke as they entered. "Looks like you're not gonna get anything else from him."

"We have enough," King said. "We only wanted a confession. It would've saved the taxpayers a lot of money prosecuting this piece of scum."

"So now what'll happen to him?" Annie asked as they left the room and headed for the main precinct floor.

Hank dropped into his chair. "I'll need your statements before long. In the meantime, Wilde will be taken to East Detention Center for the night. Likely be arraigned in the morning, then go to trial in a few weeks or months." He shrugged. "Hopefully, we can eventually get a confession from him. Maybe make a deal, but either way, he's going away for the rest of his life."

Jake narrowed his eyes. "At least he'll still have a life. That's more than I can say for any of his victims."

"He won't have much of a life," Hank said flatly.

King forced out a short laugh, almost like a low growl. "I still think I should've shot him in the back when I had a chance."

Annie spoke. "How's that officer doing? The one Wilde shot?"

"He'll be fine," Hank said. "His vest saved him, and he's been given an extended leave." He turned to King. "You can call Carter Wilde. He'll probably get a lawyer for this guy and then we can get rid of him for now. In the meantime, I'll give Lindy Metz and her parents a visit. They'll be happy to hear the news."

"We'll talk to Edgar Bragg," Annie said. "It won't bring his wife back, but it'll give him a bit of closure."

Hank nodded. He knew there was no such thing as closure, only a small measure of satisfaction that justice had been done. But the pain of losing a loved one by a senseless murder would go on forever. And that was what kept him doing his job, day after day.

As the Lincolns turned to leave, he said goodbye and promised to see them soon, then pulled his chair into his desk. Now he was faced with the massive job of building the case against Wilde. It was pretty cut and dried, but it still meant mounds of paperwork had to be done before he could turn it over to the crown attorney for prosecution.

CHAPTER 18

Wednesday, 4:28 p.m.

IZZY WILDE WASN'T the least bit happy with the way things had turned out. From his point of view, his troubles all went back to Lindy Metz. She'd been a tiger, that was for sure, and he wished he'd had a gun with him. Even a knife. Then the meddling witness would've been dead, the girl would've gotten what she deserved, and he wouldn't be in this hellhole.

He took another glance around the holding cell and convinced himself it could be worse. At least it wasn't filled with the kinds of people he'd heard about. There was only one other guy occupying the twenty-by-twenty room. Some bedraggled idiot who appeared to be drunk was sleeping it off in the far corner.

But once he got to wherever they planned to take him, it might be a whole different matter, and he quaked in fear. Was it true what the nasty cop had told him? Was he destined to be some fat greasy convict's lover? He'd sooner die, and he vowed never to succumb to such a vile practice. He'd slit his own throat before he'd allow himself to suffer that kind of humiliation.

He adjusted his position on the uncomfortable metal bench. From where he sat, he had a full view of the doorway leading into the area the holding cells occupied. He was waiting. Waiting and hoping his brother had summoned a lawyer who could at least tell him what fate awaited him. Maybe get him out of this dump. But he wasn't sure if Carter would even come through for him. His brother had always been unpredictable that way.

He should've planned things better, but he'd been so eager—.

Izzy lay back against the solid concrete wall and closed his eyes. He felt his mother's hand on his brow, telling him to relax and everything would be all right. Her tone was soothing, barely a whisper, a whisper only he could hear.

"Relax," she said in an angelic voice. The sound filled him with peace—a calming peace.

He looked up into her warm, dark brown eyes. She always made him feel better. That morning he'd skinned his knee, but she'd kissed the pain away. And when Carter was mean to him, she always took his side, and it made him feel special.

What he loved most about her was that she was always there. Even when his father had left them when Izzy was a

few months old, his mother had been closer to him than
Carter. Where was his brother now? He'd gone fishing with
his friends, but Izzy didn't care. Mother was here. His
mother. All his. Forever.

He breathed quietly, comfortable in the pure and
wholesome tranquility his mother's presence always brought.
She was all he needed.

Metal slammed against metal. Something screeched and
Izzy sprang up, startled. A uniformed officer walked toward
him, leering at him, while another one stood behind, holding
a baton.

Where was his mother? She'd left him.

Again.

"Stand back from the doors."

Izzy slunk back and dropped down onto the rigid cot.

The door clanged and rattled. Metal screeched again.

"Stand up and turn around."

He did as he was told, his eyes on the floor while the
officer handcuffed his wrists behind his back.

"Sit down."

He sat and watched as the officer clamped a pair of leg
irons to his ankles. The other cop stood by, slamming his
baton into the palm of his hand, an evil grin twisting his ugly
face.

"Where you taking me?"

No answer, just a sharp command. "Stand up."

Izzy stood.

The other cop stepped forward, and with an officer on
each side holding his arms, the prisoner was prodded from

the cell, then taken through the metal door and up a set of concrete stairs.

A warm blast of air struck him when a door at the top of the steps opened. He squinted in the light of the blazing sun as he was prodded through the doorway. The smell of hot asphalt filled his nose, mixed with fumes spitting from the tailpipe of a large cube van directly in front of him.

"Watch your step."

The leg irons were drawn to their limit as Izzy navigated three steps and found himself in a windowless cubicle. It was nothing more than one of a handful of three-by-three boxes partitioned off in a cube van. He sat on the hard iron bench and the door squealed shut behind him.

He looked around his portable cell. The walls were covered with once shiny sheet metal, now caked with dried slime—probably spewed from the mouths of irate prisoners. Air came through a mesh-covered vent above his head. Another piece of sturdy mesh covered a dim light on the wall opposite the door.

The vehicle jolted forward. They were taking him to prison now. Terror of the unknown filled Izzy, and he shook, afraid and alone. The chains holding the cuffs to his wrists and ankles rattled in the stillness. A cry escaped his lips—a pleading for someone to stop the pain, to stop the torture he felt.

"Shhh. You'll be okay now. I must go. I have a visitor and I can't keep him waiting. You stay here and rest and I promise to be back soon."

Izzy nodded at his mother. "Don't be long." He begged her with his eyes. "I'm afraid."

She smiled, and it warmed him. "I won't be long." She breezed from the room and Izzy laid his head back and closed his eyes, comfortable in the knowledge she'd be back soon. She always was. And she always would be.

He didn't know why she had so many different visitors, mostly in the evening, but she'd told him once it was business. She was smart that way. But sometimes he wondered. He was ten years old now, and though at times he thought it might be something bad she was doing, he banished the thought from his mind. Not his mother. It was only business.

Then a sudden explosion threw him violently forward. The vehicle bucked and bounced, finally landing on its side. The wall of his room became the floor, the door above his head. The light went out. A gun fired. Again and again. A muffled voice shouted something. More than one voice.

What was going on? It sounded like the vehicle had been blown up. Was there a fire? Would he perish? Where was his mother?

Something rattled at the door above him. Metal snapped. A bolt scraped back. The door swung up, slammed backwards, and a face peered over. The man turned his head and shouted, "This one ain't him."

"Check them all. He's in here somewhere."

The face disappeared and more banging came, then a voice called, "Here he is."

"Help. Get me outta here," Izzy called.

Silence.

He stared up at the doorway. "Please."

Someone scrambled up the side of the vehicle. A face appeared in the doorway—the same face—then a pair of hands dropped a bolt cutter. It slammed into the wall by Izzy's head, bounced, and came to rest at his side.

The man vanished, and all was quiet except for the sound of Izzy's breathing and the cool breeze whispering across the open doorway.

Freedom.

He struggled to his feet, his head now in the open air, the bolt cutter gripped in one hand. A pickup stood fifty feet away, and three men dashed toward it. One had the remnants of leg irons fastened to his ankles. Izzy watched in awe as they jumped in the vehicle, then spun around and drove out of sight.

He turned his attention to getting loose. Sitting down, he managed to maneuver the bolt cutter into position. He put all his weight into it and heard a snap. His hands were free. After that, it was a simple matter to cut the irons from his legs, and he scrambled from the cell.

Dropping onto the asphalt, he studied his surroundings. He stood at the edge of a narrow highway somewhere outside of the city. The men who'd ambushed the vehicle had chosen the location well.

The sturdy vehicle had held together, but now lay on its side, the front severely damaged. Izzy crouched down and looked through the bulletproof windshield. One of the officers struggled to open the door. The other one lay still, blood trickling from a wound in his head.

It was time to get out of there before help arrived. He'd been given a second chance, and he was determined to make the best of it.

CHAPTER 19

Wednesday, 6:00 p.m.

JAKE SAT ON THE COUCH in the living room, leaning forward, his mouth wide open. He stared at the TV screen, unable to believe what he was seeing and hearing.

He glanced over at Annie, curled up in her favorite chair, studying a book on crime prevention. She swung her feet to the floor and dropped the book into her lap, her wide-eyed attention now on the same unbelievable story.

According to the report, a custom-designed transport vehicle had been carrying a handful of prisoners to East Detention Center when an explosion occurred. It was determined to have been caused by a grenade or similar device tossed in front of the vehicle as it slowed for a curve. The TV screen showed the vehicle on its side surrounded by police cars, their red and blue lights flashing.

Officers and investigators milled about taking photos and

examining the scene. A siren sounded in the background, its scream lessening until finally silenced.

The newscaster continued, his report stating two prisoners had escaped. One was identified as a long-sought-after drug lord, Victor Salaz. A deep undercover operation had resulted in his capture along with several of his underlings two days before. The second fugitive was a suspected murderer named Isaiah Wilde who had been apprehended earlier that day.

Two other prisoners had remained secure. The newscaster stated the police were unsure at this point whether or not the successful attack had been carried out for the express purpose of freeing one or both prisoners. He warned the public that whatever the case, two dangerous fugitives were on the loose.

"It's obvious the intent was to free the drug lord," Jake said, disgust in his voice. "No one would go out of their way to free Wilde. I doubt he has a friend in the world. He just got lucky."

Annie didn't appear to hear the comment, her eyes still glued to the television.

The report continued, stating the two officers transporting the prisoners had been taken to the hospital. One had suffered minor injuries, and it was expected he'd be released shortly. The other had sustained head injuries, and it was unclear at this point what the extent of those injuries was. Neither officer was available for comment.

Photos of both escapees appeared on the screen. The voiceover of a police spokesman announced that a manhunt for the prisoners was being organized. All available officers, along with tracking dogs, would be used. He urged members of the public to report sightings of either fugitive to the police at once.

Annie finally found her voice. "We've got to do something."

"He could be anywhere. If he's with the other escapee and his pals, they might shelter him. At least for the time being."

Annie shook her head. "Why would they care about him? They might've given him a lift, but I suspect they would soon dump him. They're professionals, and he's too unstable." She paused and sat back. "I'm sure he's on his own again."

"So we're back to the same unanswerable question. With no friends that we know of, where'll he go, and how'll he get there?"

"And will he find another victim?" Annie said, her face masked with concern.

Jake wondered the same thing. With Wilde being unpredictable and somewhat vindictive, was his own family in danger? It was doubtful Wilde would do anything so obvious, especially now with the reality of prison life impressed on him, but Jake wasn't going to take any chances.

And surely Hank had already contacted Lindy Metz and her parents, warning them to be cautious in case the killer decided to seek revenge.

When the office phone rang, Jake looked at Annie. She sat unmoving and seemed not to hear it. Jake went to the office and picked up the receiver.

"Lincoln Investigations. Jake speaking."

"Too bad all your hard work ended up nothing." It was

the voice of Izzy Wilde, and he spoke slowly, a mocking tone to his words.

Jake's body tensed. He took a sharp breath and held it a moment, uncertain what to say. "It's not over yet," he said at last.

"You're right about that. It's just beginning. But it'll be over soon."

Jake motioned frantically to Annie from the office door. She cocked her head, then stood and came toward him.

Jake covered the receiver with one hand, lowered it, and spoke in a loud whisper. "It's Izzy Wilde."

Annie stopped mid-stride and widened her eyes.

"Where are you?" Jake said into the phone, not expecting an answer.

Wilde replied with a burst of laughter.

"Are you at your brother's?" Jake asked. Another useless question, but he was at a loss for words.

More laughter, then Wilde said in a flat voice, "Carter ain't gonna help me. You know better than that. I was counting on him, and he didn't even find me a lawyer."

"You're gonna need a lot more than a lawyer," Jake said through gritted teeth.

"You'll never even get close this time. My friends were good enough to release me, and believe me, I've got some powerful friends."

"Why're you calling me?" Jake asked.

"Just a warning is all."

Jake frowned. "What kind of warning?"

"To leave me be. I'm doing what I have to, and I'll do it as long as I need to."

"To what end?"

"To stop them wicked women who surround me and taunt me." Wilde's voice rose in pitch, and he spoke rapidly, taking short quick breaths. "Traitorous unfaithful leeches. I gotta put a stop to their lies and deceit." He was panting now. "I'll make them leave me alone."

Jake spoke in a calm, soothing voice. "Why now? Why after all these years?"

Wilde screamed. "Because she's back." Jake lowered the phone as the manic voice continued. "She's back and I gotta stop her!"

When the screeching voice stopped, Jake raised the phone to his ear. "Who's back?"

"Evil is." Wilde clenched his teeth. "I gotta stop it."

The line went dead.

Jake hung up the phone and turned to a speechless Annie. "He's nuts."

Annie nodded. "And volatile. There's no telling what he might do next."

"He mentioned his friends," Jake said. "Some powerful friends he's with."

Annie shook her head adamantly. "He's lying to throw you off. The intent of the hijacking wasn't to release him."

"I'm sure you're right."

"I'm right," Annie said. "Like I mentioned before, they'd sooner shoot him than put up with him."

Jake sat in the swivel chair behind the desk, leaned back, and sat still a moment, staring out the window. Finally, he said, "One thing I noticed during the phone call. When Izzy's calm, he appears to think and talk rationally. At least to some degree. But when his emotions take over, whether it's fear, or maybe anger, then he gets out of control."

Some time ago, Jake had made sure all conversations on the business line were recorded. It had come in handy in prior cases, and now he hoped his conversation with Izzy Wilde would be helpful in tracking the maniac down again.

He spun the chair around, fiddled with a few buttons, and managed to transfer the brief dialogue onto a flash drive. The call had shown up as an unknown number, so it was likely a dead end, but he'd get the drive to Hank ASAP, and Callaway would extract anything useful from it. If there was anything useful.

He tucked the drive into his shirt pocket and stood. "I'm sure Hank's aware of Wilde's escape. I'll see if I can get ahold of him." He removed his cell phone from his belt and touched speed dial.

"Detective Hank Corning."

Jake filled Hank in on the call with as few words as possible and hung up. "Hank said he'll send an officer to pick up the recording right away."

Annie sat in the guest chair, her hands in her lap. Her face showed signs of worry and apprehension. "What about his warning? Do you think it was a direct threat aimed at us?"

Jake's brow wrinkled in thought, and he shook his head slowly. "I don't think so. If he's in a rational mood, he won't come close to us. But nonetheless, I'd sooner err on the side of caution. There's no telling what might set him off."

Annie tugged at her bottom lip a moment. "I'll have to

give this a lot of thought. Sometimes I can put myself in their head and figure out what they might do, but in this case, I can't even imagine what's in his warped mind."

"I know one thing that's in his mind," Jake said. "He plans to kill again, and we need to figure out who, how, and where."

CHAPTER 20

Wednesday, 7:11 p.m.

HANK SAT AT HIS DESK with his head back and his eyes closed, attempting to formulate an immediate plan. He was frustrated, now faced with redoing a task that had already been brought to a successful conclusion.

Four hours ago, he had contacted Lindy Metz and her parents with the good news of Izzy Wilde's capture. When he'd received the disturbing report of Wilde's escape, he had arranged for a security detail to safeguard the Metz family.

It seemed like the entire precinct had swung into action. All available officers had spent the last couple of hours combing the area of the escape in an attempt to track down both fugitives. The K-9 unit had been deployed, and a citywide search had commenced and would continue until the escapees were back in custody.

The madman was on foot, but for how long? Though Wilde didn't seem to be especially cautious, he was resourceful, and he'd no doubt round up some form of transportation before long. There was a chance he might bring his last vehicle back into use. The hunt continued for the gray sedan, but unless it'd been abandoned in a public location, finding it seemed like a long shot.

An officer had picked up the recording from the Lincolns, and Hank had listened to it several times. It was now in the hands of Callaway, and the whiz would analyze it in detail. If there was anything to be found that might lead to the whereabouts of the fugitive, Callaway would find it.

A trace on the call had turned up negative; Wilde had used a burner phone. Exactly where the phone had been purchased, Hank didn't know, but all retailers in the area would be alerted in case Wilde was in the market for another phone.

Hank feared Izzy Wilde might be true to his word and resume his unpredictable murder spree. His phone call pointed in that direction, and the killer seemed eager to get underway at once. The sad fact was, though the city had been exposed to the news of the fugitives on the run, there were always those who paid very little attention. For many, it didn't affect their lives, and they would never consider themselves at risk.

But Izzy was crazy, and Hank faced the problem of anticipating the volatile killer's next move.

He opened his eyes as Detective King wandered over and dropped into a chair opposite Hank. "We've had no luck on the search yet," King said. "I talked to the drug unit, and they're optimistic about finding their guy. They're familiar with all his known associates." He shook his head. "But Wilde has no associates."

"Just his brother," Hank said.

"You think he's gonna contact his brother?"

Hank shrugged. "You got a better idea?"

"Nope," King said with a yawn. "I got nothin'."

Hank wasn't surprised. Though King came up with something helpful on occasion, more often than not, he was content to follow Hank's lead. "I think we should pay him a visit."

"Carter Wilde?"

Hank nodded and stood. "I know he's reluctant to turn his brother in, but I think we can get him to help us in case Izzy contacts him. We have to prepare for any and all possibilities."

"What about a warrant? Force him to comply?"

"We don't have the time, and even if we did, a warrant won't guarantee his cooperation. It could just make him resistant."

King removed his cap, finger-combed his hair back, and dropped his cap back on. He shrugged a shoulder, stood, and motioned toward the front doors. "I'm right behind you."

Hank led the way from the building and they got into the Chevy. In a few minutes, they pulled into the parking lot of Carter Wilde's apartment building on Red Ridge Street. According to Carter's file, he drove a dark blue 2002 Subaru. Hank was pleased to see it was parked in its reserved spot not far from the front door.

He drove up and down the rows of vehicles, looking for a

gray sedan. There were two. He called in the plate numbers, then, satisfied the owners lived in the apartment building, he parked in a visitors' slot behind.

The two cops walked to the front of the building and entered the lobby, and Hank pressed 101 on the panel. Carter didn't seem surprised to hear from them, and he buzzed open the security lock at once. He stood in the doorway of his apartment, watching as the cops crossed the main lobby.

Carter had a somber look on his face, and he tightened his lips and shook his head slowly. "I heard the news," he said as they approached. He stepped aside and waved the cops into his apartment. "I was apprehensive at first, but I must say, I was surprisingly relieved when I heard Izzy had been caught." He sighed. "I've had some time to do some soul-searching, and I need to face reality. He might be my brother, but I realize now how dangerous he is."

The detectives went into the living room and took a seat on the couch. Carter worked his cane, making his way to his easy chair. He settled into it and exhaled a long breath. "I know why you're here," he said. "I'll do whatever I can to help." He paused and narrowed his eyes. "On one condition."

"What's the condition?" Hank asked.

Carter looked down a moment, massaged his game leg thoughtfully, then raised his head. "My brother has always been a little … odd. He needs help. I want you to promise he'll get some help and you won't lock him away somewhere." He paused and looked at Hank earnestly. "He's my brother. I care about him."

King seemed about to speak, but Hank silenced him with a look and a guarded frown. Carter Wilde was in a precarious position. It appeared the man was torn between doing the right thing and loyalty toward his brother.

"I'm sure Izzy will undergo a mental assessment," Hank said. "That's par for the course. But I can't guarantee what the finding will be. If he's found fit to stand trial, then I have no recourse. Once we bring him in, our job's done, and any further decisions are out of my hands."

Carter pursed his lips, his eyes on Hank's. Then he nodded and spoke in a low voice. "I understand." He took a deep breath and seemed to be thinking. Finally, he said, "All right. You have my full cooperation. I expect you'll bring him in eventually, so it might as well be before he hurts anyone else."

"What we're asking is very simple," Hank said. "We want your permission to monitor your phone calls, but more importantly, if your brother contacts you, we want your help in bringing him in."

Carter emitted a light sigh and nodded in agreement.

Hank slipped a business card from his breast pocket and held it out. "You can get me on my cell any time."

Carter took the card, set it on a stand beside his chair, then narrowed his eyes at Hank. "Will you promise to be careful not to harm him? Not to shoot him?"

Hank couldn't make a promise like that. The safety of others was always his prime concern. He said, "No one in the department is trigger-happy. The last thing we want is to draw our weapons."

Carter nodded again.

"If your brother contacts you for help, offer him whatever he wants," Hank said. "Arrange to meet him if necessary. Promise him money, food, or transportation. Anything it takes to set up a meeting. And then contact me right away. Night or day."

Carter looked down, straightened a pant leg, and flicked away a piece of lint. "I'll do my best."

Hank stood and stepped toward Carter, holding out his hand. "Thank you for your cooperation. Someone will contact you immediately to get the monitoring set up. It'll involve installing some software on your cell phone and tapping your landline."

Carter shook Hank's hand and reached for his cane.

"Don't bother getting up," Hank said. "We'll see ourselves out." He turned to King, who'd stood, and the detectives left the apartment.

On the way to his vehicle, Hank made a call to the sergeant in charge of the manhunt. The dogs had lost the fugitive's trail a couple of miles from the area of the escape, but one thing was certain—Wilde was heading back toward the city.

Neighborhoods had been canvassed, hundreds of citizens had been questioned, and any and all possible leads were being followed up. Thus far, Wilde was nowhere to be found.

Right now they were in a wait-and-see situation. Until Izzy Wilde made another move, or the manhunt turned up a lead, there wasn't much he could do.

CHAPTER 21

Wednesday, 8:44 p.m.

IZZY WILDE WORMED HIS way through a row of cedar hedges. The safety of the forest lay behind him, a narrow unkempt lawn in front. He squinted in the growing darkness. Yellow crime scene tape was tacked across the front door of his house. Further down, the old shed had received the same treatment.

He couldn't tell if the buildings and property were being watched. Would they waste their manpower to guard a place they knew he'd be insane to return to? Probably not. There were no police cars in sight, the only vehicle being his old broken-down pickup resting alongside two other useless cars on the front lawn. None of them would do him any good.

He couldn't tell from his vantage point, but he assumed they'd carted away his only serviceable vehicle from the garage. But it didn't matter. He still had the old gray sedan waiting for him, hidden in plain sight not far away.

But he wasn't here for transportation. He had to get inside the house. He needed a change of clothes; the orange jumpsuit he now wore wasn't something he wanted to be seen in. He could get fresh clothes anywhere, of course, but what he needed most was to get the stash of money he had hidden in a safe place.

"This way," his mother said. She stood on the lawn, not twenty feet away, beckoning toward him. "It's safe," she called, and he knew he could trust her. He could always trust her.

He worked his way out of the bushes, and keeping low, he scurried across the lawn to the side of the house. The basement window, dead center of the building, hadn't closed right for some time. With one well-aimed kick, the window swung open, and he slipped inside, landing with a soft thud on the floor of the musty basement.

He felt his way across the darkened room, took the dusty wooden steps up, and stopped to listen, his hand on the doorknob. He breathed lightly, carefully, then, satisfied no one was on the main floor of the house, he turned the knob and the door creaked open. It stopped with a dull thump, bouncing against the side of his mother's china cabinet.

Izzy took the final step up, eased into the kitchen, and glanced around. Things were pretty much the way he'd left them. There was evidence that drawers and cupboards had been searched, but after a cursory glance, it didn't appear anything of value was missing. It didn't matter much anyway; he wouldn't be coming back here to live.

The living room looked the same as well. His mother's

favorite chair sat facing the television. The couch where she'd loved to nap was still under the front window, the ragged carpet strewn in front of it.

He took another quick look around and headed up the stairs to the second floor. He stopped short at the top and frowned. His bedroom door was open. He'd always kept it closed. They must've rifled through his room as well, and he hoped they hadn't found his stash of emergency funds.

He stepped inside and moved past his bed to an ancient dresser on the far wall. He slipped the bottom drawer fully out, then reached a hand into the cavity and smiled. A couple of sharp tugs worked loose a packet of money, neatly bound with an elastic band. He stood and tossed it onto the bed.

As long as he didn't have to keep on buying new cars every day, the funds would last him a good long time. He didn't trust banks, and he was glad he'd kept some money aside for a rainy day. And it certainly was a rainy day.

He knelt down and reached into the cavity again, this time removing a small pistol. He smiled grimly, stood, and tossed it onto the bed beside the money.

He turned to the task of finding a suitable wardrobe. The cops had taken his favorite running shoes from him, replacing them with a canvas pair. He kicked them off, then stripping off his police-provided jumpsuit, he tossed it aside and rummaged around in his closet.

He came up with a nondescript button-down shirt and a pair of faded blue jeans and put them on. He found a pair of worn running shoes at the back of the closet and slipped them on, and then, from a shelf above the row of clothing he'd never wear again, he found a baseball cap. He worked it onto his head, then stepped back and admired himself in the full-length mirror.

He looked like an average Joe. He grinned at himself. But better looking.

He grabbed the packet of money and slipped it into his side pocket, then tucked the pistol behind his back, secured in place by his belt. Looking around the room, he decided it might be better if no one knew he'd been here. He might have to come back again. He worked the drawer into place, then bundled up his former attire and stuffed it all under the bed.

He moved to the doorway and stopped short when he heard a voice—his mother's soft voice. She was coming up the stairs. His smile disappeared when a man spoke in a low tone. His mother giggled and Izzy frowned.

He stepped behind the door and watched through the crack as his mother led the stranger across the hallway and into her bedroom. She closed the door, and Izzy took a careful step into the hallway, disquieted, and unsure what to think.

He hadn't felt well today and had come home from school early. He knew his mother had a lot of male friends, but he was fourteen years old now, and had seen and heard enough to know what was going on was more than friendship.

Curious and disturbed, he put his ear to the door of his mother's room. Low voices sounded from the other side.

He suppressed his guilt for spying on his mother in her bedroom, but he had to find out what was going on. He knelt with care in front of the door and pressed his eye to the keyhole. His mouth widened as his mother kicked off her shoes, tossed her hair, and removed her dress while the stranger watched.

Izzy closed his eyes a moment, ashamed and embarrassed to see his mother that way. Then, overtaken by curiosity, he opened them again and watched the troubling scene, scarcely daring to breathe lest he be found out.

He recoiled as the filthy visitor reached out and put a hand on his mother, fondling her. Izzy's eyes popped and his blood boiled.

His mother's dark brown eyes shone as she stood and subjected herself to his vulgar touch. He stroked her long black hair, caressing it with his fingers, touching her in forbidden places.

Then she held out a hand and spoke. The visitor stepped back, removed his wallet, and dropped some bills on the nightstand.

Izzy gasped. His mother's head spun toward the closed door, her hair twirling around her throat. Her dark brown eyes seemed to bore into his and he dropped down, catching his breath. His heart pounded as an unfamiliar anger welled up inside him.

The awful truth hit him, and he recoiled in shock. His wonderful mother was a prostitute. She sold herself to any man who came along. And she was a liar. The times she'd soothed him when he was sad, or held him when he was lonely and said she loved him, were all a lie.

She was a whore. A filthy whore.

Anger, sadness, and despair overtook him, and he stumbled to his feet and raced down the stairs.

He jumped the last three steps to the landing and heard a door open. A voice called—the voice of a strange woman—mocking him, taunting him. "Izzy, dear? Is that you?" It wasn't soft and loving anymore. It was cruel and evil. It was the voice of a woman who had sold herself for a pittance. Her soul in exchange for a few dollars.

She was detestable and loathsome and he hated her. Hated her for what she'd done to their family. She'd chased his father away many years ago, then, like the spawn of Satan, straight from the depths of hell, she'd destroyed what love he had once felt for her.

All gone.

He needed to find Carter. Carter would know what to do. His brother had always been there for him. He wondered if Carter knew what their mother was. He couldn't possibly know.

He burst through the front door of the house and tore across the lawn toward the trees. He had to get away from there. Away from that woman and the house she had desecrated.

He had to get to the gray sedan.

CHAPTER 22

Wednesday, 10:12 p.m.

TANYA ARBUCKLE SLID HER handbag toward her, thumbed through her wallet, and dropped a five-dollar tip on the bar. She often came to Benny's after work to relax and nurse a drink or two and, as usual, it seemed like most of her time had been spent fending off the advances of men twice her age.

Was that all she could attract?

Not that she was homely, but she was exhausted and didn't look her best—whatever that was. And the type of guys who'd been eyeing her weren't the kind she'd ever consider spending an evening with, never mind sharing a drink with in a gloomy dive bar.

At twenty-six years old, she'd given up all hopes of finding a decent man long ago.

It seemed like all the good ones were taken. The story of her life.

And anyway, she wasn't here to meet anyone. She'd dealt with enough people during her long day tied to the cash register, and she wanted peace and relative quiet away from her dead-end job. The couple of drinks she'd had were enough to do the trick, and it was time to head home. She had to get up early in the morning.

She spun her stool around and dropped to her feet, avoiding eye contact with a couple of drooling patrons who thought they still had a chance with her. Crossing the dingy room, she pushed open the solid wooden door and stepped into the warm night air.

Two guys leaning against the brick wall at the side of the door abruptly stopped their conversation and leered at her.

"Need someone to walk you home?" one of them asked. The other guy laughed and flicked his cigarette butt into the gutter.

Tanya raised her head without answering, turned her back on them, and headed down the sidewalk. A few moments later, she glanced over her shoulder. They were still watching her, their laughter and catcalls fading away as she hurried toward home.

One of these days she hoped to get out of this neighborhood, but for now, the small apartment three blocks away was all she could afford.

She sighed. Maybe one day.

Hearing a vehicle behind her, she turned her head as a gray sedan pulled to the curb beside her.

The driver rolled down his window and flashed a toothy smile. "Excuse me, miss."

Tanya stopped and turned toward the vehicle. "Yes?"

"I'm looking for this address," he said, waving a piece of paper out the window. "Can you help me?"

Tanya stepped toward the vehicle, reached for the paper, then gasped as the man's hand shot out and seized her wrist. As a scream welled up inside of her, he forced the door open, pushing it against her body as he jumped out. A sweaty hand went over her mouth, the other gripping her long black hair, and her cry for help died inside.

She struggled, but she was no match for the strong arms holding her from behind.

"Stay still. I ain't gonna hurt you," he hissed in her ear.

She had no intention of succumbing, and she continued to claw at his hands and wrists. Then something went around her neck. It felt like a rope, or maybe a belt, and she fought for air. Then her eyes dimmed and her body weakened, until finally, she felt herself sinking into his arms as her mind went blank.

It was hard to tell how long she'd been unconscious, and as her mind cleared, she became aware of a rocking motion. She was in a car. He'd dumped her into the trunk of his vehicle.

Her breathing became rapid and shallow as panic filled her. She wanted to scream, but she was unable to take a deep breath. She tried to calm herself down, to control her shaking, to think. Where was he taking her? What was he going to do to her?

She put a trembling hand to her throat. Whatever had

almost choked the life from her earlier was gone. Perhaps he wasn't trying to kill her. At least, not yet.

Her heart raced. She was sweating and felt dizzy. Not from the close air inside the trunk, but from fear. Fear of the unknown. Fear of what she might face at the end of the journey.

She took a deep gasping breath and held it, closing her eyes against the blackness of her surroundings, exerting all her willpower to force herself to calm down.

As she fought to control her panic, she scrambled to find something to protect herself with. He must've planned this with care; the trunk was empty. She lay on her back, trying to come up with a plan as the car continued on, taking several turns, speeding up and slowing down. After a few minutes, the vehicle came to a stop, then backed up and stopped again, and the engine died.

The car door opened and footsteps sounded beside the vehicle. A metal door scraped open behind the car. He'd backed up to a building somewhere.

The trunk swung open and she looked up, unable to move as renewed trembling filled her body.

He reached out a hand. "Let's go."

She lay still and turned her eyes away, clasping her hands in front of herself, unable to move, speak, or scream.

He grasped her under the arms and dragged her from the trunk, forcing her to her feet.

With a sudden burst of courage she spun around to run, stopped short by his grasp on her hair. He tugged her toward him and pointed to the doorway.

"In there," he said.

Overcome with rage, Tanya swung her free hand and raked his face with her fingernails. He stepped aside, grasped her wrists, and turned her around, wrapping his arms about her chest.

She was helpless—clamped in his grip as he propelled her toward the waiting door. She'd done her best and was determined to not give up, never to succumb.

He pushed her through the doorway, stepped inside, and slammed the door behind him.

"Downstairs," he said, panting to catch his breath.

He twisted her arm behind her back, his other hand around her throat, and prodded her down a concrete stairway.

Her ankle gave out and she stumbled. He lost his grip, and she fell down the last half dozen steps and lay on her back. He glared at her, his face twisted into a sneer as he came down the stairs toward her.

She rolled, staggered to her feet, and limped across the floor, glancing around the concrete-walled room. There were no windows, and no doors except one—the one at the top of the stairs.

He stood back and watched her, his arms folded, as she looked frantically around for a weapon. Her eyes widened at the sight of a cot along the far wall. It was covered with a white sheet, a pillow at one end, and she recoiled in horror when she realized what it meant.

He was going to rape her.

She spun to face him, terrified and unable to breathe.

He laughed, a low guttural, mocking sound. "It's not what you think," he said, dabbing at his injured face with the palm of one hand. He looked at the blood, gave a short chuckle, and raised his face toward her. "You shouldn't have done that."

Tanya narrowed her eyes and gritted her teeth. "Touch me again and you'll get even worse."

His smirk vanished. "Turn around. Don't look at me again."

She didn't move.

He went to a table in one corner, his eyes on her face as he moved. He picked up a knife, stroked a finger across the blade, then held it up.

"Turn around or I'll take your eyes."

She glanced around the room, then at the knife, her eyes frozen on the sharp tip of the blade. Her bravery vanished as he twirled it in his hand, leering at her. Her shoulders slumped, and she turned around slowly, defeated, her head down.

He stepped behind her and she felt the tip of the knife on the back of her neck.

"Lie down."

Tanya moved to the bed and lay on her back, turning her head to watch as he went to the table and picked something up. She averted her eyes when he spun back and came toward her.

"Put your hands beside you."

She trembled and laid her arms at her sides, careful not to look at his face.

He fastened a cable tie around each of her wrists and secured them to the side rails of the bed. Then he bound her feet with a rope, ran it off the end of the cot, and tied it to the frame.

He stood back a few feet, mumbled something to himself, and then gave a low chuckle.

"I'll be back," he said. His footsteps sounded on the stairs, the outer door slammed, and Tanya was alone. Alone and terrified.

CHAPTER 23

DAY 4 - Thursday, 7:35 a.m.

HANK PUT HIS BREAKFAST dishes into the sink, ran some warm water over them, and glanced out of his apartment window. He had hoped to be awakened in the night with the news of Izzy Wilde's capture. No news had come, and he was now facing another day with Wilde on the loose.

The evening before, Callaway had installed the software on Carter Wilde's cell phone, and the landline tap was in place. Every call would be recorded and monitored live at the precinct. Hank had left notice to contact him at once if Izzy called his brother.

It might be a long shot, but it could break things wide open if the plan worked.

He checked his service weapon, grabbed his briefcase, and left his apartment. On his way to the precinct, he gave King a call. The detective was still at home, but he was expecting to leave shortly.

Hank's heart sank when he neared the precinct. A postal delivery truck was pulled up in front of the building. He looked at his watch. It was much too early for mail delivery. He parked his vehicle and strode around to the front and up the steps, fearing the worst.

Hank stepped inside and glanced toward Diego's office. Luke Rushton was leaned forward in a chair, carrying on a conversation with the captain. The detective's fears intensified when he spied a familiar-looking box on Diego's desk, the lid flipped up. From where Hank stood, he saw bold red handwriting on the outside of the package.

He went to Diego's office and stepped inside without knocking. Even before looking into the box, the look on the captain's face told Hank what the package contained.

A glance confirmed his suspicion. It was a lock of long black hair nestled in white tissue paper.

Diego leaned back in his chair and gave a long drawn-out sigh before speaking. "It appears we might have another victim, Hank."

Hank glanced at Rushton. The postman was hunched forward in his chair, his cap in his hand, his eyes darting back and forth between Hank and the captain.

"Was it in the same mailbox?" Hank asked him.

Rushton turned toward the detective and shook his head. "Same area. Different box."

Hank looked at the captain. "And no fingerprints on the carton?"

Diego shrugged one shoulder. "Just Luke's."

Hank gave a slow nod, his eyes unfocused, his mind turning to the events of the day before. Wilde had promised there would be more victims, and the box on Diego's desk showed the butcher hadn't been frightened out of carrying on with his horrific plan.

Diego broke the silence. "Luke, how far was this mailbox from the other one?"

Rushton scratched his head. "A couple blocks away."

"How many mailbox locations in the area?"

"One about every couple of blocks on the main streets. Less in the residential areas."

Diego looked at Hank. "I want officers to watch every mailbox in the area for as long as it takes."

Hank nodded. It wouldn't be hard to find a few officers willing to pull all-nighters. They could always use the overtime pay. "I'll get on it, Captain."

"It's early, but nobody's called in a homicide yet," Diego said. "It'd be great if you could find this guy before that happens, Hank. In the meantime, I'll get this down to the lab and see if they can tell us anything. It's possible this is another lock from the first victim."

"I'll do my best," Hank said, but knew in his heart his best wouldn't be enough to save what he suspected was another victim. He nodded at Rushton and made his way to his desk.

~*~

ANNIE WENT INTO the office and pulled up to the desk. She had a single-minded determination—to find Izzy Wilde before he struck again.

The fugitive's victims seemed to fit a specific profile, but Annie didn't want to take any chances. In the past, she and her family had been targeted by the very ones they'd been trying to track down.

Jake had taken Matty and Kyle to school. It was only a couple of blocks from the house, but Jake had gotten into the habit of dropping the boys off each day if they were working on a case like the current one. Once inside the school, they would be safe. The building was locked down during school hours, and visitors were screened before entry was allowed.

As her iMac whirred to life, she heard the Firebird in the driveway. In a couple of minutes, Jake poked his head into the office.

"Thought I'd find you here," he said.

Annie shrugged. "We have a job to do."

"Any ideas?" Jake pulled up the guest chair, eased into it, and slouched back.

Annie shook her head. "We know who we're looking for. Our problem is in figuring out where he is."

"If he buys another car, he's gotta be smart enough not to use the same method. But just in case, the police are monitoring all the local ads for anyone matching Wilde's description."

"He might steal the next one," Annie said. "One thing we know—he needs some transportation."

"He might've hung on to the gray sedan," Jake suggested.

"With the police on the lookout for it?"

Jake grinned. "He's not the brightest guy we've come up against."

Annie leaned forward, dropped her elbows on the desk, and cupped her hands under her chin. "So, if you were Izzy Wilde, what would you do? Where would you go?"

Jake frowned. "Are you calling me dumb?"

Annie chuckled. "Not at all. But try to think simple for a couple of minutes."

Jake laid his head back, looked at the ceiling a moment, then said, "I'd have to find a woman with black hair and dark brown eyes."

"Where?"

Jake shrugged. "The supermarket. Library. Maybe at the mall."

"Too much light," Annie said. "Chances are, he'd stalk his victims somewhere where he wouldn't be recognized."

"How about a restaurant or a bar?"

Annie snapped her fingers. "I think you might've hit it."

"A restaurant?"

"No. A bar."

"Phil's is a restaurant," Jake said. "That's where he found Olivia Bragg."

"It's also a bar," Annie said.

"It's early morning. Even if you're right, he won't be on the prowl right now."

"No, but perhaps this evening. I'll suggest it to Hank. He has enough manpower to cover every bar in the area."

Jake pursed his lips. "Where does he hang out during the daytime?"

"One thing I know," Annie said. "When he tried to kidnap

Lindy Metz, he had every intention to kill her. That means he had a place lined up to do it."

"If he intended to shave her head, he'd need a place with electricity." Jake crossed his arms. "Unless he used scissors."

"According to Hank, her head appeared to be shaved with a razor. It could have been cordless, already charged."

"Okay, then, where would he be?"

"That's the question," Annie said.

Jake leaned forward, a deep frown on his brow. "Wait a second."

"What is it?"

He jumped to his feet. "Grab your bag. I have an idea."

Whatever Jake's idea was, it seemed urgent; he was already halfway out the front door. Annie dashed to the kitchen, grabbed her handbag off the counter, and followed him out.

The passenger-side door of the Firebird was hanging open, and Jake revved up the engine, waiting impatiently for her.

Annie locked the house door, raced down the sidewalk, and jumped into the vehicle. "Where're we going?" she asked as she fastened her seat belt.

The Firebird roared from the driveway and turned left. "Carter Wilde's."

Annie was puzzled. Wilde might be unpredictable, but he wasn't foolish enough to visit his brother. She looked at Jake. "I asked you to think simple. This might be a little too simple."

Jake laughed. "Not Carter's apartment. But I think Izzy might be somewhere in the building."

"How'd you come to that conclusion?"

Jake spun the steering wheel and the car shot onto Main Street. He glanced in the rearview mirror, curved around a slow vehicle, then took a left turn down a side street before answering.

"Remember the day I saw him there? I've been mulling it over, and I don't think he was going to visit his brother. I know the guy's a bit of a dimwit, but I doubt he'd show up there unannounced. If we can believe Carter, his brother never contacted him. And anyway, Carter wasn't home at the time." Jake paused and glanced at Annie. "I think he had another reason to go there."

Annie hung onto the dash as the vehicle took another sudden turn. "You think he's using one of the apartments?"

Jake glanced at her and grinned. "Nope. That would be too obvious, and any disturbance might be heard by the tenants." He hugged the steering wheel and peered through the windshield. "Hold on. We're almost there."

"You think he might be using the basement?" Annie asked.

Jake whipped past a line of parked cars and eased down Red Ridge Street. "Either the basement, or another room nobody uses. His brother's the superintendent, so Izzy could obtain access if he wanted to."

Annie added, "And since Carter has a bad leg, he doesn't get around so well. He might never go to the basement."

"Now you got it," Jake said. He touched the brakes and pulled to the side of the street.

The apartment building loomed to their right. Annie reached into the backseat, retrieved a pair of binoculars, and scanned the parking area. In a moment, she said, "All clear."

Jake eased the vehicle into the lot, idled up to the side of the building, and stopped. He shut the engine off and turned to Annie. "Let's go take a look."

CHAPTER 24

Thursday, 9:17 a.m.

JAKE STEPPED OUT OF the Firebird and glanced around. Two rows of tenants' cars were lined up in designated spots to his left, the parking area extending around and behind the building. A woman pushed a stroller toward her waiting vehicle. Another car was leaving the lot and turning onto the quiet residential street.

There were several gray sedans, but it was doubtful that Izzy's car was among them. Jake had no idea whether or not the fugitive would be using the same vehicle, or even if he still had it.

"Let's go behind the building," Jake said to Annie as she closed the car door and rounded the front of the vehicle.

They walked to the rear of the property and scanned their surroundings. A couple of overflowing dumpsters were pushed up against the back fence. Most of the visitors' parking spots remained empty, no doubt too early in the morning for socializing. A bicycle was chained to a post protruding through the asphalt near a patch of weeds that had somehow managed to thrive.

Annie pointed toward the rear of the apartment building. "There's a door."

They moved toward the center of the structure and stopped in front of the metal door. Jake tested the knob. It was locked.

"Did you bring your tools?" he asked.

"Right here," Annie said, pulling a small leather case from her handbag. She flipped it open, glanced at the lock, and removed a pair of odd-looking tools from the case.

Jake watched with interest as Annie went to work. She had practiced her technique on a large variety of locks, and he knew she could open just about any pin tumbler lock in record time.

And she did. He heard a click and Annie said, "Got it." She turned the knob with caution. The bottom of the door scraped against concrete as she inched it open and peeked in. She pulled her head back, looked at Jake, and whispered, "There's a light on down there."

Jake grasped the knob and eased the door further open. A set of concrete steps led down into a lighted basement—no doubt the furnace and electrical room. A steady humming came from below as an industrial-sized air conditioner pumped cool air throughout the building.

Jake crouched and glanced down the steps. The stairway was walled on both sides, a concrete floor at the bottom, and a view of a massive electrical panel against the far wall. Jake motioned for Annie to follow behind, and he went inside, easing down the stairs.

He stopped on the bottom step and peered around the corner. A chair sat in the center of the room, wisps of hair on the floor around it. A pair of scissors sat on a nearby bench, more rope on top. Long locks of black hair were taped to the wall above the bench.

A cot had been set up against one wall, and his eyes widened when he saw a female figure lying on it, her head turned toward him. Even from where he stood, he noticed the girl's eyes were filled with terror.

When he stepped into full view, she spoke, her uncertain voice coming out as a breathless moan. "Help me."

Jake glanced around the room and then turned to Annie, two steps behind him. "Call the police."

He rushed to the cot and crouched beside the trembling girl. Her hands were tied to the sides of the bed, her feet lashed together and fastened to the end.

But the most horrifying thing was that her head had been completely shaved. There was no doubt this was one of Izzy Wilde's victims, and if they hadn't gotten here when they had, she would've ended up like the girl in the park.

Jake tackled the knots as Annie called the detective and filled him in.

The girl's arms were now freed, and Jake turned to the cord binding her feet.

"Hank said a car'll be here right away," Annie said, hanging up the phone.

The final rope fell free, and Annie helped the trembling

young woman sit on the edge of the bed, then sat beside her, her arm around her shoulder.

"What's your name?" Annie asked.

"Tanya." Tears of relief flowed as the woman looked at Annie. "Tanya Arbuckle."

"Let's get her outside," Jake said.

"Not so fast," a voice said behind Jake.

Jake spun around. Izzy Wilde stood at the bottom of the stairs, facing their way, a pistol in his hand. A faint smile touched one corner of his mouth. "It was nice of you to come here. Now I don't have to look for you."

Jake edged sideways, away from the girls, attempting to put space between him and Annie. He needed to make himself the target. If someone was gonna get shot, it might as well be him.

"Stay still," Izzy said in a shrill voice, swinging the gun toward Jake. "I'll shoot you if I have to."

"The police are on their way," Jake said in a calm voice.

Izzy's eyes narrowed and he looked toward Annie and Tanya, then turned the gun their way. "Stand up."

Jake took a step forward, and the gunman swung the weapon back. "Stay still."

Jake dropped his arms to his sides, his hands knotted into fists, ready to pounce if it appeared the would-be killer intended to fire toward Annie.

"Stand up," Izzy repeated, a manic look in his eyes. He licked his lips and raised his voice. "Stand up."

Annie helped Tanya to her feet, her arm around the woman's shoulder.

Izzy's eyes darted back and forth, then he motioned with the pistol. "Get over there beside your husband."

Annie didn't move.

Izzy raised the weapon and sighted down the barrel, his eyes unblinking. "Now."

Annie glanced at Tanya, then dropped her arm and moved toward Jake.

"Get behind me," Jake said to Annie. "He can't shoot us all."

Izzy's face twisted into a sneer as he sidled toward Tanya. He stepped behind her and wrapped one arm around her throat, holding the pistol to her temple with the other.

The color drained from Tanya's face, and she closed her eyes, wrapping her arms around herself, her whole body trembling.

"Let's go," Izzy said, prodding the woman toward the stairs.

Jake took another step forward, careful to keep a safe distance from the gunman. The deranged killer was liable to shoot his hostage if Jake posed a threat.

Had they rescued a victim with success, only to have her murdered in cold blood in front of their eyes? He had to do something.

"Izzy, let the girl go," Jake said. "You can take me with you."

Izzy gave a quick, sharp laugh. "I don't want you. Maybe next time." His eyes gleamed. "I got what I want."

Annie took a step forward, her hands up in surrender. "Then take me."

Jake looked at Annie in horror. He knew his wife had a brave streak, but this was going too far. "No," he shouted. "Stay where you are."

Izzy backed up to the stairs and took one step up. Tanya stumbled to follow. "Don't worry," he said, his eyes on Jake. "I ain't interested in your wife."

Jake moved to the bottom of the stairs, powerless to help as Izzy backed up the steps, dragging his hostage with him, the weapon still pressed against the terrified woman's head.

Where were the police?

As soon as the unhinged madman disappeared through the doorway at the top of the stairs, Jake raced up the steps and leaped out onto the asphalt. He could hear sirens some distance away, drawing closer.

The sirens had frightened off the gunman, and he had discarded his hostage rather than chance being caught. She had crumpled to the ground not far from the exit, her head in her hands, sobbing quietly.

Jake looked around. Izzy Wilde was fifty feet away, running across the parking lot. The killer hopped a low fence, then ran behind a small building and vanished from view.

Jake followed, pounding across the pavement. He vaulted over the fence and looked around.

Izzy Wilde was nowhere in sight.

Then an engine roared and tires squealed. Jake turned. A gray sedan spun around a car, hopped over a curb, and veered onto the street. Jake raced after the vehicle, cutting across the lawn in an attempt to get ahead of the fugitive.

He reached the sidewalk as Izzy's vehicle spun past. The

driver was bent over the steering wheel, his eyes intent on the road ahead.

Jake squinted at the speeding vehicle, memorizing the license plate number—404 LVX. It was a gray Volkswagen Passat. Probably about 2005 as near as Jake could tell.

Wilde had gotten away again, but for the time being, the killer hadn't been able to claim another victim.

CHAPTER 25

Thursday, 9:52 a.m.

HANK TURNED INTO THE driveway of 1166 Red Ridge Street and pulled up behind Jake's Firebird.

Two police cars were parked near the rear of the lot, and the area was being sealed off with crime scene tape. CSI was on the way, and the basement would soon be documented in detail, much of its contents carried away for painstaking examination.

An ambulance sat idling, its rear doors open. The intended victim would be taken to the hospital as a matter of course. Assuming she was unharmed, she'd be released shortly thereafter, and Hank would take the woman's statement as soon as possible.

Hank and King stepped from the vehicle and went to the Firebird. Jake and Annie were leaning against the front fender watching the proceedings when the detectives approached.

Jake turned toward Hank and cracked a wide grin.

Hank nodded back and looked at Annie. "How'd you figure out he was here?"

Annie laughed. "It wasn't me this time. Jake figured it out." She explained the theory Jake had been working on, then shrugged. "It just made sense."

King crossed his arms and glared at Jake. "You should've called us."

Jake shrugged. "I didn't expect anything to come of it. It was just an idea, and we got lucky."

"He got away," King said matter-of-factly. "How is that lucky?"

Annie frowned at King. "Sure, he got away." She motioned toward the ambulance. "But so did Tanya."

King shrugged and gazed around the lot.

Jake handed Hank a scrap of paper. "Here's his plate number. He's driving a gray Volkswagen Passat—a sedan. Probably the same one he used before. He must've stashed it somewhere."

Hank took the paper, studied it, and handed it to King. "Get a BOLO out on this vehicle right away."

King glanced at the number a moment, then pulled out his cell phone and turned away.

"We had no idea he had kidnapped another girl," Jake said. "It caught us by surprise when we went down there."

Hank explained about the carton containing a lock of black hair that Luke Rushton had delivered to the precinct that morning. "You guys got here just in time. I'm convinced Tanya Arbuckle was destined to be his next murder victim." He looked at Annie. "Does Tanya have dark brown eyes?"

Annie nodded grimly. "Just like the other two."

"And I'm assuming she has black hair?"

"Yup," Jake said. "And it's taped all over the wall down there."

Hank's face took on a grave expression. "I'd better take a look." He glanced toward the ambulance as it pulled away. "And I'm anxious to talk to Tanya Arbuckle. I need to retrace her steps and find out where Wilde might've found her."

"She was too shaken up to talk much," Annie said. "All we could get from her is that she'd been kidnapped late last night after leaving a bar and heading home."

"Do you know the name of the bar?"

Annie shook her head.

"And Wilde is armed now," Jake added.

"He has a gun?" Hank asked.

"A pistol."

"As far as we know," Hank said with a deep frown, "he never had a gun before. He must've picked it up somewhere."

King had finished with the phone call and turned back, listening to the conversation. "It could've been in his vehicle," he said.

Hank thought about that a moment and then motioned toward King. "Let's go downstairs." He turned to Jake and wagged a finger. "Don't forget your statements."

Jake nodded and King followed Hank to the rear of the building. Hank pulled two pair of shoe covers from an inner pocket, handing a pair to King. After putting them on, they descended down the steps into the bowels of the building.

Hank took in his surroundings—the cot with the

fragments of rope still attached, the hair taped haphazardly to the wall, the chair where Tanya had undoubtedly been shaved. It was all eerily similar to the shed they'd discovered at Izzy Wilde's house that seemed like so long ago.

He took out his cell phone and snapped some photos.

"Looky here, Hank," King said. He was crouched down, digging in a cardboard box. He held up a blue plastic tarpaulin. "I'll bet he was gonna kill her here, wrap her body up in this, and then transport her somewhere else."

"Any blood on it?"

King shook his head. "Nope. I expect he planned to use a fresh tarp for each victim." He pointed to the box. "There're three of them here. All brand new."

"Any receipt in the box? Any idea where he bought them?"

King searched through the box, removing the tarpaulins one at a time. Finally, he announced, "Nope. No receipt."

Hank sighed and turned his gaze toward the bench. Beside the scissors and the extra rope lay three leather belts. It looked like Izzy Wilde had more than one victim in mind.

So far, the last two had been fortunate and had escaped with their lives. Hank wanted to make sure there were no more.

He stood back and glanced around the room again. It appeared Tanya Arbuckle had been the first victim held here. He'd intended to use this room as his new killing floor—his slaughterhouse and trophy room.

Hank turned around as someone called his name from the top of the stairs. He went to the bottom of the steps and

164

looked up. An officer was crouched on the landing.

"Hank, there's someone here who says it's urgent he speak to you. Says his name's Carter Wilde."

"Be right there," Hank said. He turned to King. "See if you can find anything else interesting, and take a few more pictures. I want to talk to Carter Wilde."

King nodded and Hank took the stairs up, stepping outside.

Carter Wilde stood behind the yellow tape, leaning on his cane, a confused expression on his face.

"What's going on here?" Carter asked. He waved toward the officers standing to one side. "They won't tell me anything." He glanced toward the street. "And what're the Lincolns doing here? Is this something to do with my brother?"

"I'm afraid it is," Hank said. "Your brother was holding a woman captive here. The Lincolns found her, but Izzy got away."

Carter's eyes bulged and his mouth gaped open. Finally, he asked, "Down there? In my building?"

Hank nodded. "How would Izzy gain access to this room?"

Carter shook his head, then narrowed his eyes and looked at Hank. "He must've gotten my keys. I keep them hanging by the door in my apartment."

"Did you see him recently?" Hank asked.

Carter shook his head. "No. Not for some time."

"Does your brother have a key to your apartment?"

"Sure, he does," Carter said. "You don't think …"

Hank finished the statement. "That he could've let himself into your apartment and taken the keys to the basement?"

Carter looked confused. "But I know the keys are there. They were there this morning."

Hank shrugged. "He could've made a copy and put the original back."

Carter nodded slowly, then drew his brows together and asked, "Is … is the girl okay?"

"She's fine."

Carter breathed a sigh of relief, then his face took on a worried look. "Detective, as much as it pains me to say it, you have to find my brother. I'm afraid he's going to hurt someone else."

"It appears he has every intention to," Hank said. "But we'll get him."

King approached, nodded at Carter, and tucked his hands into his pockets. He turned to Hank. "CSI is here."

"Okay, we'll let them do their job." Hank looked at Carter. "I'm afraid the basement's off-limits for a while. At least until we get everything documented. If there's an emergency and you need to go down there for some reason, let one of the officers know."

Carter nodded and glanced toward the doorway to the basement. "I don't understand why my brother would use that room for … his dirty work. I don't go in there much, but if the air conditioner broke down, or we needed some electrical work done, someone would have to go down there."

"I'm betting it was temporary," King said, turning to

Carter. "Do you have any idea where he might go next?"

Carter rubbed at his forehead before answering, "I can't think of anywhere."

Hank turned as a team dressed in overalls carried equipment past them before turning back to face Carter. "Contact me if you think of something."

"Absolutely," Carter said. "Please let me know if there's anything else I can do." He looked toward the basement, his lips in a tight line. "I'll do whatever it takes, Detective."

"We'll be in touch," Hank said, then looked at King. "Let's get to work."

The Lincolns had left by the time Hank and King returned to the side of the building. He'd have to contact them later to get their statements, but right now, he needed to make sure all available officers were looking for the gray Volkswagen, then he'd check on Tanya Arbuckle.

Izzy Wilde was on the run and, as far as Hank knew, had no place to hide. He prayed the fugitive was dumb enough to hold on to the Volkswagen.

Wilde was on the run, but he was unpredictable. Hank felt sure it was a matter of time before the fugitive made a fatal mistake, but unfortunately, time was of the utmost importance. Izzy Wilde was determined to carry out his mad obsession without hesitation.

CHAPTER 26

Thursday, 11:14 a.m.

IZZY WILDE POUNDED AT the steering wheel and cursed a long streak.

Life was such a never-ending struggle. It seemed like doing what had to be done was never easy.

First that devil of a woman had gotten away, leading to him getting thrown in jail. He hadn't expected such a violent response from a woman, and his face was sore where she'd attacked him, and his hand still ached where she'd bitten him like the dog she was.

As if that wasn't bad enough, the last one had gotten away when the Lincolns interfered, and he'd almost gotten nabbed again.

And he was fed up with it.

He cursed again and spun the steering wheel into the Hillcrest Mall parking lot, then drove to the rear of the lot and backed into an empty spot near a rusty chain-link fence.

He wouldn't be seen here in the employee parking area.

He didn't want to chance buying another car—at least not until he figured out how he could do it undetected—so he planned to do the next best thing.

He assumed Jake Lincoln had seen the plates on this vehicle; the big guy had been close enough. There must be a lot of gray Volkswagens in the city, and the police would stop them all, but he wasn't planning on keeping it much longer.

But it would do for now.

At first, he'd planned to lie low until nightfall, but he was desperate to satisfy the craving he felt deep inside. His mother had done a wicked thing, and he had to erase the memory from his mind once more.

And there was only one way.

But he had an immediate problem. Finding the next wicked dark-brown-eyed woman was a snap. They were all over the place. The problem was where to take her. He'd had two perfect spots, but they were overrun by cops now. He yearned to go back to the old house where he'd grown up. That was home. But they would no doubt be looking for him there, and he didn't dare.

His soul was hungry and yearned for sustenance, and he couldn't wait any longer.

He got back into his car and sat still a moment, contemplating a plan, then started his vehicle and pulled out.

He drove closer to the main doors. The mall was always busy, and there were no parking spots available. Perfect. That was what he wanted.

He pulled up to the curb, where he had a clear view of the

entrance. He searched under the passenger seat, found a small pair of binoculars, and focused them on the doors.

People came and went. Men, women, old, young, couples, kids, and his craving grew.

Finally, he lowered the glasses, licked his lips, and a smile spread across his face.

There she was.

An evil black-haired, dark-brown-eyed shrew. His eyes narrowed and his breath quickened as she walked past, casually swinging a shopping bag, paying him no mind. She walked across the lot, heading down between the rows of vehicles. He started the engine and followed.

She turned her head and glanced at his vehicle as he pulled alongside her and stopped.

Izzy wound down his window. "I'm looking for a parking spot," he said, smiling now. "Where ya parked?"

"Up there," she said, pointing to a red BMW sedan a few cars away.

Izzy pulled his vehicle just short of where she'd indicated and stopped. He sat motionless with his hand on the door handle, his anticipation growing, his hunger building, as she opened the back door, set her purchases inside, then opened the front door.

He had to time this right.

The moment she climbed inside her car and closed the door, he sprang from his vehicle.

She had her head down, no doubt looking for her keys, and she didn't see him as he hurried to the passenger-side door of her car and yanked the door open.

Her head spun toward him, her mouth dropping open. He climbed in and slammed the door, then turned to her, a warm smile on his face.

Her keys fell from her hand and rattled to the floor. She reached for the door handle.

He spoke sharply. "Don't."

She hesitated, her hand on the handle, her dark brown eyes growing wider as he lifted his shirt, removed the pistol, and pointed it her way.

"You'll be safer if you do what you're told," he said. "I ain't gonna hurt you."

She raised her eyes to his. "What … what do you want?"

"Not what you think." He grabbed her handbag and tossed it into the backseat, then motioned toward the floor. "Get the keys. Start the car."

She swallowed hard, scarcely breathing, then turned her eyes away and reached to the floor, picking up the keys. Her hand shook as she selected a key from the ring and inserted it.

"Start the car," he said. "We're going for a ride."

She looked at him and spoke, her voice hoarse as she forced out the words. "Where … are we going?"

Izzy raised the pistol. "Turn your eyes away. Don't look at me again. Ever. You understand?"

She turned her head away and nodded, then dropped her hands to her lap and stared blankly through the windshield.

She flinched when he spoke again. "Start the car."

She started the engine, then laid her head back, her hands on the steering wheel, and closed her eyes.

"Take a deep breath," he said in a soothing voice. "Don't be afraid. Just drive."

She nodded and inhaled a long breath, then opened her eyes and eased from the spot. "Which ... which way?"

He pointed.

And she drove.

He watched her as they turned onto Main Street and turned left. They were always afraid. A proper reaction, to be sure. Once they'd been caught in their evil ways and knew they had to pay, the reaction was always the same. Fear. Never remorse.

Her long black hair cascaded over her shoulders as her wicked eyes watched the road in front of her. Undoubtedly, her heart was as dark, abominable, and unrepentant as the others' hearts had been. They always were.

"What's your name?" he said, not that he cared.

"Hannah," she whispered. "Hannah Quinn."

"Keep driving, Hannah."

A few minutes later, he pointed ahead. "Turn there."

She slowed the vehicle and pulled to the right, then her voice trembled as she spoke. "It ... it's a graveyard."

"It's all right," he said with a long-suffering sigh. "I gotta visit somebody."

Hannah glanced in the rearview mirror, then pulled into the lane.

"Drive straight in," he said. "Go to the back of the lot."

She clung to the wheel and drove down the narrow lane. Gleaming tombstones protruded from the ground to their left and to their right. Fresh flowers, blooming plants, and an impeccable lawn decorated the ground above the death and decay below.

She shuddered and swallowed, her eyes straight ahead, driving deeper and deeper into the place of the dead. The pavement ended, turning into a dirt path.

His eyes roved over the well-kept grounds. No one was here. This was a place seldom visited, and it was a perfect spot for what he must do.

He motioned with the pistol. "Pull over there, Hannah."

Hannah turned the steering wheel to the left and stopped the vehicle underneath a towering oak, then sat back and let out a long, quivering breath. She glanced at him, then turned her eyes away, dropped her head, wove her fingers together in her lap, and remained quiet.

Izzy stepped from the vehicle, rounded the car, and opened the driver-side door. "Get out."

She spoke without looking up. "Can I wait here for you?"

He raised his voice and grabbed her arm. "No. Now, get out."

She climbed from the vehicle and glanced around as though considering making a run for it.

He tightened his grip on her arm. "Lie down."

Her eyes bulged. She drew a sharp breath and attempted to take a step back.

Izzy put his left leg behind her ankle, his hand around her throat, and pushed her. She fell to the ground and landed on her back, then brought her hands up as if to protect herself as he knelt beside her.

She sobbed, whimpered, and whined like a wounded

animal. Tears burst from her dark brown eyes as she glared into his.

He removed his hunting knife from a sheath at his side and held it in front of her frightened eyes, clenching his teeth. "Don't look at me."

Hannah closed her eyes and her body shook uncontrollably.

He touched the tip of his knife to her cheek and considered taking her eyes out, just for looking at him. He changed his mind. That wasn't what he'd come here to do, and time was wasting.

Izzy's mother lay whimpering on the soft bed of grass as he knelt beside her, the razor-sharp knife cropping her black hair a lock at a time, until finally, she would seduce an unwitting man no longer.

Soon she'd be dead, and her wicked ways would die with her.

CHAPTER 27

Thursday, 12:16 p.m.

ANNIE SAT AT THE DESK in the office of Lincoln Investigations, an open file folder in front of her, twirling a pen in her hand. She was relieved Tanya Arbuckle had been rescued, but the unsettling situation showed Izzy Wilde was determined to continue his killing spree.

They'd twice tracked him down, and twice been foiled in their attempt to deliver him to justice.

She dropped her pen onto the desk, sat back, and looked at Jake. He was lounging back in the guest chair, a deep frown on his face, glaring at a photo of Izzy Wilde.

"We have to anticipate his next move," Annie said. "He's running out of hiding places, and he doesn't dare use the same vehicle."

Jake tossed the picture onto the desk and shrugged. "I'm fresh out of ideas. It's unlikely he'll go near his brother again, and his house is off-limits."

"I believe he intended to use the apartment basement as his new trophy case. He seems determined to keep a lock of his victim's hair on display. If he continues, then he needs a base of operations, so to speak."

"There're lots of abandoned buildings in the city," Jake said.

"But he'll want someplace private."

Jake nodded and blew out a long breath. "And we need to figure out where."

Annie leaned forward and cupped her chin in her hand, staring at the picture of Izzy Wilde. He wasn't an unattractive man. He was rather handsome, actually. But not in a rugged way. His face was a little soft perhaps, but he had a cocky look about him without appearing threatening. Annie understood how he could approach his victims without arousing alarm. He looked harmless.

Annie was startled from her thoughts when the phone on the desk rang. She picked it up.

"Lincoln Investigations. Annie speaking."

"I told you to stay outta my business."

Annie took a quick breath and put the phone on speaker. "Izzy Wilde?" she asked.

Jake leaned forward as the voice continued. "You seem like you don't wanna give up. But you'll never catch me."

Annie glanced at the shelf behind her. A red light glowed, showing the call was being automatically recorded.

She spoke into the phone. "Maybe not, but the police will."

Izzy gave a short laugh. "Maybe they will. But not before I've finished what I gotta do."

"What is it you need to do?" Annie asked.

"I told you already." Annie heard rapid breathing on the line, then Izzy continued in a shrill voice. "Because she's back."

Annie let a few moments pass before speaking. "I understand." She hesitated. "Maybe we can help you."

Izzy had calmed down, his voice returning to normal. "It don't concern you. It's my business."

"Then tell me where you are," Annie said, her voice as soothing as she could manage. "I'll come and see you. We can talk."

"You expect me to trust you? After what you and your husband did?"

"We wanted to save the girl."

Izzy laughed again. "You did manage to do that, but there're lots more of them."

"Wait until we've had a chance to talk," Annie said. "I want to help you."

A long, hard laugh came over the line. "Afraid it's too late for that."

Annie caught her breath and swallowed hard. "What … what's too late?"

"I told you there were lots more."

Annie waited.

"She was easy to find. She trusted me and I didn't let her down." Annie could almost see his face twisted into a self-satisfied smile as he continued. "She had such beautiful long hair. It's a real shame."

Annie sat back and looked at Jake. His face was darkened

with anger as he glared at the phone. He caught her glance and raised his eyes toward hers and emitted a low growl. His hands worked themselves into fists, and he held them up helplessly.

Annie took a breath and spoke into the phone. "Did you kill another girl?"

A shriek came from the line. "She weren't no girl. She was an evil woman."

Annie's hand shook. She closed her eyes, trying to calm herself.

They'd been unable to save another victim.

She cleared her throat, then spoke in a defeated voice. "Where is she?"

"Where all dead things belong." Izzy laughed. "She's right at home now."

Jake picked up the phone and spoke into it through gritted teeth. "Where is she, you scumbag?"

Izzy hesitated, then spoke in a monotone voice. "Hey, Jake. Didn't appreciate your interference afore. I thought you'd understand. Seems I was mistaken."

Jake frowned. "Why would I understand?"

"Cause you're a man."

"What does that have to do with it?" Jake paused and lowered his voice. "Help me understand, please."

Izzy chuckled. "You've already shown me you don't. It's too late now."

Jake covered the phone and frowned at Annie. "This guy's nuts."

Annie gave a long sigh and reached for the phone. Jake set

it onto the desk and sat back again, shaking his head in exasperation.

"Izzy, tell us where the ... woman is, please," she said.

"I put her back where she come from."

Annie wanted to climb through the phone and wring Wilde's neck, but she fought to remain calm. "Where exactly is that?"

"Told you already."

The line went dead.

Annie hung up the phone slowly, and she and Jake looked quietly at each other for a few moments. Finally, Jake spoke in a low voice. "We'd better call Hank."

"And he'll want to hear this recording. Perhaps they can trace the call as well, but Wilde might've used a disposable phone."

Annie dialed Hank's number and put the call on speaker. When the detective answered, she filled him in on the phone call. "I'll get a copy of the recording to you right away," she said.

"I'll get Callaway to dissect it," Hank said, adding, "We haven't received a report of another body. Are you convinced he was telling the truth?"

"I'd count on it," Annie said.

Hank sighed. "I'm afraid you might be right." He hesitated, then added, "We found the gray sedan. The Volkswagen."

"And?"

"He left it in the parking lot at Hillcrest Mall. In the middle of an aisle. It was blocking other vehicles, and the owner of a blocked vehicle called us to have it removed, and there you have it. So, he either stole another vehicle, or worse still—"

Annie interrupted. "He carjacked someone."

Hank took a deep breath and let it out slowly. "It appears you might be right."

"Anything of interest in the car?" Jake asked.

"They're still going over it," Hank said. "But we found a pair of binoculars on the front seat and a couple of unused burner phones in the backseat. There's no doubt it's his car. Early forensic reports indicate his prints are all over it, and there's evidence someone was in the trunk. Until we find out who his latest victim is, he has a fresh vehicle."

"Where did he get the Volkswagen?" Annie asked.

"He bought it privately online. From an obscure bulletin board. Somehow we missed that one in our search. There're so many places to pick up used vehicles, but Callaway's still on it." Hank sighed. "Additionally, we have word out to all of the bars and restaurants in town to be on the watch, but we can't be everywhere."

"Your manpower's stretched pretty thin," Annie said. "There're not enough officers to cover all of the possibilities."

"You're right about that," Hank said, adding, "But we're one step behind him. Canvassing has uncovered where he found Lindy Metz. We obtained video footage from 7-Eleven showing she'd stopped for a drink on her way home, so he's not limiting his search to bars and restaurants."

"And now he's targeting people at the mall," Jake put in. "But who was she, and where is she?"

"I don't understand why he called us," Annie said. "He appears to be taunting us."

"He's not hiding his actions," Hank said. "That's for sure. Sometimes this type of killer wants to be caught, and perhaps that's why he sends packages of the victim's hair to us, as well as calling you. He might have a subconscious need to tell someone what he's done."

"But he didn't tell us where she is," Jake said. "Only that he put her back where she belongs."

Annie tilted her head to one side and pursed her lips. "Back where she belongs," she repeated. "Where does she belong?"

"Maybe he took her home," Hank said.

"But where's home?" Annie asked. "Since we don't know who she is, and if he's trying to give us a hint, that hardly helps."

Jake snapped his fingers, a faint grin replacing his frown. "I know where she is."

Annie looked at Jake and waited.

"He's killing his mother over and over, right?"

Annie nodded.

"Hank, where's his mother buried?" Jake asked.

The rustle of papers came over the phone and then Hank said, "Northtown Cemetery."

Jake sat back and crossed his arms. "That's where you'll find the victim."

CHAPTER 28

Thursday, 1:10 p.m.

HANK CONTACTED DISPATCH immediately, and the two cruisers closest to Northtown Cemetery were sent to inspect the property. He hoped they were dead wrong about there being another victim, but his instinct told him Jake had been correct in his speculation.

He pushed back from his desk and hurried into the break room. King was lounging as usual, polishing off a blueberry muffin and washing it down with a cup of coffee.

Hank poured a mug of the black sludge, dumped in lots of cream and sugar, and pulled back a chair across from his partner. "We might have another body," he said as he sat and laid his arms on the table.

King set his empty cup down and gave Hank a quizzical look.

Hank brought King up to speed on the latest, finishing with, "I'm waiting for a call to tell me the bad news."

And then his phone rang.

A body had been found in the cemetery.

Hank sighed, clicked off his phone, and pushed back his chair. He dumped the rest of his foul-tasting coffee into the sink and turned to King. "Let's go."

King wolfed the last bite of his muffin, tossed his cup into the wastebasket, and followed Hank from the break room.

Ten minutes later, Hank drove through the massive wrought iron gates of Northtown Cemetery. A quarter mile away, near the back of the sprawling cemetery, a couple of police cruisers were visible. As the detectives drew closer, first responders could be seen stretching yellow crime scene tape around the immediate area.

The medical examiner, as well as CSI, would be arriving soon. He'd wait for Nancy's official pronouncement, but Hank was pretty sure he knew what was waiting for them.

He stopped fifty feet away and pulled in beside a cruiser, and he and King got out. Hank turned as he heard a familiar rumble and spotted a red blur from the corner of his eye. Jake's Firebird was coming down the lane toward him.

The vehicle pulled in beside them and Jake and Annie got out.

"Jake was positive he was correct, so we decided to come here," Annie said with a sigh, glancing toward the tape. "This is one time I wish he'd been wrong."

Hank wished so too, but he didn't say anything. He turned as the forensic van bumped down the lane. It was followed by the coroner's van, and both vehicles pulled in and came to a stop.

The CSI team got out of their vehicle, and investigators unloaded equipment, lugging it to the crime scene. As he strode past, lead investigator Rod Jameson nodded at Hank and mumbled, "Morning, folks."

Hank turned to Detective King. "We'd better take a look." They donned foot covers, then ducked under the tape and picked their way across the lawn and approached the body.

The victim was a young woman, maybe midtwenties. She lay on her back with her arms at her side, face up, perpendicular to a headstone. Her head was a few inches from the stone and, as far as Hank could tell, the body was in the exact position of the corpse six feet below.

Hank looked at the inscription on the headstone. "Debra Anne Wilde." Izzy's mother.

His eyes roved around the grassy area. Ten feet away the ground was littered with the victim's hair. Long black locks ruffled in the breeze.

The grass around the hair was trampled, and Hank presumed it was where the victim had been shaved and strangled. He took a picture of the area.

Many of the surrounding graves had vases of flowers or colorful plants in various stages of decay surrounding the stones. Other than the flawless grass the caretakers tended to, the grave of Mrs. Wilde looked forsaken, and Hank noted the conspicuous absence of any flowers near the headstone.

Medical examiner Nancy Pietek stepped under the tape and worked her way through the short grass, greeting the detectives before crouching beside the body. She examined the leather belt around the woman's neck, felt the skin of the victim, and examined the bulging dark brown eyes and gaping mouth.

She stood and announced what Hank already knew. "The cause of death is asphyxiation by strangulation."

"How long ago?" Hank asked.

"I'd say no more than an hour." She pointed. "There're some defensive wounds on her arms, so it appears the vic was conscious at the time."

Hank nodded. Without a doubt, Izzy Wilde had called the Lincolns immediately after the killing.

He knelt beside the body and examined the pockets of the victim's jeans. Some loose change, nothing else. No ID.

A delicate gold chain hung around her neck, the end tucked behind her yellow-and-white striped t-shirt. Hank worked it out and snapped a picture of the small pendant it supported.

King's cell phone camera clicked as he took a photo of the headstone. He moved over and shot a picture of the hair and the surrounding area.

CSI was documenting the scene with photos as well. Evidence cones were being set up in several places. Hank moved over to where an investigator was crouched down several feet away, examining a set of tire tracks in the grass.

"Tracks tell you anything?"

The investigator looked up at Hank and shook his head. "Not much. By the depth of the impression into the soil, it was most likely a light car. Normal-width tires." He pointed. "Some footprints over there." He swung a hand across the area. "You can see where the car pulled in, then backed out again."

Hank felt certain Izzy would be using the victim's car, and until they found out who she was, it would be impossible to determine exactly what kind of car he was driving.

He glanced around the area. There were no cameras. He'd done a visual check when he had first entered the lot, and there didn't appear to be any surveillance at the gate, either. Not unusual for a cemetery.

He went back to where King was standing, his arms folded, watching an investigator crouched by the body. The investigator was employing a fingerprint scanner, and he stood and looked at Hank. "No match in the system for her prints."

Hank nodded. He hadn't expected there would be.

He turned to the sound of another vehicle rumbling down the lane. The Channel 7 Action News van pulled to a stop beside the coroner's van, and Lisa Krunk hopped from the passenger-side door. On the other side of the vehicle, the cameraman, Don, had opened the back door and was in the process of swinging his camera equipment onto his shoulder.

Without doubt, Lisa had found out about this latest murder through the police scanner Hank knew she had in the van. He sighed and went to meet her. He'd have to give Lisa some kind of a statement.

King had noticed the new arrival and followed Hank, and the two cops ducked under the tape and waited for her beside the Firebird.

Lisa smiled her wide smile as she approached, her cameraman close behind, the red light already glowing. "Good afternoon, Hank," Lisa said. She nodded at the Lincolns, then flashed a smile at King.

Hank nodded, King grunted, and Jake and Annie remained quiet.

Lisa glanced at Don, then held the microphone under her thin, sharp nose and spoke. "Detective Corning, what can you tell my viewers about what happened here today?"

As much as Hank disliked Lisa, he was the face of RHPD at the moment, and he chose his words with care. "We've discovered the body of an unidentified female, approximately twenty-five years old. Investigators are in the process of examining the scene."

"Detective, is this another murder by Izzy Wilde?"

"There're some indications it might be. However, it's too early to make any solid claims." Hank hesitated. "I'd like to remind the viewers, however, that Izzy Wilde is still at large. Please call Crime Stoppers if you should see him or suspect you know where he is."

Lisa turned to face Annie and spoke into the mike while Don trained his camera on the Lincolns. "The presence of Lincoln Investigations indicates to me this case is related. I happen to know they were instrumental in the original capture of Izzy Wilde." She poked the mike at Jake.

Jake frowned at the microphone. "We aren't privy to all that goes on within the police department. We were hired by a third party and are here because of the possibility of a relationship between the two murders."

Lisa swung the mike over toward Annie.

"You'll have to refer any further questions to Detective Corning," Annie said.

Hank took a step forward and Lisa swung the mike his

way. "I'll make a further statement when we know more," he said. "That's all for now."

Lisa turned away and looked at the camera. "We'll keep you updated on this story as it unfolds. For Channel 7 Action News, I'm Lisa Krunk."

The red light went out. Lisa clicked off the mike and turned to Hank. "Thank you, Detective," she said, another fake smile taking over her face.

Hank nodded and Lisa left, Don following at her heels.

Hank heard a faint zipping sound coming from fifty feet away. The victim's body was being placed into a body bag, and soon she'd be carried away for further inspection at the capable hands of Nancy Pietek.

But for now, Hank still had no idea who the Jane Doe was. Nor did he have any solid clues as to the whereabouts of Izzy Wilde.

CHAPTER 29

Thursday, 2:05 p.m.

JAKE WATCHED LISA KRUNK climb into the van and it zipped away, kicking up clouds of dust as it made its way from the cemetery. No doubt the pesky newswoman had gone to bother someone else for the time being.

Always striving to get the best of any situation and outdo her so-called competition, Lisa was tight about giving out information, but she seemed to expect everyone to bow at her feet. Jake had no doubt that in her characteristic attempt to create a sensational story, she'd be sticking her nose into the case again before long.

Jake turned back and spoke to Hank. "We didn't get a look at the body. Was she ...?"

Hank nodded and glanced over to where CSI was finishing up with the scene. "Just like the last one." He looked at Jake and spoke in a monotone voice. "Shaved head and choked to death with a belt. Just over an hour ago. Just before he called you."

Annie slipped a flash drive from her handbag and handed it to the cop. "Here's the recording of his call."

Hank took the drive and rolled it over and over in his fingers while he spoke. "Callaway had no luck in tracing the call. Wilde used a disposable phone. No GPS." He held up the drive. "Let's hope he has better luck with this." He tucked it into his shirt pocket and removed his cell phone. "Do you want to see a photo of the victim?"

"No, thanks," Annie said. "We'll take your word for it."

"I assume she has black hair and dark brown eyes?" Jake asked.

Hank nodded slowly. "Just like Olivia Bragg, Lindy Metz, and Tanya Arbuckle." A faint smile touched his mouth. "I make it a habit to memorize the names of the victims." He took a deep breath, a glint of anger showing in his eyes. "I need to find out the name of this one."

Jake knew Hank felt the same way he did about the victims. They weren't just victims, they were real people with real lives. And they all have names, families, and friends. Thankfully, Lindy and Tanya survived their ordeal, but Olivia and Jane Doe deserved to be remembered. Not just by those who knew them, but also by those who didn't.

Hank crossed his arms and mused, "I wonder if we'll get a package in the mail tomorrow. Somehow I don't think so. I believe sending a lock of the victim's hair to the precinct was

Wilde's way of announcing what he'd done. Goading us, maybe."

"If he doesn't, then his MO has changed," King said.

"Maybe," Hank said. "But he still kills his victims in the same way and for the same warped reason. Yes, this time was different. At least for him. His first three abductions took place after dark. This one was in broad daylight. His MO has changed somewhat, but in his mind, it's justified."

"He was angry," Annie said. "Angry that Tanya was rescued, and he couldn't wait for some kind of revenge."

King motioned toward the crime scene. "Or he couldn't wait to kill his mother again."

"Both times that he called us," Jake said, "he repeated the same thing. 'She's back.' And he has to keep killing her over and over."

"Do we dare hope this is the final one?" Annie said. "Perhaps this time he feels he returned her to her grave."

Nobody had an answer.

Finally, Jake spoke. "I assume Izzy hasn't called his brother yet."

"Nope. Carter Wilde doesn't get many personal calls, but we're monitoring all of them. So far, nothing." Hank scratched his head. "He's unpredictable. That's the problem. We have no idea what he's gonna do next or where he's gonna go."

"Even unpredictable people can be predictable," Annie said. "For example, he has to eat. He likely has to buy gasoline for the vehicle. He has to sleep somewhere."

"We're doing our best to cover those areas," Hank said.

"But this small city seems much larger when we have to be everywhere at once."

Annie continued, "We have to assume he'll be searching for another victim eventually."

"So what's his next move, Annie?" King said.

Jake looked at King, wondering if the cop was being his usual cocky self or not. The look on King's face told Jake it was a serious question.

"I think he's satisfied for today," Annie said. "He's gonna look for someplace to hide out. He'll park in some out of the way place, get some sleep, maybe something to eat, then tomorrow ... who knows?"

"The problem with that is, we don't know what he's driving."

Hank spoke up. "And that's why we need to make it our first priority to find out who this Jane Doe is."

"We might have to wait until she's reported missing," King said. "We can't be showing a photo of a dead woman on people's TV screens, and we can't canvass the entire city in a few hours."

"No," Hank said. "But we can hold a press conference and ask people to call in if they suspect a young woman's missing. I'll make sure 9-1-1 puts every call through, whether the person has been missing forty-eight hours or not."

"There might be another way," Annie said.

They all looked at Annie and Jake grinned to himself. His wife should've been a cop. She was always coming up with a brilliant idea.

"There might be surveillance at the mall," she said. "If it

caught a glimpse of her or her vehicle, it might tell us something."

"We tried that as soon as we found the gray Volkswagen," Hank said. "Nothing turned up." He squinted and rubbed the back of his neck. A moment later, he snapped his fingers and said, "But I still think you're on to something."

"Oh?"

Hank nodded. "We know what our victim looks like now, and we know what she was wearing."

He pulled out his cell and hit speed dial. In a moment, he said into the phone, "Callaway, I want you to arrange to get any camera footage you can from every store in Hillcrest Mall. Everything from ten this morning until noon. We need to take a look at it all ASAP. It's urgent." He hung up the phone. "If she bought anything at all, we'll find her."

"There was no camera footage outside the mall?" Jake asked.

"Nothing that showed the area where the kidnapping took place," Hank said. He dialed another number. "Nancy, I need a close-up picture of our Jane Doe's face as soon as you can make her look normal." Hank nodded and said, "Thanks, Nancy." He hung up and slipped the phone back into his pocket.

"Let's hope something turns up," King said. "That's all we got."

"If it leads to finding out what car she was driving," Hank said, "then we'll be one step closer to finding Izzy."

"Good thinking, Annie," King said, and Jake thought it

was rare praise coming from a cop whose accolades were few and far between.

"We'd better get going," Hank said, turning to Jake. "Let us know if you have any more ideas."

Jake nodded. "Of course."

Hank went and spoke to Jameson for a minute. When he came back, he and King got into the Chevy. It clanked to a start, and the two detectives drove away.

Annie looked at her watch and opened the passenger-side door of the Firebird. "Matty'll be home soon. We'd better get going, too."

Jake got in behind the steering wheel, brought the engine to life, and turned to Annie as she buckled her seat belt. "One thing I noticed. So far, Wilde has been operating in the northern half of the city."

"Maybe because it's closer to home for him."

Jake backed out, then pulled ahead and drove up the lane, turning onto the street. He glanced at Annie. Her brow was in a tight line. She was probably trying to come up with another brilliant idea. "You don't think he'll chance going home again, do you?"

"I doubt it. Not now. I expect the place is being watched."

"Yeah, I guess you're right." He looked over at Annie again. "What's on your mind?"

"I'm afraid he's not going to wait. He's going to make another attempt to kidnap someone else soon." She sighed. "Perhaps he won't, but people's lives—women's lives—are in danger."

Jake reached over and patted Annie on the leg. "I

understand how hard this is on you, but everyone's doing the best they can."

Annie gave Jake's hand a squeeze. "I hope our best is good enough. And soon enough." She pointed out the windshield. "Now get your eyes on the road and your hands on the steering wheel. We're no good to anyone if we end up running into a tree."

CHAPTER 30

Thursday, 2:35 p.m.

WHEN HANK AND KING arrived back at the precinct and went inside, Captain Diego was standing in his office doorway. He beckoned them over, then stepped back inside and dropped with a sigh into his high-backed leather chair behind his overflowing workload.

Hank went into the office, his eyes automatically zooming in on Diego's desk, half-expecting to see another delivery. There wasn't.

He took a seat, leaned forward, and looked at the captain. Diego appeared exhausted. The stress of the last few days showed as bags under his eyes, and Hank assumed the mayor had been rubbing him the wrong way again. The city mayor expected miracles from RHPD, but steadfastly refused to support a budget increase.

"What's up, Captain?" Hank asked.

"You tell me." The captain sat back, straightened his dark

blue tie, and looked back and forth between Hank and King.

King leaned against the filing cabinet and crossed his arms. "No ID on the victim, but there seems to be no doubt it's the work of Izzy Wilde."

"I want to hold a quickie press conference," Hank said. "We have to find out who she is."

Diego nodded. "I'll get it set up for three thirty." He made a note on a pad in front of him.

"Even if we find out who she is before that, it's still important," Hank said, explaining what he hoped to find through the mall security video. "We need to warn potential victims, especially anyone who fits his profile."

Diego leaned forward. "The narco squad has apprehended two men suspected of the prisoner transport assault. They admitted to being the ones who organized it, but they won't give up Salaz. And if they can be believed, they have no knowledge of who Wilde is. Their intention wasn't to free him. They only wanted Salaz."

"I never expected they would be any help," King said. "Wilde is on his own, and no self-respecting narco would give a crazed killer the time of day, let alone go out of their way to free him."

"That's a bit of good news, at least," Hank said and tilted his head to one side. "Is there anything else, Captain? You look a little worried."

"Not worried, just apprehensive. It's nothing that concerns you," Diego said. "You're doing your job."

"Try me," Hank said.

Diego took a deep breath and let it out slowly. "Needless

to say, the news of today's murder is unsettling, and I'd hate to think we were negligent in any way in allowing Wilde to escape."

"No one was negligent, Captain. There were unforeseen circumstances, and no one can be held culpable."

Diego nodded and steepled his hands under his chin. "I'm sure you're aware of how easily public opinion can be swayed. A lot of good men have been forced to retire for a lot less."

"I'll think of something for the press conference to set the record straight," Hank said.

"Run it by me first, Hank."

"Will do."

"And get this maniac before someone else is killed. Every officer is at your disposal. Keep me informed."

Hank assured Diego he would, and they left the office. The captain had no reason for concern. He was just overstressed. Diego was well respected among the men, and Hank was pretty sure everyone would have the captain's back if crunch time came.

"Call me if you need me," King said, shuffling toward the back of the room.

Hank went to his desk, set his briefcase beside his chair, and picked up a folder sent from the ME's office. He flipped it open.

He recognized the photo inside as that of the victim. The leather strap had been removed from around her neck, and her mouth was now closed. Considering the woman was dead, she looked about the best she could.

Hank hurried over to Callaway. Another photo of Jane

Doe lay on the desk, and the young whiz was staring at his monitor. He tapped his keyboard, rubbed the strain from his eyes, and looked up as Hank approached.

"We were able to get a lot of footage," Callaway said. "I'm still going over it. Not all of the stores have cameras, so it's hit and miss. So far, no luck."

Hank went around and stood behind Callaway. He leaned in and watched the monitor as Callaway restarted the video, playing it in double time.

Hank scrutinized each person who came in and out of stores, paid for purchases, or walked up and down aisles. He strained to see the face of the woman in the photo. Each time Callaway switched to a video from another store, Hank prayed it would help them reveal the true name of Jane Doe.

In a few minutes, Callaway sat back. "That's the last one from inside the stores. All we have left is some footage from around the mall."

"Let's watch it all," Hank said. "Start with anything near the east entrance doors."

Callaway cued up another video and Hank glared at the screen. According to the timestamp, it was late morning, and the mall wasn't all that busy. A few stragglers came and went. Finally, Hank half-shouted, pointing at the monitor. "Stop. That's her."

The young cop stopped the video, backed it up, and paused it. Hank strained to see. "She's wearing a yellow-and-white striped t-shirt and blue jeans. Can you zoom in a bit?"

Callaway zoomed in on the woman's face. "It's not very clear. That's about the best you're gonna get."

The image was pixelated, but long black hair framed a face Hank was sure was the right one. He wasn't much for malls, but he'd been to Hillcrest Mall many times in the past, and he knew the layout. "Zoom back again," he said.

Callaway zoomed back.

Hank pointed. "Zoom in on the bag."

Callaway did.

"That's a Cranston's shopping bag she's carrying," Hank said. "I'd recognize it anywhere. And I know exactly where that shot's from. She just left Cranston's."

Hank looked at the timestamp. It read 11:18 a.m. He pulled out his cell phone, got the number for Cranston's Department Store, and dialed. He asked to be put through to store security, and in a few moments, a man answered, "Security. Chris here."

Chris was a good friend of the Lincolns, and Lincoln Investigations had done some work for Cranston's in the past. Consequently, Chris was on a first-name basis with Hank, well aware of who he was. Hank identified himself and was acknowledged by a robust greeting, and he got down to business.

"Chris, this is urgent," he said. "A woman made a purchase from Cranston's sometime between eleven ten and eleven eighteen. I need to know who she is. Will you check credit card records from your east checkouts during that period?"

"No problem. Hold on a few minutes."

Hank drew up a chair and dropped into it. He stared blank-eyed at the monitor, positive they were on the right track, and hoping the woman had paid by credit card. He was desperate to find out this woman's name.

In a few minutes, Chris came back on the line. "During that time frame, there were three purchases on credit cards made by Cranston Club members, and well as two from nonmembers."

"Give me the names of the members." Hank grabbed a pen from Callaway's desk and flipped over the photo of the victim. He poised the pen and waited.

"According to the names from their club cards, we have Sarah Mitchell, Hannah Quinn, and Teresa Gonzales."

Hank scribbled down the names. "Thanks, Chris. You've been a big help. I'll talk to you later." Hank hung up. He hoped Jane Doe was a member of Cranston's. Otherwise, he'd need to get a warrant to obtain the credit card numbers of any other purchasing customers in order to get their names. He didn't want to waste that much time.

Callaway eyed the names and did a search on the DMV records for Sarah Mitchell.

Hank looked at the photo of a fifty-something woman and his heart sank.

Callaway did another search, this time for Hannah Quinn.

Hank's eyes popped and a grim smile spread across his lips. "That's her. That's our Jane Doe." Hank slugged Callaway on the shoulder. "Good job. Any vehicles in her name?"

Callaway did another search and printed out the records, and Hank took the printouts back to his desk. He was elated at finding out who she was, but he was heartbroken for the family of the woman who now had a name.

And the uncomfortable task of notifying the victim's loved ones always fell to him.

He put a BOLO out on Hannah Quinn's red BMW sedan. It was less common than the vehicle Izzy had used previously, and now that they had the plate number, it was just a matter of time before the car was spotted.

Hank looked at his watch. The press would be gathered on the front steps, and he was already a few minutes late. He'd have to put off contacting Hannah's family until after the press conference.

He grabbed a sheet of blank paper and a pen and jotted down some notes. This would be a short conference. All he wanted was to warn the citizens of Richmond Hill, then get back to the urgent job of tracking down a killer.

CHAPTER 31

Thursday, 3:35 p.m.

ANNIE SAT BACK IN HER comfortable chair and stared at the TV screen, her mind sinking into thought as a commercial ran. Channel 7 Action News had broadcast Hank's news conference live. The cop's short address on the front steps of the RHPD building had contained little more than an alert to the city advising caution. Hank hadn't taken any questions.

She wondered how many people would see the conference at this time of day. No doubt they would rerun it several times as a news alert, and the story would take a prominent place on the six o'clock news, but until then, most of the black-haired, dark-brown-eyed, female citizens of the city would remain uninformed and at risk.

Jake swung upright from a lying position on the couch, switched off the television, and rubbed his bristling hair back. He looked at Annie. "Hank didn't mention Jane Doe, but I'll bet the red BMW he asked people to watch for is hers. I'm surprised he didn't call us."

"He didn't have time," Annie said. "And I feel helpless sitting here with nothing to go on, and no idea in the world where Izzy might be."

Matty looked up from where he was lying on the floor, a pillow behind his head, a comic book rolled up in his hand. He had a worried look on his face. "Uncle Hank said women with dark hair should be careful. Kyle's mom has dark hair."

Jake spoke. "We'll talk to her, but I'm sure she's fine. She has light brown eyes."

That seemed to satisfy Matty, and he flipped his comic open again, soon absorbed in reading about the latest adventures of Batman.

But this wasn't Gotham, there were no superheroes here, and Annie wanted to do something before another unknown victim got a deadly taste of Izzy Wilde's mad obsession.

She reached to the stand beside her chair and picked up a file folder, flipping it open. She leafed through the scant evidence they had on the Izzy Wilde case for the hundredth time. Each time she'd hoped something would pop out at her, but it never did. There wasn't a whole lot to go on.

She sighed, dropped the folder back onto the stand, and stood. "I'm going to see Chrissy for a few minutes." She turned to her son. "Matty, stay inside, please. You can go and see Kyle if you want, but make sure you stay inside their house for now."

Matty looked up and frowned. "I don't have dark brown eyes."

Annie laughed. "Just stay inside."

Though Izzy Wilde had called Lincoln Investigations twice, each time warning them to stay away, his warnings never came across as a direct threat toward her or her family. She didn't feel they were in any imminent danger, but she decided it was always more sensible to play it safe.

She went to the kitchen for her handbag and walked out the front door, then stopped short at the sight of Lisa Krunk strolling up the path toward her.

The newswoman had a wide smile pasted on her unattractive face, and she waved one hand casually, the other hand gripping a cordless microphone. Don followed dutifully behind, the camera on his shoulder. The red light wasn't on.

"Good afternoon, Annie," Lisa said as she approached, the forced smile still stuck to her face.

Annie smiled politely, stepped off the front porch, and waited.

Lisa stopped three feet away, the mike at her side. "I just came from the news conference," she said. "I want to put together a piece for the six o'clock news, and I was hoping to ask you a few questions."

"I don't know any more than what you already have," Annie said. "Detective Corning would be your best source."

"Hank doesn't have time for any questions right now. He shooed me away when I tried to talk to him."

Annie wanted to shoo her away as well, but she remained polite. "I assume he gave you all he had at the press conference." Annie paused, then asked, "What do you want to know from us?"

Lisa hesitated, then said, "I'm interested in getting an interview with Izzy Wilde. I've talked to his brother in the past, but he feels it would be impossible to connect me up with Izzy." She cocked her head, and her voice took on an uncharacteristic begging tone. "I'm certain you and Jake are working on some leads, and I want to make a deal with you."

Annie frowned. "What kind of deal?" Lisa's deals usually ended up being one-sided, with Lisa coming out the winner.

"I want to interview Izzy Wilde. In return, Lincoln Investigations would get full credit for assistance." She paused and said in an offhand manner, "I'm sure you could always use the publicity."

Annie didn't want that kind of publicity. Besides, they had as much business as they could handle. She raised her chin an inch and glared at Lisa. "We don't know where he is. If we did, we would tell the police first."

Lisa was too self-centered to feel embarrassed by her unethical request. She continued, undaunted. "I thought you might have some idea."

"None," Annie said. She turned when she heard the door open behind her. Jake stepped out onto the porch, a deep frown on his face as he looked at the camera, then back at Lisa.

Lisa looked calmly at Jake and explained what she wanted. He gave the same response as Annie. "We don't know where he is. Sorry, we can't help you."

Annie put her hands on her hips. "You'd have a better chance if you drove around looking for a red BMW," she said. "We have nothing for you."

Lisa glared back, stuck her nose in the air, and spoke in a condescending tone. "I'm going to find him eventually," she said. "And when I do, I thought you might be interested in being the ones who brings him in."

"We don't care who catches him," Jake said. "And if you come across him, you'd get more goodwill from the police if you contacted them rather than trying to interview a killer."

Lisa narrowed her eyes. "Are you saying I'm not interested in justice?"

"It looks that way, yes," Jake said. "Sometimes I have to wonder what's the most important to you."

Lisa cocked her head, undeterred. "The story is the most important. I'm a journalist."

Annie gave an exasperated sigh and rolled her eyes. Lisa had a warped sense of right and wrong. Without some integrity, she was destined be a two-bit hack forever rather than the investigative journalist she thought herself to be.

Lisa crossed her arms. "Are you telling me you don't want to be interviewed on camera?"

"That's exactly what we're saying," Jake said. "We've nothing to tell you, and nothing that'll help you or the police find Izzy Wilde."

Lisa stared tight-lipped a moment and then nodded at Don, and they strode back to the van and got in. It edged from the curb and disappeared down the street.

Annie looked at Jake and shook her head. "I swear that woman's losing her mind."

Jake laughed and followed Annie back into the house. "I thought you were going to Chrissy's."

"Just give me a minute to calm down." She hurried into the living room as her cell phone played a jingle. It was Hank.

"I might drop by a little later if you guys're gonna be home," the cop said.

"We'll let you know if we go out," Annie said. "If it's a social visit, why don't you bring Amelia with you?"

Hank paused. "We might end up talking business."

"I'm sure it wouldn't be the first time you discussed your job with Amelia. She probably wants to know you value her opinion enough to involve her."

"Yeah, you're probably right. I'll see how things pop."

"Did you find out who Jane Doe is?" Annie asked.

"I did—with Callaway's help. We figured it out from the mall's security recordings, and with the assistance of Chris at Cranston's. The woman's name is Hannah Quinn, and I'm about to pay her husband a visit. Then I have a few things to do, but if all goes well, I'll see you in two or three hours."

Annie hung up. She didn't envy Hank his assignment. She told Jake the news, then went to see Chrissy. In case her best friend wasn't up on the latest, Annie wanted to warn her there was a killer on the loose.

CHAPTER 32

Thursday, 5:15 p.m.

HANK SAT QUIETLY IN the driveway of the house where Hannah Quinn used to live. Things had gone pretty much as he'd expected. Hannah's husband had just gotten home from work, and the man had been shattered at the news of his wife's murder. Hank had watched out-of-control tears flow down the devastated man's face.

But the thing that broke Hank's heart was finding out the couple had a two-year-old child. A baby girl.

Hannah's mother had been taking care of the toddler while Hannah went shopping, and Hank was thankful the child hadn't been with her mother at the time of the abduction. One senseless death was bad enough, but two, especially that of a child, was unthinkable.

Sometimes Hank hated this job.

He started his car and backed from the driveway, leaving the wretched man behind. Out of his sight, but not forgotten.

Hank had seen a lot that would be burned into his mind forever. Some things never went away.

He drove to the precinct, contemplating the burden he carried. It was his decision, of course. No one had forced him to be a homicide detective, but he'd made a choice what seemed like so long ago. His consolation was in finding justice for those who'd been victims of others.

He wondered if he was taking it all too personally. He'd been taught to separate the job from his feelings. Many a good cop had ended up driven half-insane—victims of PTSD—by burying themselves too deeply in their jobs, unable to separate their personal lives from the heartbreaking events that surrounded them on a daily basis.

And though he wasn't much for booze, he understood why a lot of cops turned to the bottle more often than they wanted to admit.

Maybe he should talk to someone about it. Though he didn't want to burden Amelia with his troubles, perhaps Annie had been right. Amelia was probably the one he should talk to.

Could be he was too soft. Perhaps he should be a little more callous like Detective King; nothing seemed to concern his partner for long. Hank wasn't sure which was worse.

Or perhaps King kept it all bottled up inside. Sometimes one never knew for sure until it was too late.

Yes, he'd talk to Amelia.

He pulled into the parking lot behind the precinct and went to the front of the building. He climbed the steps, feeling a little better. Thinking it through helped somewhat, and as he strode through the doors and into the precinct, he vowed to renew his efforts in finding Izzy Wilde.

But he didn't know where to start.

Thus far, the red BMW hadn't been spotted, and though Izzy's face was now known to many of the inhabitants of the city, no one had reported a sighting.

As he passed Diego's office, he glanced inside. The captain was leaning over his desk, a pile of paperwork in front of him, and Hank was reminded his boss had the weight of the whole precinct on him. If Diego ever retired, and Hank was offered the captain's job, he'd turn it down flat. He didn't feel cut out to handle that kind of pressure.

Besides, he didn't want to spend the rest of his career behind a desk. As gut-wrenching as this job was sometimes, he couldn't see himself doing anything else, and it gave him a sense of fulfillment when a case came to a successful conclusion.

He spun his head when he heard someone call his name. It was Callaway, and the young cop was frantically waving him over.

Hank hurried to Callaway's desk. "What's up?"

Callaway sat back and slipped his headphones off one ear. "It's Wilde," he said. "He finally contacted his brother. He wants to meet."

Hank sat on the edge of the guest chair and leaned forward, dropping his arms onto the desk. "When did he call?"

"Just now. Two minutes ago."

"And when does he want to meet?"

"He didn't say exactly. Carter told him he'd have to think about it first. Izzy sounded desperate, and he said he'd call back in a few minutes."

"He hasn't called back yet?"

"Not yet."

"I'll listen to the recording in a minute," Hank said. He pulled out his cell phone and called Carter Wilde. The man answered right away, and Hank gave his name. "I assume you're still willing to help us?"

"I am, Detective. I was about to call you. Did you intercept my brother's phone call?"

"Yes, we heard the call and I want you to meet him. When he calls back, find out where he wants to meet. Don't sound too eager, but make sure you agree. I can have a team surround the area in less than half an hour. We'll be monitoring the call."

Carter agreed and Hank hung up and looked at Callaway. "Were you able to trace the call?"

The young whiz shook his head. "It was too short."

Hank stood. "Is King here?"

Callaway cocked a thumb over his shoulder. "I think he's in the break room."

Maybe that was King's secret. Perhaps Hank should spend a little more time in the break room. Sure, and then the job would never get done.

He hurried down the hallway and found King slouched back in a chair, his legs crossed at the ankles as they rested comfortably on the tabletop. Hank told King about the call.

His partner looked disappointed. "I was about to call it quits for the day. Head home."

Hank frowned. "Not until the job's done."

King shrugged and took a sip of coffee. "What do you want me to do?"

Though King was a slacker at times, Hank knew his partner could get a job done in short order when he applied himself. Unfortunately, those times were rare. Hank had finally discovered that although King would never be a leader, a good nudge in the right direction usually got him moving.

"I want a SWAT team briefed on the operation and ready to move at a moment's notice. This might be our only chance to get this guy, and I don't want to mess it up."

King slipped his legs off the table, finished his coffee, and rose to his feet. "I'll get right on it."

Hank hurried back to Callaway's desk, where Wilde's prior phone call was cued up and ready for Hank to listen to. But he didn't have time. Izzy was calling his brother back.

"Can you meet me?" Izzy was asking. "It's important. I wanna see you again, and I need some stuff."

Carter gave an exaggerated sigh. "What do you want?"

"I need some extra clothes. Your stuff will fit me all right. And I could use a new vehicle."

"I can't get you a vehicle," Carter said. "You'll have to make do with what you have, but I'll bring you some clothes. Anything else?"

"How about some food?"

"I'll see what's in the fridge. I'm sure I'll find something." Carter paused. "Where do you wanna meet?"

Izzy hesitated, then said, "I got the perfect spot picked out. Secluded and not busy at this time of day. Meet me at Richmond Valley Park. I'll be at the rear of the park, over by the tennis courts. I'll be watching for you."

There was a long pause, then Carter said, "I can be there by six thirty."

"Six thirty is good. And, Carter, make sure nobody follows you."

"Who's gonna follow me? They're after you, not me."

"Just be careful. You never know what the cops might be up to."

"Of course I'll be careful," Carter said. "Do you think I wanna get charged for aiding and abetting a fugitive?"

Hank smiled. Carter was playing his part to perfection.

"I guess not," Izzy said.

"Then I'll see you soon."

The line went dead and Hank sprang into action. He popped his head into Diego's office, gave him a brief version of recent events, then went to find King.

His partner was on the phone, standing at his seldom-used desk. "We're ready to roll," Hank said. "We have a location."

Fifteen minutes later, a vanload of the best was on the move. The team parked a quarter mile away, and elite officers approached the area in silence, taking up covert positions on all sides. A sniper watched through his scope from a vantage point fifty yards away. No one would get past—in or out.

Hank and King would hang back out of sight until the arrest was made, monitoring the operation on two-way radios. Too many cops increased the odds of being seen, and

Hank wanted the team to do their job and make a clean capture.

Minutes went by.

Hank looked at his watch. Carter would be arriving near the tennis courts before long. The man had been briefed on what to do—relax, meet his brother as planned, and let the team take care of the rest. They knew what to do.

Word came over his radio. Carter had parked his vehicle on the road and was on his way to the designated meeting place. There was no sign of Izzy yet, but Carter was four minutes early.

The radio went silent and Hank waited.

~*~

IZZY WILDE CROUCHED in the grass, high atop a hill, two hundred yards behind the tennis courts. He had watched the team move in through high-powered field glasses purchased specially for the occasion. The proprietor of the army surplus store where he'd bought them had been happy to make a sale, and anyway, the guy had been too drunk to recognize who he was doing business with.

It was one of his favorite stores, and it was the same place where he'd purchased his hunting knife earlier that day. Today, he'd taken the occasion to buy a scope for his rifle at the same time. Then a trip out of town, a few practice shots, and he had the scope adjusted pretty well. Not perfect, but good enough for his purposes. He had no pretense at being an expert.

Izzy couldn't tell how many cops there were—likely not more than a handful. He could make out two at the moment. One lay flat on his stomach, peeking around a tree not far from the tennis courts. Another one hunkered down behind a concrete garbage container on the other side of the courts. He assumed more were nearby.

He didn't care how many there were. He only wanted one. From his distance, he didn't expect to hit anyone, anyway. He wasn't good with a rifle. But hit or miss, if he got a clean shot, he was gonna take it.

They thought he was stupid. They thought he took foolish chances by calling Carter on the phone when it was obvious to him they would be bugging his brother's calls. And he'd made sure to keep the conversations short. He didn't want them to trace the call and find his position. And now, he'd show them a thing or two. He wasn't stupid.

The location where he waited patiently had been chosen simply because he held an advantage here. His plan was to pound off a few shots, then head back down the other side of the hill, where his beautiful red BMW awaited.

He raised the rifle, propped the barrel on a jutting rock, and squinted through the scope. His dear brother was hobbling across the lawn, heading toward the tennis courts. Izzy watched him stop and glance around, then drop the shoulder bag he was carrying onto the ground beside him.

Then Carter eased himself to a sitting position on the grass, laid his cane beside him, and waited.

Izzy adjusted his view toward the cop who thought the tree was going to protect him. Should he aim for the cop's head? Or maybe for his back? He'd be wearing a vest. A shot to the back wouldn't do much, though it was a larger target and would give him a better chance of hitting something.

But it didn't matter much. This was all just a warning, anyway. Just to show them who was in control.

He aimed for the cop's back, held his breath, and squeezed off five shots.

It was time to scram. He'd find out later if his handiwork had amounted to anything or not.

CHAPTER 33

Thursday, 8:18 p.m.

JAKE SETTLED INTO a chair, a leftover chicken drumstick in one hand, a napkin in the other, and pulled up to the kitchen table across from Annie.

His wife was relaxing, nursing a cold drink after spending the last two hours hunched over her computer. She'd just finished up a background check for a client and emailed the summary files. There wasn't much they could do about the Izzy Wilde case at the moment, and she liked to keep up with their regular flow of more mundane tasks. That was their bread and butter, a regular income they could count on to keep the company afloat.

They were still under retainer to Edgar Bragg, but the funds he had supplied would soon run out. By looking at the distraught widower's lifestyle, Jake assumed the man couldn't keep payments up indefinitely. Whether they were paid or not, Jake and Annie were committed to bringing Izzy Wilde to justice. Always the compassionate one, Annie would insist on it.

He had tried to get ahold of Hank a little earlier, but the cop hadn't had time to talk. He'd mentioned something about a stakeout and the possibility of catching Wilde. Jake was anxious to hear more about the operation, and especially how it had turned out. He was pretty sure Hank would've contacted him immediately if he had any good news to report.

When the doorbell rang, Jake jumped up and tossed the bare chicken bone into the garbage bin, wiped his hands, and hurried to the door.

He peeked through the peephole. Hank stood outside on the porch, his hands in his pockets, gazing around the neighborhood. Jake opened the door sporting a wide grin and invited his best friend in.

Hank stepped inside and greeted Jake with a handshake, following him into the kitchen. He dropped wearily into a chair, smiled at Annie, and yawned loudly.

"You look like you could use a cup of coffee," Annie said. "Jake just made a fresh pot."

"Yes, please. That and a good long nap."

"I wouldn't mind a cup while you're up," Jake added.

Annie poured three mugs of coffee and brought them to the table along with cream and sugar. Hank fixed his up with cream and a long stream of sugar, took a sip, and stretched.

Jake had waited long enough. "What's the news?" he asked, looking at Hank.

Hank sighed deeply, set his cup down, and dropped his

arms on the table. "We thought we had Izzy Wilde. He'd arranged to meet his brother in Richmond Valley Park. With Carter's help, we surrounded the meeting spot. Izzy must've sensed a trap, or perhaps it was all a game to him, but he was waiting for us."

Annie leaned in, a troubled look on her face. "Waiting for you?"

"He fired several shots from a good two hundred yards behind our line. Wounded an officer in the leg. Only an experienced sniper could expect a hit from that distance. I'm surprised he even came close."

Jake frowned. "He got away?"

Hank nodded. "Clean away. We scoured the entire area where the shots came from and finally found five shell casings atop a knoll. There's a small road at least a quarter mile beyond that. We assume he made his getaway using that road. Officers are still searching the area, but I'd bet he's long gone. No doubt still driving the red BMW."

"How's the officer?" Annie asked.

"He'll be fine. It wasn't more than a flesh wound. They took him to the hospital, bandaged him up, and sent him home. It'll be desk duty for him for a while."

"What do you think Wilde was trying to prove?" Annie asked. "That he's smarter than you?"

"Maybe he's continuing to taunt us," Hank said. "I don't think he intended to kill any of the cops. He'd be a real fool to take a chance like that not knowing he had a reasonable chance of hitting anything."

"Maybe he *is* a fool," Jake put in. "That's been my theory all along."

"I think he's insane," Annie said. "His phone calls to us attest to that. Any mere mention of his mother sends him off on a raving diatribe."

"Whatever else he is," Hank said, "he's a menace who must be stopped. If he's widened his targets to include anyone, especially police officers, then it appears no one's safe now. He's become even more unpredictable."

"Hi, Uncle Hank." Matty strolled into the room and greeted Hank with a fist bump. He sat beside his father and looked curiously at the cop. "You look tired, Uncle Hank."

Hank laughed. "Good observation. In fact, I'm worn right out."

"Can't you get some sleep?"

Hank laughed. "Cops don't sleep."

Matty looked at Hank in disbelief, then chuckled and slid off his chair. "I'm pretty sure they do," he said, then wandered into the living room. The sounds of the television soon wafted into the kitchen.

"We had a visitor today," Annie said. "Lisa Krunk thinks we know where Izzy Wilde is. She's determined to interview him, and she wanted to make some kind of deal with us."

"What kind of deal?"

"She thought if she mentioned Lincoln Investigations favorably in one of her news stories, it would be good for our business."

"She's always trying to stay ahead of the pack," Hank said. "I hope you didn't offer to help her."

"Not a chance," Jake said. "We have nothing for her anyway. She left in a huff."

Annie turned the conversation to a more serious matter. "Tell us about Hannah Quinn."

Hank looked even more tired, defeated perhaps. His shoulders drooped and he stared at his hands a moment. Finally, he looked up, a distant look in his eyes, and took a long breath. "Twenty-five years old. Leaves behind a husband and a two-year-old girl."

Annie remained silent, but Jake saw the anguish in his wife's eyes. He knew what she was thinking. She always felt deeply for the victims of senseless crime, and her heart would be breaking in two, not only for the father, but for the toddler as well.

At the moment, Jake felt only anger. He had a good idea what Hannah Quinn's husband would be going through right now. The man's future would be filled with despair, and the girl would grow up knowing little about who her mother was. It was almost an unbearable thought.

There was silence in the room for a while. No one had anything to add, and though none of them had ever met Hannah Quinn, they quietly mourned for her and her family.

Annie turned to Hank and broke the stillness. "Did you give any more thought to what we talked about? About discussing things with Amelia?"

"I did," Hank said, forcing a faint grin. "And you're right. I need someone I can let this all out on. It's great to talk to you guys, but I've decided to let Amelia in on a little more of my world." He looked at his watch. "She's expecting me by nine, so I'd better get going. I need to take a little break. There's nothing I can do right now, and I'm sure I'll be the first one to get a call if anything pops."

Jake stood and saw Hank to the door. He stood in the doorway and watched the cop back out of the driveway and head away.

It was getting dark out, and Izzy Wilde was still out there in the darkness somewhere. The lunatic's first three kidnappings had all taken place after the sun had set, and Jake was concerned. Izzy still had a vehicle, and if the police had no success in locating him in the next hour or two, there might be news of another mindless slaughter in the morning.

CHAPTER 34

DAY 5 - Friday, 7:21 a.m.

LISA KRUNK HAD AWAKENED with one ambition. The same thought that had plagued her sleep, causing her to toss and turn throughout the night, was still foremost in her mind.

She had to get the story.

Due to her unparalleled investigative skills, Channel 7 had offered her some prime-time slots a couple of times recently. Her knack of getting to the heart of any story, combined with her exposés on a variety of timely topics, had guaranteed she was predestined for bigger and better things.

It was just a matter of time before she was recognized nationwide, certain to stand alongside the greats who'd gone before.

It all took guts, determination, and perseverance.

And she had that in spades.

There was always a story. One just had to ferret it out, then elaborate and embellish and, with her editing skills, it would come together into a masterpiece worthy of her adoring fans.

And right now, the story was all about Izzy Wilde.

It was disturbing that the Lincolns had brushed her aside without so much as hearing her proposal. She often went out of her way, not only to assist them in their investigations whenever possible, but to aid the local police as well, and it made their curt dismissal of her even more unbelievable.

Detective Corning wasn't much better, barely giving her the time of day unless it suited his agenda.

She was on a first-name basis with the lot of them, and it just wasn't fair.

But today was another day, and she was determined to make the most of it. Her public relied on her to bring them high-quality stories day after day. It saddened her that many of her well-crafted reports, though often commanding the top spot on the evening news, were soon forgotten by the next day. The never-ending flow of mundane pieces that other so-called reporters littered the news with saw to that.

She sighed at the thought and resolved to outshine them all.

It was essential she look and feel her best for the day ahead. She downed a bottle of instant breakfast drink, dropped one more for the road into her bag, then tended to her appearance. It was important to her how she looked on camera.

She brushed down her long black hair, touched up her red lips, and admired herself in the full-length mirror hanging on the bathroom door. She looked great.

Hurrying back to the living room, she brushed aside the curtain and peered out. Don would be arriving soon, and her faithful cameraman would wait for her at the curb seven floors below.

She thought perhaps she didn't give her cameraman enough credit. Sure, anyone could do his job, but he was loyal to her, devoted to his work, and always willing to jump when she demanded it.

She made a point to consider giving him a small bonus this Christmas.

The ringing of her cell phone startled her. She raced to the kitchen and rifled through her handbag, then pulled the phone out and looked at the caller ID. It was an unknown number.

"Lisa Krunk," she said in the most businesslike voice she could manage.

She heard breathing on the line and she frowned. It must be one of her multitude of fans, no doubt calling just to hear her voice.

"Who's this?" she demanded.

"Ms. Krunk?" It was a man's voice.

"Yes."

The voice continued. "I understand you wanna speak to me."

She caught her breath. She had a pretty good idea who was calling. From the research she'd done on the case, she recognized the distinct voice of Izzy Wilde. Her heart pounded. This might be the break she needed. It seemed too good to be true, but here it was.

She took a deep breath to calm her excitement, then spoke in a relaxed voice. "Mr. Wilde. I'm anxious to talk with you."

"What do you wanna talk about?" It sounded like an innocent enough question, spoken in a casual manner.

Lisa struggled to think. She had a million questions, and every one of his answers was bound to produce more questions. But she detested phone interviews. She needed things to be close-up and personal. She needed to look her subjects in the eye, to see deep into their souls, and trust her instincts to take the interview into a profitable direction.

"I'd like to meet with you," she said, then held her breath.

Izzy gave a short laugh. "Why would I wanna do that?"

"Because you have a story," Lisa said. "Everyone has a story they need to tell. And I'd very much like to hear yours, and I believe the people of this city would love to hear it as well."

"I keep up with the news. My story's on the front page and on every television."

Was she losing him? She stroked his ego. "But that's not your real story. Your fans would prefer to hear about the real you."

"My fans?" It wasn't really a question. It was more of an acceptance of a truth dawning on him. Perhaps recognition that his work hadn't gone unappreciated. He took a quick breath. "Do you think so?" His voice showed some enthusiasm now.

She had him interested. "Of course," she lied. She bit her lip, then continued with what he wanted to hear.

"Everywhere I go, I hear from people who admire you for your accomplishments."

"You do?"

Was he swallowing her line? She hoped he was gullible enough. She continued pouring out the verbal charade. "I'm a bit of a fan myself."

She closed her eyes and waited for his reply.

He remained silent. What was he thinking?

Finally, he spoke. "It ain't safe. How do I know I can trust you?"

She thought quickly. He was nibbling at the hook, and she couldn't afford to lose him now. Now that it was so close. So close.

"I'll come alone," she said. "We must trust each other. Can I trust you, Izzy?"

"Of course you can trust me. But that ain't my concern. I worked long and hard to keep ahead of them cops. I'm not about to give up everything."

"It's for the fans, Izzy. Think of your fans."

There was more silence, then Izzy answered at last. "All right. Come alone."

"I will."

"No camera."

She hesitated. "No camera."

"You'd better not try to betray me," Izzy said. "I'll be watching and waiting."

"I won't betray you." She paused and spoke breathlessly. "Where do you want to meet?"

"I'll call you back. Get into your car and head south down

Main Street, then wait for my call. I'll guide you. I need to be careful."

"I understand. And please, call me Lisa. All my friends call me Lisa."

"Fine, Lisa. I'll call you back in fifteen minutes."

The line went dead. Lisa dropped her arms to her side, laid her head back and closed her eyes. She breathed deeply for a while, her heart beating in time with her pounding pulse.

She finally calmed down. It was time to get ready.

She peeked out the window. Don was waiting for her. She rang his number. "I have to go somewhere by myself this morning, Don. I'll call you back again when I need you."

Lisa hung up and watched as the van pulled from the curb and left the lot.

She hurried to the bedroom, rummaged through a drawer in her nightstand, and found her old cell phone. She turned it on. The battery was getting weak, but it would do. She dumped it into her handbag along with her other phone, then grabbed her apartment keys and headed out, locking the door behind her.

Her rarely used silver Toyota waited for her in the underground parking. She climbed in, started the engine, and took a deep breath, hoping she was doing the right thing.

She convinced herself she was and backed from the slot, then headed for Main Street.

She looked at her watch. It'd been almost ten minutes since she'd talked to Izzy. He'd be calling her back soon.

As she pulled onto Main, she was overtaken with a feeling

of extreme nervousness. Her mouth felt dry—she should've brought some water—and her hands were sweating.

Maybe she was being foolish after all.

There was a reason she'd brought her extra phone. It was just as a precaution, but her forethought might serve a dual purpose—to show her goodwill and, of course, to ring up some points toward future favors.

She pulled both phones from her handbag, laid her main one on the passenger seat, then dialed a number with the other.

CHAPTER 35

Friday, 8:54 a.m.

JAKE'S IPHONE RANG.

He removed it from his side pocket and looked at the caller ID, a frown deepening across his brow. What did Lisa Krunk want now? Was she calling to apologize? He chuckled. Fat chance. She probably had more demands—something else she wanted from them.

He sighed lightly and answered the call, struggling to remain patient. "Yes, Lisa."

"Jake, I have a great opportunity for you." Lisa seemed out of breath, with a noticeable quiver in her voice as she continued, "I have to make this fast. I'm on the road, and I don't have much time to explain."

Jake glared at the phone, then put it on speaker and went into the office, where Annie sat at the computer. She sat back as he dropped into the guest chair, leaned forward, and set his cell phone on the desk between them.

"I'm listening," he said.

Lisa continued, "I've secured an interview with Izzy Wilde, and when I'm finished, I want to do my civic duty and have him arrested."

Jake looked up at Annie. His wife's eyes were widening at she stared at the phone in disbelief. He knew she was thinking the same thing he was. Lisa had gone too far this time. He knew she'd do just about anything for a story, but this was craziness.

"How did you manage that?" Jake asked.

"I had mentioned it to his brother. They must've been in contact with each other, and he's agreed to the interview."

Jake knew Lisa was unaware that the police had been monitoring Wilde's calls. He realized if there'd been some contact between the brothers, either it was in person, or Carter had another phone.

Annie leaned forward. "You need to call the police, Lisa."

Lisa raised her voice and spoke adamantly. "No." She took a deep breath, then said flatly, "I need this."

"Then why're you calling me?" Jake asked.

"I want to give you the opportunity to catch him. But not until I'm done with the interview. I owe you that much."

"You don't owe us anything," Annie said.

"I want to show there's no ill will between us, and I don't hold any hard feelings toward either one of you." Lisa sniffed and continued, "And it's a win-win situation for everyone. I get the interview, you get the credit, and the police get their man."

"And this is all out of the goodness of your heart?" Jake asked.

"Yes. That and perhaps for future consideration."

Jake rolled his eyes and a grim smile appeared on his lips. With Lisa, there was always a catch. As much as he disliked her most of the time, he didn't want to see her get into a potentially dangerous situation.

"Izzy Wilde is armed," Jake said. "And you know very well we aren't allowed to carry weapons. What can we do against an armed man? You need to let the police handle it."

There was silence for a moment. Finally, Lisa said, "You can call the police after I'm done with the interview, and you'll still get the credit."

Jake knew Lisa wouldn't cooperate unless she got a promise from him not to call the police. If he agreed, at least they would have something to go on. Otherwise, she would shut them and the police out completely. He had no choice. "Fine," he said. "You have a deal. How'll I know when you're done?"

"I have two phones. Wilde will be calling me on my main line to tell me where to meet him. In case something goes wrong, I'll leave this phone on and you can listen in."

"Where are you?" Annie asked. "Is this going down right now?"

"I'm on Main Street heading north," Lisa said. "I'm on my way to interview him now."

"Is Don with you?"

"I'm alone. In my own vehicle. Wilde doesn't want the interview on camera."

The faint sound of a ringing phone came through the speaker.

"That's him calling now," Lisa said, her voice breathless again. "Don't say anything."

Jake and Annie leaned in and strained to hear the conversation.

"This is Lisa," they heard her say.

Lisa must be holding her two cell phones together. Jake glared at his phone as Izzy Wilde's voice came low and clear over the line. "Are you heading north?"

"Yes, I'm on Main," Lisa said.

"And you're alone?"

"Yes."

"Remember, I'll be watching you. If you double-cross me, it won't end well for you or anyone else who gets involved."

"I'm alone," Lisa repeated. "I give you my word. We have to trust each other, remember?"

"I remember. And you're sure nobody's following you?"

"I've been in this business a long time, and I'd know if I was being followed. Besides, no one else knows about our meeting."

That appeared to satisfy Wilde, and he spoke again. "What're you driving?"

"A silver Toyota Corolla."

"Then keep driving. Let me know when you get to Magnetic Drive. It's in the old industrial area."

There was silence for a few minutes, and the Lincolns waited quietly lest any words spoken carried through to Izzy's ear and alerted him.

Finally, Lisa spoke. "I'm coming up to Magnetic Drive now."

"Turn left when you do, then drive slow and keep to the right."

"I'm turning left." Lisa's voice quivered with excitement now.

"Pull in behind unit six forty-eight, then park and wait for me. You can hang up now."

In a moment, Lisa's whispered voice came over the line. "Jake, are you there?"

"I'm here."

"Did you get the address?"

"Yes. I'm familiar with the area."

"It's an old building. The whole area looks deserted. Garbage all over the place. A couple of rusty cars. It's eerie."

Jake glanced at Annie as she leaned in toward the phone and said, "Lisa, you still have a chance to get out of there before it's too late."

"I'll be okay," Lisa said. "I know what I'm doing. And if anything goes awry, I have a canister of pepper spray in my bag."

Annie's voice took on an uncharacteristic tone of concern for Lisa Krunk. "Please be careful. Izzy Wilde is an unstable and dangerous man."

"I can take care of myself."

They waited in silence a few minutes and then Lisa whispered, "He's coming now. I have to hide the phone in my handbag. Hopefully, you'll still be able to make out what's being said. I'll let you know when I'm finished and clear."

The distinct sound of a car door opening came over the phone, then a voice said, "Follow me."

"Where're we going?" It was Lisa speaking.

"You'll see." There was silence, then Izzy spoke again. "Give me your handbag."

"It's just my personal stuff."

A muffled voice was covered by a rustling sound. Then Izzy said, "Why do you have two phones?"

"I want to record our conversation."

Izzy spoke in a rough voice. "You don't need to record it. You can write it down or memorize it."

Jake and Annie looked at each other in alarm as the line went dead. The call had been terminated.

Jake picked up his phone, hung up, and poised his finger over the redial button. "Should we call her back?"

Annie frowned and pursed her lips. "I don't think so," she said at last. "We don't want to arouse suspicion. That stupid woman's in enough danger as it is."

Jake dropped his cell phone into his pocket. He stood and paced a moment, considering the situation. Finally, he stopped and turned to face Annie. "I think we should call Hank."

Annie shrugged. "You promised Lisa you wouldn't involve the police until she let you know."

"But if something goes wrong, I wouldn't want to feel we're responsible."

"We're not responsible," Annie said. "Lisa's a big girl. She's nutty, but it's her decision."

"Then we'll give it half an hour," Jake said. "Whether or not Lisa's in danger, we don't want Izzy Wilde to get away again. There's no guarantee he'll stick around after she leaves.

I don't think he's that dumb. By giving him the chance to escape, she's putting the lives of others at danger."

Annie pressed her lips together in a straight line, a light frown on her face. "Lisa has put us in a tough situation," she said. "If we call the police and they surround the place, he might hold her hostage. And if he feels she's trying to double-cross him, he won't be in a good mood."

Jake considered that a moment. "I'm sure Hank knows how to handle it, and they're not gonna go in there guns a-blazing. The last thing he'll want is a hostage situation. They could be ready to go in as soon as Lisa comes out. That way nobody gets hurt, and Wilde would be trapped."

Annie nodded and looked at her watch. "We'll wait for half an hour. If we haven't heard back from Lisa by then, we'll call Hank and let him take care of it."

CHAPTER 36

Friday, 9:22 a.m.

LISA KRUNK CLUTCHED her handbag in one arm as Izzy Wilde held the other, guiding her across the pitted asphalt.

Her pepper spray lay on the ground where he'd flung it in disgust after searching her bag. The two cell phones she had depended on were helplessly out of reach, tucked safely in Izzy's side pocket.

She had only her wits to get her through this.

She clenched her teeth to keep them from chattering, unsure why she was so nervous. She'd been in the presence of killers before, and as long as she hadn't given them any reason to turn on her, she'd always managed to come out without harm.

If Jake kept their agreement about not calling the police, and Izzy Wilde didn't smell a double-cross, she'd be fine.

But the thing that bothered Lisa the most was that unit 648 where she had met Izzy was well behind them now.

They'd crossed the adjoining properties and were now three or four buildings away from the initial meeting place. If Jake called the police eventually, she hoped they could find Wilde before he got clean away.

As much as she wanted this interview, letting Wilde escape after it was over was outside of even her moral compass. And without a cell phone, it could be a problem.

She turned her head toward her escort and demanded, "Where're you taking me?"

Without looking her way, he nodded his head toward a nearby building. It was run-down like the rest of the units on this forgotten street. Businesses had moved lock, stock and barrel to the more prosperous west side of town, where commerce was growing and land was cheap. One day, this area would be plowed under and rebuilt as the latest and greatest in family living. But for now, it was isolated and unwanted, the temporary hideout of a fugitive.

A bright red BMW was parked diagonally in the alley beside the unit, its shiny exterior in sharp contrast to the dirty concrete-and-steel buildings on either side.

The rear door of the unit they now veered toward hung open. A pair of windows high above were darkened by aging and faded newspaper.

"Inside," Izzy said, releasing her arm and prodding her through the open doorway.

Lisa stepped into the dim room and squinted, aided only by a stingy amount of sun that seeped around the newspaper covering the windows or through cracks in the walls of the outdated building.

As her eyes became accustomed to the feeble light, she could make out a small table at one side of the vast room. Hard-backed chairs sat one on either side of the table, an unlit candle in the middle.

Izzy pointed to one of the chairs. "Sit there."

Lisa sat down, laid her handbag in her lap, and watched as he sat in the other chair and leaned forward, his arms on his knees, and studied her.

"You're very brave," he said at last, then chuckled. "Either that, or very stupid."

"You have no reason to hurt me," she said.

He shrugged. "Maybe not."

She didn't like the sound of that, but she fought her misgivings. "Do you mind if I take notes?"

He shook his head. "Go ahead."

Lisa pulled a small notepad and pen from her handbag, poised the pen, and cleared her throat.

He interrupted her train of thought by standing abruptly. He reached into his pocket and removed her cell phones. "It's just a precaution," he said, dropping them onto the floor.

She gasped as he brought a heel down hard, destroying a cell phone. He pounded repeatedly with first one foot, then the other, until both phones were well beyond use.

"I'm sure you can afford another one," he said, taking a seat. He smiled. "Now, where were we?"

She raised her eyes to his and remained silent.

He waved a hand toward the ruined phones. "I know those things have some kind of tracer in them. I can't have anyone finding you if they come looking."

She glanced toward the open door on the other side of her killer, then trained her eyes back toward his and nodded. "I understand."

He smiled again, this time showing yellow teeth, unbrushed and unattractive. "What I meant to say was, I can't have them finding *me*. You're free to go any time you want."

Lisa gave him an uncertain nod. "Thank you." She glanced around the room again. "Is this where you've been staying?"

He laughed. "This spot's just for the occasion. I got lots of other places I can go."

Lisa hesitated, then asked, "Mr. Wilde, tell me about your desire to kill women. What drives you?"

An unknown glint came into his faraway eyes, the smile now gone from his face. "It's the evil," he said. "It keeps coming back."

Lisa scribbled in her pad. "Evil? What kind of evil?"

He shrugged. "It's all around me sometimes, and there's only one way to get rid of it."

"And how do you get rid of it?"

"Kill it."

Lisa hesitated. She needed to be careful not to set him off. "Like you killed Hannah Quinn?"

He raised his voice, causing her to shrink back. "Just like Hannah Quinn."

Lisa took a breath. "Why now, after all these years since …"

Izzy laughed hard, the laughter dying away to a snort as his face twisted into a sneer. "Since my mother died? You can say it." His voice sharpened. "Because she's back. That's why. I fought it for many years. Fought the memory of what she did to us." He leaned in, his voice becoming shriller. "She destroyed our family. Drove away my father. Then Carter and me. All because of ..." His eyes took on a pained look. He breathed long and deep, then sat back and remained silent, glaring at her.

A moment later, he leaped to his feet, cleared his throat, and crossed his arms. He scowled down at her. "Tell me about my fans," he said.

Lisa wanted to know more about his mother, about his father and brother, and what drove him to kill. But he was getting into a frenzy, and she wanted him to calm down. She thought hard, searching her mind for the right thing to say— what he wanted to hear.

She looked up into his darkening face. "Your fans," she said, still devising a line she could feed him. "I get phone calls and emails. They want to know more about you. They appreciate what you're doing, and that's why I'm here." She paused and took a breath, waiting for his response.

Without moving his eyes from her face, he took a step back and sat on the edge of the chair. A faint smile appeared on his lips, then a grin that morphed into a smirk as he continued to leer at her. "You're lying," he said in a sharp voice. "I have no fans." He leaned forward, his eyes widening, then he bared his teeth and screamed, "I have no fans. You're a liar? A filthy liar. Just like my mother."

Every muscle in Lisa's body tensed. This was getting out of control. She glanced toward the door again, calculating her odds of escape should his verbal barrage turn physical. Her odds didn't look good.

"I'm sorry," she said, biting her lip. "Please, forgive me."

He stood to his feet and leaned forward, gritting his teeth. "That's what she said." He paced in a small circle. "That's what she always said." He stopped in front of her and leaned over, his face inches from hers. His breath was foul, and a rasping sound came from his throat as he breathed rapidly. She shrank back into the chair as he screamed, "Sorry don't do it no more."

Lisa began to panic, her eyes darting back and forth as she looked for a way of escape. There was none. He had her boxed in, too close for her to move. She could only glare into his fiery eyes, remain silent, and pray he'd calm down.

"The police know I'm here," she said.

"Then why ain't they coming to rescue you?"

She had no answer.

Izzy grabbed her arm and wrenched her to her feet. "Why'd you do this? Why'd you do this to Father? And to Carter? And to me?"

She tried to break free, but he held on tighter. She kicked uselessly at him as he dragged her toward the wall. Her eyes popped when he picked up a pair of scissors, held them close to her nose, and spoke through clenched teeth. "Now you have to pay for what you did."

He pushed her backwards, forcing her against the wall. She stood helpless and terrified, her dark brown eyes transfixed on the razor-sharp scissors. He removed his hand from her arm and stroked her long black hair. "This is the cause of it all," he said, his voice almost calm. "And your eyes. Your eyes have seduced for the last time."

In a sudden burst of panic, she struck out at him with both fists. He laughed and seized her by the wrists, the tip of the scissors brushing her cheek.

She screamed, knowing her cries would go unheard, but it was all she had.

He forced her to the ground and straddled her as she struggled in vain, unable to free herself from the full weight of his body holding her down.

Then the tears came and she closed her eyes. She lay defeated and still, listening to the soft snip, snip, snip of scissors in her ear.

CHAPTER 37

Friday, 9:42 a.m.

ANNIE TAPPED HER fingers impatiently on the desktop, and each second that ticked by caused her anxiety to build. It wasn't just her concern for Lisa's safety, though that was troubling enough, but Izzy Wilde was on the loose and, unless he'd cut his interview with Lisa short, they knew exactly where he was. And time was wasting.

Jake seemed restless as well. He'd paced the office, then wandered into the living room and ended up circling through the kitchen and back to the office. Round and round. And each time he'd appeared, he gave her an edgy look and circled again.

But now he sat slouched back waiting for the allotted minutes to pass, the chair groaning under his weight as he fidgeted with his hands.

They both jumped when the phone on the desk rang. Annie beat Jake to it, scooping up the receiver.

"Lincoln Investigation. Annie speaking."

"Annie, it's Carter Wilde." He sounded worried, and he spoke with an uneasy hesitation.

Annie leaned forward and looked at Jake, then set the phone on the desk and put it on speaker.

"Hello, Mr. Wilde," she said politely.

Carter Wilde got right to the reason for his call. "I'm rather concerned about my brother, and I might've done something foolish."

The caller seemed in no hurry to elaborate, so Annie asked, "What did you do?"

Carter took a deep breath and continued, "Last evening, I got a package delivered to my door. I opened it up and found a disposable phone and a note from Izzy inside."

"I assume you notified the police," Annie said.

A long sigh came over the line before the caller answered. "Perhaps I should've. I considered it and, in hindsight, maybe it would've been the best thing. But after I read the note, I changed my mind."

Jake furrowed his brow and glared at the phone impatiently. "What did the note say, Carter?"

"It was a short note stating he wanted to talk to me. It appears that after the incident in the park, Izzy was positive I was being watched and my phone line was being tapped. So he sent me the disposable phone and asked me to call him right away."

"And I assume you did?" Annie said.

"Yes, I called him right away. He accused me of double-crossing him by notifying the police earlier. Which I did, but I didn't tell him that. I think I convinced him otherwise."

Jake frowned. "Are the police unaware of what you're telling us?"

"Yes. They're still tapping my lines, but I'm calling you on the disposable phone." There was silence a moment and then Carter continued, "I'm in a quandary here. I'm torn between doing the right thing and my brother's safety. I want him caught, and hopefully he can get some help, but he's armed now, and he won't surrender without a fight." Carter sighed. "He's getting increasingly violent, and he sounded distraught on the phone. In short, I'm afraid he'll get himself killed if the police get involved. Suicide by cop, perhaps. He's becoming more and more unstable."

Annie understood Carter's position, though she wasn't concerned about whether or not Izzy Wilde got shot. She only wanted him stopped by whatever means it took. And she was anxious for Lisa. "Mr. Wilde," she said, "are you aware your brother had consented to an interview with Lisa Krunk?"

Carter cleared his throat. "Unfortunately, I let it slip when I was talking to him. I mentioned she wanted to interview him, and he sounded interested in the possibility. And that's the real reason for my call. Did he happen to phone her, and did she follow up on it?"

"Yes," Jake said. "He called her this morning and arranged the interview. They're together now. She's reckless sometimes, and she might be in danger."

"I never wanted that to happen, but she was insistent, so I foolishly mentioned it to him." He paused and let out a quivering sigh. "She's rather a remarkable woman, and I didn't want to disappoint her. It was foolhardy, I know, but I didn't consider the possible consequences."

"And what do you expect us to do?" Jake asked.

"I need your help. I'm desperate. I tried to call my brother again this morning, but he's either not answering, or he discarded the phone."

"I believe we know where they are," Annie said. "Lisa called us and told us exactly where she was headed."

Carter breathed a sigh of relief. "That's what I was hoping. I couldn't convince Izzy to tell me where he is, but I assumed if Ms. Krunk had taken Izzy up on his offer, she'd find a way to let someone know where she was going. Seeing how much she wanted the interview without any police involvement, and given your close relationship with her, I guessed it would be you rather than them."

"And you thought we would give you his location?" Annie asked. She glanced at Jake and studied his face.

"Mrs. Lincoln, I believe if I knew where he was, and I could talk to him face to face, I could convince him to surrender."

"What makes you sure we haven't notified the police already?"

"I didn't know for sure. But I assumed Ms. Krunk wouldn't want you to. At least, not right away. I'm familiar with her and her brand of reporting, and she seems willing to do anything for a good story."

"Mr. Wilde," Annie said, "the police want a peaceful outcome as well, and if they feel it'll help, they'll let you talk to your brother. If he surrenders, so much the better."

"I can't chance it." Carter paused and took a deep breath. "Please try to understand. He's my brother. And if I can convince him to give himself up, then Ms. Krunk will be safe. I can't bear the thought of anything happening to either one of them." He paused before adding, "But if I'm not successful, there's no harm done, and we'll call the police. But I have to know I gave it my best shot, and I'm asking for your understanding and cooperation."

Annie sat back and looked at Jake. After a moment, he nodded his head, his eyes telling her they were in agreement. She leaned forward and spoke with hesitation into the phone.

"We'll tell you where he is … with one condition."

"Yes?"

"We'll go together. If you're unsuccessful in getting him to surrender, we'll call the police." Annie had serious misgivings and had come to her decision with reluctance. She hoped she was doing the sensible thing.

Carter hesitated, and Annie heard him breathing on the line. Finally, he said, "All right. You have a deal."

CHAPTER 38

Friday, 10:17 a.m.

WHEN JAKE PULLED THE Firebird onto Red Ridge Street, Carter Wilde was waiting by the curb in front of his apartment building. Jake pulled to a stop and Carter climbed into the backseat, laying his cane on the floor beside him. He straddled the hump and leaned slightly forward, looking between the bucket seats.

Annie had turned sideways, and she smiled a hello and observed their anxious passenger. He had lines of worry about his eyes, his brow a permanent frown.

Carter spoke with noticeable concern in his voice. "I hope we're not too late."

"We'll find out in a few minutes," Jake said as he touched the gas. The Firebird spun from the curb and pulled a U-turn. Jake glanced into the backseat. "I sure hope you know what you're doing."

Carter gripped the seat in front of him. "Just get us there safely, and I'll take care of it."

Jake broke a few speed limits and made record time getting to the semideserted industrial area. He turned onto Magnetic Drive, drove a quarter mile, slowed down, and strained to see the fading street numbers.

"There's six twenty," Annie said and pointed up the street. "We're looking for six forty-eight. It's the next complex."

"We'll park at six twenty and walk over," Jake said, touching the brakes. He swerved into the driveway and eased the car toward the rear of the unit, coming to a stop behind the building.

They climbed from the vehicle and Annie looked across the rear of the property to the building beyond. She pointed. "I think that's Lisa's car. It looks like one I've seen her driving a time or two."

"We're in the right place," Jake said grimly. He looked at Carter. "Let's do this."

Carter nodded and the three crossed the property. Jake detoured to Lisa's Toyota and peeked inside. He gave a shrug and joined the others again. "That's her car, all right. She's got a police scanner in the dash."

Annie strode ahead, moving silently to the far end of the unit. She peered around the side of the building. Garbage littered the alley between the two buildings. Old newspapers rustled in the morning breeze. A faint odor of something rotting in the heat stung her nose, but Izzy's vehicle was nowhere to be seen.

She went back and joined the two men, who'd approached

the rear of the building. Jake scaled a water pipe, then swung over and gripped a crumbling windowsill, pulling himself up. He scraped away a patch of grime and peered inside, then shook his head and dropped to the ground.

"No one there," he said.

Annie spun around and glared back toward Lisa's car, her hands on her hips. The newswoman had definitely met Izzy at this secluded spot. Why else would her vehicle be here? She frowned. Perhaps he'd driven her elsewhere.

Jake must've read her mind. "I don't think they've gone far. If they left, wouldn't they have taken Lisa's car?" He waved a hand toward the deserted complex. "And this is a perfect place to do his killing."

"He might be in one of the other units," Carter said, pointing with the tip of his cane.

Annie agreed. "In case he was double-crossed." She gazed down the long, wide swath of asphalt that ran along the rear of the adjoining buildings. Lisa and Izzy could be in any one of them.

Jake strode toward the next building, Annie and Carter close behind. The unit had a similar window, but no water pipe to climb. Annie tried the rear door. It was locked.

The lack of a water pipe didn't deter Jake. He had found a steel barrel, and he lugged it over and positioned it quietly under the window. He climbed up, peered in the window, and dropped back down.

"It's empty as well," he said. "We'll try the next one."

They crossed the graying asphalt toward the next building. Annie went ahead, past the unit, and peered around the corner.

A red BMW shone in the morning sun.

Izzy was still here.

Somewhere.

She edged toward the empty vehicle and peeked inside, half-expecting Izzy Wilde to pop around the corner. There was some bubble pack on the floor of the backseat. Probably from the burner phone he'd purchased. There were no weapons to be seen, and unless his rifle was in the trunk, he no doubt had it with him.

Annie glanced uneasily around, then hurried to the rear of the building, where the two men moved with caution toward the unit. She told them of her discovery. "He's either in this one or the next one," she said.

Carter pointed toward the rear door of the building and whispered, "The door's slightly open."

"I'll take a look," Jake said, holding up a hand of caution. "You two stay here." He eased toward the door and stopped, a hand on the knob.

Annie held her breath as Jake pushed the door inwards an inch or two and peered through the crack. A moment later, he pushed the door open and disappeared inside.

Annie exchanged a look with Carter, then hurried to the door, Carter directly behind. She stopped in the doorway. Her mouth dropped open and her eyes bulged.

It was Lisa Krunk.

Even without the long black hair Lisa had once so proudly worn, Annie would recognize that thin, sharp nose anywhere.

She stared at the fearful sight of the newswoman propped up in a metal chair, long locks of hair scattered about the floor around her. She was bound and gagged, her dark brown eyes filled with relief. Tufts of hair stuck out at odd angles where it'd been cropped short.

Jake slipped the gag from the woman's mouth, then worked at the cord that held her firmly to the chair.

Annie stepped closer and stopped in front of Lisa. She leaned over, her hands on her knees. "Are you all right?" she asked.

Tear tracks burrowed through Lisa's heavy makeup, running down her face toward her chin. She blinked away a tear and nodded. "I'm okay."

Jake tossed the now loosened rope aside and helped Lisa to her feet. Annie stood and quietly watched a sight she thought she'd never see. Her husband had his arm around the frightened woman's shoulder as she cried against his chest, her sobs of relief filling the empty room.

Carter seemed unsure what to do or say. He stood back, his hands in his pockets, and watched the scene unfold. Finally, he stepped closer, put his hand on Lisa's shoulder, and spoke gently. "I should never have told Izzy you wanted to talk to him. I'm sorry."

Lisa nodded in recognition of his apology, then freed herself from Jake and stood back. She raised her head and dabbed at her watery eyes, then looked at Carter, forcing a smile. "It's not your fault. I should've known better."

Annie scanned the large room with her eyes. There was no doubt Izzy was gone. Perhaps their arrival had scared him off before he got a chance to finish what he came to do. They might've gotten here just in time.

She turned to Lisa, who'd composed herself somewhat. "When did Izzy leave?" she asked.

"A few minutes before you arrived." Lisa sniffled and glanced nervously toward the door. "But he said he'd be back."

"His car's still at the side of the building," Jake said. "But there's no sign of him."

Carter was absently nudging at an empty soda can with his foot. He gave it a solid kick, sending it tinkling across the concrete floor, then he took a deep breath and pulled out his cell phone. "I think I'd better call the police. I can't ask you to wait any longer. It's gone too far." Annie heard the distinct 9-1-1 tone as he dialed. He put the phone to his ear, then wandered away, intent on his conversation.

Annie felt certain if Izzy wanted to get as far away as possible, he would've taken the BMW. Or if he wanted to make a clean getaway and stay under the police radar, perhaps Lisa's car. She had no doubt he was in the vicinity, perhaps watching the building from some safe hideaway. His rifle might be trained on the back door even now.

"They'll be here right away," Carter said at last, turning back. "I told them Izzy Wilde's in the area, probably armed, and certainly dangerous." He sighed deeply and tucked his phone away. "I think we'd better leave."

A slamming door caused Annie to jump. She spun her head toward the far end of the vast area. Izzy Wilde appeared to have exited a small room fifty feet away. He raced across the floor away from them, dodged around a stack of cardboard boxes, and vanished through an open doorway leading into the front offices of the building.

Jake leaped into action, streaking across the floor toward the fugitive.

Carter hesitated a moment and then turned to Annie. "You two stay here and wait for the police. We'll get him." Then he turned and followed Jake as fast as his game leg would carry him.

CHAPTER 39

Friday, 10:31 a.m.

JAKE SPRINTED INTO the front section of the unit and came to a quick stop. He glanced up and down the dim hallway, where a row of three closed doors, probably leading into offices, lined the narrow passageway. To his far left, a pair of tempered-glass doors led outside.

But Izzy Wilde was not in sight.

Carter stepped into the hallway behind Jake, breathing rapidly in an attempt to catch his breath. He leaned on his cane and pointed to the exit doors. "Out there."

"Check the offices," Jake called over his shoulder as he raced to the door. He tugged on the handle. It was locked from the inside. Was Izzy still in the building? He spun back and poked his head into the nearest office.

It was empty, with no obvious signs of an exit. Light

streamed through large windows facing the front of the building—windows that weren't made to open. He tugged on the door of a small closet. Empty. He looked underneath a broken-down desk. Nothing.

He ran back to the hall and into the next room. It had the same layout as the last one, but Izzy wasn't in there, either. He hurried back to the hallway in time to see Carter disappear into the last room.

Jake dashed down the corridor and followed.

It was a much larger office, brightly lit from sunlight streaming through wall-to-wall windows. At the front of the room, a metal door hung open a few inches.

Jake brushed past Carter, dodged a chair, and pulled the door inward. He scrambled outside and looked in both directions. There was no sign of the fugitive. He raced to the corner of the building. The BMW sat in the same position as before. He glanced back as Carter eased himself through the doorway and hobbled toward him.

"He must've circled around back," Jake said. "I'll take a look. You stay here."

He galloped down the alleyway between the two buildings and stopped short at the rear of the BMW.

The trunk hung partially open. Izzy had come this way.

Flipping the lid up, he peered inside the now empty trunk. What'd been in there a short time ago? Whatever it was, Izzy wanted it bad enough to pause mid-chase and grab it. Perhaps a weapon. Maybe his rifle.

He left the trunk open and sped to the rear of the unit, poking his head inside the back door. Annie and Lisa sat comfortably on wooden crates, facing each other, engaged in quiet conversation.

The girls were safe, but where was the fugitive?

Carter had made it up the alley, and he gasped for air as he hurried toward Jake and stopped. "I have to come with you," he managed to say between short breaths. "If you find Izzy, I need to be there."

Jake shrugged and glanced to his left. Lisa's car stood three units away. Izzy could've escaped in either vehicle had he wanted to, but he didn't seem to be in any hurry to get away.

The killer had to be close by. What was he up to?

"I wanna find him before the police come," Carter continued. "Now that he has no hostages, they'll be more liable to shoot him on sight." He shook his head vigorously. "I can't let that happen."

"We'll have to search every building," Jake said. "But I'm pretty sure he's armed. He stopped to get something from the trunk of the BMW. Possibly the rifle he used to shoot at the cops."

Carter frowned and gazed toward the adjoining building. "We're going to have to be careful, then. He won't shoot me, so we should stay together as much as possible."

"Suits me," Jake said with a shrug. He motioned toward the next unit with a wave of his hand. "We'll check that one first."

Jake glanced toward the BMW as he scurried past the alley. It was still there, untouched. He crept to the rear entrance door of the unit and twisted the knob. Locked.

He stood back and surveyed the rear of the building. A window, similar to the ones in the other units, was well out of his reach. He frowned at a rotting skid leaning against the wall close by.

He dragged the skid over, propped it up under the window, and tested his weight on one of the fragile slats. It groaned and threatened to let loose, but held. He lessened the weight on the slats by wedging his fingers in the cracks between the bricks, and managed to haul himself up. He gripped the windowsill, eased higher, and squinted through the grime.

His eyes roved around the room and then grew wider.

Izzy was inside the building.

The interior layout of the unit was similar to the others, and the fugitive paced back and forth near the front door leading to the offices. He held a rifle in one hand and walked with his head down as if thinking.

Jake dropped to the ground and turned to Carter. "He's inside, but the door's locked."

"He must've gone through the front," Carter said with a furrowed brow. "Or perhaps there's a side door."

"He's armed. A rifle." Jake frowned and glared at the building. "What I'd like to know is, why's he still hanging around? He knows we're looking for him. He should be long gone by now."

"He's crazy," was Carter's answer. "He's not thinking straight."

"I think we should wait for the police," Jake said. "He'll be trapped in there, and there's no way he can shoot his way out. How much ammunition could he have?"

Carter hesitated. "Give me one last chance. I'll go to the front. There's gotta be a way in. If I can talk to him, I think I can get him to surrender. You watch the back door in case he tries to run."

Jake shrugged. "We'll give it a whirl."

Carter limped toward the corner of the building, then went out of sight down the alleyway. Jake waited a few moments and then climbed back up the skid and peered through the window.

Izzy had stopped pacing. He sat on the floor, leaning against the wall, his head down. The weapon lay on the floor beside him.

As Jake continued to watch, the door leading to the offices eased open and Carter stepped inside. Izzy grabbed the rifle, then sprang to his feet and stood still. He held the weapon in a firing position, watching his brother approach.

Carter stopped ten feet from Izzy and spoke a few words, and the fugitive seemed to relax. He lowered the rifle a few inches and stuffed his free hand into a pocket.

The brothers carried on an animated conversation for two or three minutes, then Carter motioned toward the rear of the unit. Izzy turned his gaze in the direction his brother had indicated, and though it was doubtful he saw Jake, the killer's eyes seemed to burn into his.

Then the unexpected happened. Izzy turned back to Carter and shrugged, then took a step forward and surrendered the rifle. Carter shouldered the weapon, and the two headed toward the rear of the unit.

Dropping to the ground, Jake hurried to the back door and waited. In a moment, the door swung open and Carter motioned him inside.

Izzy's eyes popped and he turned to his brother. "You double-crossed me." He took a step away, his head moving back and forth between Jake and Carter. "I knew I couldn't trust you."

"You're gonna be fine, Izzy," Carter said. "You have to trust me."

Jake stepped in, crossed his arms, and glared stone-faced at Izzy. The fugitive avoided his eyes and glanced around as if looking for an escape route.

"The police are on their way," Jake said. "Don't try to run."

Izzy glanced at Carter, his eyes unblinking as he stared for a few moments. Then a smile touched one corner of his mouth, and he turned toward Jake and gave a short laugh. "It ain't over yet."

Jake looked at the killer. Deep lines etched his thin unshaven face. He appeared beaten down, yet he still retained his cocky attitude. "I'm pretty sure it is," Jake said.

Carter shrugged. "Izzy might be right."

Jake looked at Carter in confusion and then turned his gaze toward Izzy.

Carter spoke again. "Sometimes my brother gets out of control. I told him not to hurt Ms. Krunk, but he wouldn't listen." He turned to Izzy. "I didn't double-cross you, you idiot."

He took a step back, brought the rifle into firing position, and aimed it at Jake. "No, my dear brother, I didn't double-cross you. I've been on your side all along."

CHAPTER 40

Friday, 10:45 a.m.

JAKE STARED WIDE-EYED at the barrel of the gun in Carter Wilde's hand. Pieces of the truth dawned in his mind. It appeared Carter wasn't only in on the killing spree with his brother, but he might be the instigator.

Jake put his hands halfway up and glanced at Izzy, who seemed to be confused.

Carter addressed his brother in a sharp voice. "If you'd have listened to me from the start, little brother, we wouldn't be in this mess. I told you to leave Ms. Krunk alone."

Izzy dropped his head and spoke in a whispered voice. "She made me do it. She starting talking about that evil witch, and I ... I couldn't help myself."

"You have to learn to control it," Carter said. "You're a little bit slow, Izzy, and you need to learn to wait until I give you the go-ahead. And not before."

Izzy shrugged and raised his eyes. "I thought you would

enjoy this one. She ain't like the rest. She's strong-willed and feisty."

Jake glanced at the rifle, calculating his chances while the brothers were engaged in an argument. The odds didn't look good.

Carter seemed to know Jake's thoughts. He took another step back and raised the rifle. "Don't make me shoot you yet. Not here."

Jake crossed his arms and glared at the elder brother. If Carter wasn't planning on shooting him now, then he might have time to make a move. The opportunity would be bound to come, and Jake planned on making the best of it.

"One thing confuses me, Carter," Jake said. "Why'd you drag Annie and me here? Why not go about your merry killing spree and stay away from us?"

Carter laughed. "Oh, there're lots of good reasons for that. I wanted to shoot you both when I had the chance, but I needed you. Maybe I'll tell you why before I kill you. Maybe."

Perhaps Jake would get a chance to make his move. Or perhaps not. But he had to try, and he needed to stall for time. "Why not tell me now?" he asked.

Carter squinted at Jake. "All right," he said at last. "If you must know." He waved a hand toward Izzy. "My dim-witted brother saw your phone number on Ms. Krunk's phone. It seems she'd been talking to you during her drive to meet him. She was obviously safeguarding herself, and I assumed she told you where she was heading. Right after Izzy gave Ms. Krunk a haircut, he called me. Then I called you and had to half-beg you not to contact the police. I couldn't afford that."

"Couldn't you have told Izzy to leave without involving us?"

"When I talked to him, he accused me of betraying him and hung up on me. He wouldn't answer my calls after that." A strange look appeared in Carter's eyes and then faded away. "I was worried about Ms. Krunk."

"So you needed us to find her and set her free?"

"Yes, and you did it in record time." He shrugged. "But I also needed you to help me find Izzy." He looked at his brother with a scowl. "He can't take care of himself. So, unfortunately, I had to come with you to protect my dumb brother from getting caught."

"I'm sorry, Carter," Izzy said. "It ain't gonna happen again. I wouldn't have run from you if I knew."

"No harm done. We can clean this up easily." Carter laughed, tossed his cane aside, and stood upright. "I guess I don't need that anymore."

The man's limp was a lie like everything else he had said and done.

"The police are on their way," Jake said, frowning at the cane.

Carter feigned surprise. "Oh. Did you call them? I'm pretty sure you didn't." He shrugged one shoulder and looked at his brother. "I know I didn't. Did you, Izzy?"

Izzy frowned and shook his head.

"They monitored your calls," Jake said.

Carter grinned. "I took care of that little problem as soon as they started tapping them. Throwaway phones are cheap enough. Izzy and I have been in constant contact ever since."

He snickered and aimed down the barrel of the rifle. "Bang! Bang!" He lowered the weapon. "I think I'm gonna enjoy this."

"Then you might as well get it over with," Jake said.

"Soon enough." Carter lifted his shirt, revealing a pistol tucked into his waistband. He removed it and handed it to Izzy. "Go watch the girls while I take care of this guy."

Izzy took the gun, hefted it in his hand, and feigned a shot toward Jake.

"Go now," Carter said. "Do what I say." He pointed a stern finger. "And don't hurt Ms. Krunk, whatever happens. Do you hear me? She gets to go free after this is all over."

Izzy nodded. "What about the other one?"

"Only if she gets uppity. I'd rather do it myself. Just don't let them leave." He pointed toward the back door. "Go. I've got work to do."

Izzy breathed on the gun and buffed it on his sleeve, then sighted down the barrel. A grin twisted his face, then he strode out the back door, closing it softly behind him.

Jake had to make a move, and make it soon. Annie was in imminent danger, unmindful of what was going on in the nearby unit, and unaware a madman was on his way toward her. And Izzy Wilde was nuts.

"You don't have to worry about your wife," Carter said in an offhand manner. "At least, not yet. My brother doesn't have the guts to kill anyone."

"The girl in the park, and the one in the graveyard—?"

"Both girls were my handiwork," Carter said. "He catches them and I do the deed. Shaving their head's an added touch he likes to do." He shook his head. "He's strange, you know. He even mailed a box of hair to the cops a couple of times. Said it makes him feel better. Has a thing about black hair and dark brown eyes. Claims it's because our mother had the same, and he thinks he sees her everywhere." He threw his head back and laughed. "The nut even insisted on shaving our mother bald before I killed her."

"They said you were at a friend's house."

Carter shrugged. "I was. But with all those people hanging around, it wasn't hard for me to sneak away for a few minutes."

Jake stalled for time, digging for something else to say. Anything that would catch the killer off guard. "A lot of people thought your father killed your mother," he said. "According to some of the reports."

Carter looked at Jake with a close-lipped smile. "My father? That's a good one. He's buried deep in the backyard. Came snooping around when he found out my mother was dead. Wanted to take the house away from us." He shook his head. "Never. Wasn't his." He sighed lightly.

"So you killed him?"

"Had to. The man was no good, anyway." Carter had a faraway look as he continued. "But I owe him a lot. He's the one who taught me how to keep women in their place." Carter laughed. "At first, I wasn't too keen on seeing him beat my mother up all the time, but he made me watch, and after a while I saw how much fun it was. Then he let me join in." He chuckled. "Mom put a quick stop to it after my father left. Temporarily, that is. She eventually got what she deserved for driving him away and tearing the family apart."

Carter took a deep breath, lowered his eyes, and Jake leaped forward. He collided with the gunman and both men fell heavily. Jake spun his head to face Carter. The man lay on the floor, an expression of pain on his face, still clinging to the gun as though the thing was tied to his arm. Jake rolled sideways as a shot rang out.

"Stop."

Jake turned his head. He'd miscalculated the maniac's agility. The barrel of the gun was inches away, the shooter's finger on the trigger.

"Get up."

Jake kept one eye on the gun and climbed to his feet.

Carter scrambled backwards like a clam, then he stood up and stepped back. He gripped the rifle in one hand and brushed himself off with the other, keeping a wary eye on Jake. "Next time I'll kill you on the spot." He nodded toward the door. "Now get going. I'll take care of your wife later."

Jake didn't move, still stalling for time, waiting for another opportunity. "What about Lisa?"

Carter chuckled. "Ms. Krunk thinks I'm a hero, and Izzy knows exactly what to do. After I'm done with you, I'll join my brother, then I'll manage to rescue Ms. Krunk. Knowing her, she'll run when she gets the chance." He shrugged. "Then I'll take care of Annie and be gone before Ms. Krunk manages to get the police here."

Carter patted the rifle, then laughed long and hard. "Then I'll truly be her hero, and Izzy'll still be on the run. Just like before. He'll get the credit for killing the two of you like he wants, and I'll continue to protect him. Then Ms. Krunk and I will be free to pursue a relationship."

The thought of Lisa in a relationship with Carter Wilde would've made Jake laugh under different circumstances. But right now, it was a matter of life or death, perhaps for both him and Annie. "You can't protect your brother forever," he said. "Once the police get ahold of him, he'll talk."

"I doubt that. You see, my little brother looks up to me. He's always wanted to be like his older brother, but he doesn't have the nerve to draw blood. That's my job. But in his sick mind, he believes it's him. And who's gonna think otherwise?" He touched his temple with his forefinger. "He's nuts."

Jake glared into Carter's fiery eyes, then down at the weapon in his hand. He'd underestimated Wilde a moment ago. If he got another chance, he wasn't about to blow it again and get himself shot.

"And now, it's time to get this over with," Carter said, motioning toward the front of the unit with the rifle. "Ms. Krunk is waiting for me."

CHAPTER 41

Friday, 11:12 a.m.

ANNIE STOOD AND GLANCED at her watch for the umpteenth time. It'd been more than half an hour since Carter had called the police, and though response times were often slow, she'd expected to hear approaching sirens by now.

She looked over at Lisa, pacing the floor twenty feet away. The newswoman ran a hand over her bristling hair. It didn't help. Her attempts to lessen her bizarre appearance by turning up her collar hadn't made a difference, either. Annie stifled a smile and turned away.

The rear door of the building slammed open and Annie spun around. Izzy Wilde stepped inside, brandishing a pistol in one hand. He stopped, his lips twisted into a sneer, and aimed the weapon at Annie.

"I'm back," he said in a mocking tone.

Where was Jake? And Carter? Surely her husband couldn't be far behind the fugitive.

Annie raised her hands halfway up and stepped back as the gunman moved closer. Then he stopped and turned toward Lisa. Annie's eyes followed his gaze. The woman was beyond fear, beyond anger, and she appeared ready to disregard all danger to herself as she strode bravely toward the killer.

Izzy swung the gun toward Lisa, his finger on the trigger. "You better stay back."

Lisa's common sense took over. She came to a stop ten feet from Wilde and crossed her arms, her eyes burning with hatred.

Annie glanced toward the open door. It was twenty feet away, but there was a possibility she could make it through safely before Izzy could react. She banished the thought. It would be cowardly to leave Lisa alone at the mercy of a sadistic fiend.

She took a couple of careful steps sideways, attempting to put distance between her and the gunman.

Izzy spun back toward her. "Stand still," he said, his voice a low growl. "There's no reason not to shoot you."

Annie stopped and raised her chin. "You wouldn't be able to get both of us."

Izzy frowned, his deep-set eyes sinking even further into their sockets. "Maybe not, but you wanna take a chance?"

"Jake'll be here soon," Annie said in an unsure voice.

Izzy laughed. "Jake ain't coming. He's a little busy."

"Your brother isn't protecting you anymore," Annie said.

"And he has your rifle." She looked at the pistol again. Where'd it come from? As far as she knew, he hadn't been carrying an additional weapon earlier. He might've had it stashed behind his back.

And where was Carter?

Izzy's grin became a sneer, and he opened his mouth to speak, then closed it again. Then he snickered, almost like a cackle. It ended as a snort, then his face sobered and he waved the weapon toward Lisa and spoke with a low snarl. "Get over here. I want you two together so I can keep an eye on you. Any funny stuff and I'll shoot you both stone dead."

Lisa hesitated, then raised her nose and strode toward Annie. She stopped, turned her back to the wall, and glared at Izzy, who moved in and stopped a few feet away. Lisa stood unmoving, her hands on her hips, a defiant expression on her face.

What was he waiting for? Something was out of place. If he was going to kill them, why was he hesitating? Annie glanced toward her handbag, sitting on the floor beside the crate where they'd been resting earlier. Her cell phone was in her bag, along with a small container of pepper spray, both hopelessly out of reach.

Izzy followed her glance. "The police ain't coming."

What was he talking about? Did he know something she didn't, and was that why he still had a cocky attitude? He didn't seem in any hurry to make an escape before the police arrived.

Annie frowned and a feeling of dread washed over her.

Something had happened to Jake.

Izzy continued, "I called the cops back and canceled the call. Told them it was a false alarm." He smiled. "Oh, and I guess you're wondering about Carter and your husband." He waved a hand. "They've gone the other way." He shrugged. "I expect they'll be back, and then I'll clean up this little mess you made."

Izzy was lying. Annie was sure of it. And there was something he wasn't telling them. Something that didn't make sense about the situation.

Lisa spoke. "I told my cameraman to call the police if I wasn't back by eleven. He knows where I am."

Izzy chuckled. "You can't fool me. I didn't give you the location until you were driving here, and the only person you talked to on the phone on the way here was Jake. Ain't nobody knows where you are."

Lisa took a step toward him. "Then why not finish the job now?"

Izzy's gun hand wavered and he stepped back. "Can't yet."

"Lisa, don't," Annie said.

Lisa paid no attention and took another step forward. "Why not?"

"Just can't, that's all." He glanced toward the door, then raised the pistol and sighted down the barrel toward Lisa. His hand shook, and his eyes darted back and forth between Lisa and Annie. "Both of you. Stay back."

Izzy's eyes showed an uncharacteristic uncertainty. His voice trembled and he shuffled backwards.

Annie soon discovered Lisa had noticed Izzy's odd demeanor as well. Without hesitation, Lisa dashed forward and made a perfect closed-fist swing toward the startled man's jaw. Her fist connected with a crunch and Izzy went to his knees. The pistol hit the floor and bounced out of reach.

The killer blinked and shook his head, then dove for the weapon. Annie moved in. Her foot connected with the pistol and sent it clattering across the concrete floor.

Lisa pounced on her dazed foe, utilizing all of her pent-up anger as she beat mercilessly at him with her fists. He attempted to ward off her blows with one hand while the other reached for his attacker's throat. His fingers tightened, and Lisa gasped and struggled for air.

Annie dove for the pistol, then spun into a crouch and rammed the barrel of the gun into the side of Izzy's head. "I'm not afraid to shoot you."

Izzy's hand slackened and fell away from Lisa's throat. He emitted a low growl and lay still, fear growing in his eyes as he trained them on Annie's determined face. He breathed heavily, not daring to move.

"You can get up now," Annie said to Lisa. "He's not going anywhere."

Lisa glared at the subdued killer, then, panting for air, she came to her feet and attempted to compose herself.

Annie stood and backed up to a safe distance, keeping the weapon trained on the man's head.

"It ain't over," he said in a low voice as he stood and glanced toward the door. "It ain't over yet."

Annie pointed. "Sit against the wall and keep your mouth shut."

Izzy cast her a look of hatred, then slunk toward the wall

and sat down. He leaned his head back against the concrete, his hands resting on his bent knees, and remained quiet.

Annie turned to Lisa. "Can you handle a pistol?"

Lisa nodded and gave Annie a wry smile. "I'm pretty sure if I pull the trigger, anything standing in front of the gun will get a bullet in it."

Annie chuckled and handed her the weapon. "Good enough. Watch him while I call the police."

Lisa took the gun, wrapped her finger around the trigger, and aimed it at the man who had tortured her. "Look who's in control now," she said.

Izzy turned his head away a moment, then looked back at Lisa and cowered against the wall as she moved closer.

"I have half a notion to shoot you now," the angry newswoman said in a menacing tone. "Who would care? No one would know it wasn't self-defense, and there's no doubt I'd get away with it." She gave a short laugh. "Besides, I might enjoy it."

"You wouldn't dare."

"Try me. You'll soon find out."

Annie studied Lisa's face and concluded it was an empty threat. However, if Izzy attempted to escape, Annie felt sure there was a distinct likelihood the furious woman could follow through on her warning.

Annie figured she wouldn't lose any sleep over it either way.

She recovered her handbag and dialed Hank's number. When the cop answered, she gave him a rundown on what had transpired in as few words as possible. Hank promised he'd contact dispatch and get them to send a car at once. He was a few minutes away and would be there shortly as well.

Annie dialed Jake's number, and her concern deepened when the call went to voicemail. She hung up and turned to Lisa. "I need to find Jake." She pointed at the cowering killer. "You can shoot him if you need to."

Lisa stood stock still, her legs anchored in an immovable stance. She held the gun motionless, aimed at the killer's heart, with a cross between a determined smile and a look of victory on her face.

Annie turned and sprinted toward the door. Jake was out there somewhere, and she prayed he was safe.

CHAPTER 42

Friday, 11:31 a.m.

JAKE GLANCED BACK OVER his shoulder. His mind was whirling as he tried in desperation to find a way out of this deadly situation. Not only was his life in danger, but Annie's was as well.

Carter Wilde prodded Jake in the back with the muzzle of the rifle. "Turn around and keep moving."

Jake turned back and continued along the front of the units. His wife was in the rear of the next building with a crazy lunatic, and there was nothing he could do to help her. His one hope was that Carter had spoken the truth when he had said Izzy had never killed anyone. If that remained true, Annie might be safe for now. But not for long.

"Stop. Down the alley."

Jake stopped and looked to his left. The red BMW sat between the two buildings, its trunk still open.

"We're going for a ride," Carter said.

"Great," Jake said, looking over his shoulder at the gunman. "I've never driven a BMW."

"You're not driving. I am."

"With a rifle in your hand?"

"I expect you'll be too dead to care," the killer said, a sneer twisting his mouth. He motioned with a tilt of his head. "Get moving."

Jake hesitated and weighed his options. There weren't many. If Carter planned on shooting him here, then transporting his body to who knows where, his only recourse was to make an attempt to disarm the gunman. Soon. But the killer was being cautious, keeping back a safe distance, the gun never wavering.

"Get a move on."

Jake turned and walked down the alley toward the BMW. If he made a run for it, perhaps he could manage to get the vehicle between him and Carter before the killer had a chance to aim and shoot.

Carter appeared ready for any reaction, and he wasn't taking any chances. "If you run, I'm gonna shoot you." He poked Jake with the muzzle. "You're not gonna fool me a second time."

Jake was in a grim situation, and he had to make a move. It was better than giving up, and at least he'd stand some kind of chance.

"Around behind the car," Carter said. "Get in the trunk."

So that was it. Once he was in the trunk, Carter would shoot him, then finish his pretense of freeing Lisa. Annie would then be at the cold-blooded killer's mercy, and Jake shuddered to think of the consequences should his feeble plan fail.

Jake went to the rear of the car and turned his back to the open trunk. Carter moved around to face him, staying a few feet out of Jake's reach.

"Turn around. Get inside."

It was Jake's last chance to do something. If he got shot in the process, he was determined to bring the killer down before he succumbed to the bullet. He tensed his leg muscles and studied Carter's eyes, ready to spring at the first sign of a lapse in the killer's concentration.

Carter lessened Jake's odds by taking a step back. He raised the rifle, closed one eye, and sighted down the barrel. "I'll give you three seconds before I shoot."

Jake caught his breath, his attention drawn from the killer's eyes a moment. He smiled grimly to himself and took a deep breath.

"You win," he said. "I'll get in the trunk, but first I have to tell you something you'll be interested in. It's about your mother."

Carter frowned. His curiosity was aroused, but his suspicions were raised. He eased back two more feet, then opened both eyes and lowered the rifle a couple of inches. "What is it?"

Jake raised his arms slowly and intertwined his fingers above his head.

The killer glared, his frown deepening. "What're you doing?"

Jake had no final speech, and nothing to say regarding Carter's mother. His intent was not to make a final move, or even to stall for time, but to distract the gunman and force him to keep his attention on Jake's curious movement.

And Jake only needed a few seconds.

That was all it took for Annie to make her final leap forward and bring a three-foot length of pipe down onto the killer's head.

Carter's breath shot out in a whoosh as he crumpled to the ground, the rifle slipping from his grasp.

Jake dove for the weapon and retrieved it. He stood and glanced at the murderer in the dust at his feet, then turned to his wife and grinned down at her. "Nothing like leaving it to the last second," he said.

Annie tossed the pipe aside and shrugged, then wrapped her arms around him. "I had to do something," she said. "I'm tired of you always being the hero." She looked up into his eyes. "But I'm confused. What went on here?"

Jake filled her in quickly on Carter's revelation. "And so it turns out," he said. "Izzy and Carter were in this whole thing together."

Carter moaned and rolled over, one hand favoring the growing welt on the back of his head. He moaned again and struggled to his feet, his wild eyes filled with hatred as he glared at the Lincolns.

Jake raised the rifle. "I hope your head hurts."

The murderer growled from his throat but remained still.

Jake turned his attention back to Annie. "How'd you get away from Izzy?"

"You can chalk that one up to Lisa. She attacked him and half-killed him with her fists. She has the pistol, and she's keeping a close watch on him now."

"I'd better call the police," Jake said.

"They're already on their way."

Jake chuckled. "Then let's take this scumbag inside and wait for them."

Annie dialed Hank's number. "Where are you?" she asked, then listened a moment and said, "We're in the alley between the first two units." She hung up. "We might as well wait here. Hank's about thirty seconds away."

Carter looked around in desperation.

Tires squealed and Jake looked up the alley toward the front of the building. Hank pulled the Chevy up to the alley entrance and climbed out. The cop waved a hand when he saw them, then drew his weapon and strode their way.

Carter swore a long streak, then turned and dashed in the opposite direction.

Jake spun around and raised the rifle. "Stop." He paused. No matter what kind of a scumbag Carter was, he couldn't shoot an unarmed man. Especially in the back. He lowered the weapon as the killer disappeared from sight.

Carter was headed the other way, away from the unit where his brother was, and obviously determined to put as much space between him and his pursuers as possible.

Hank ground to a stop and pointed toward the direction the killer had gone. "You follow him. I'll circle around front, and we'll see if we can cut him off."

"We'll get him," Jake called over his shoulder as he sprinted after the killer, Annie close behind him.

CHAPTER 43

Friday, 11:45 a.m.

CARTER WILDE WAS IN a dire predicament. He had a cop on his trail, the Lincolns were probably chasing him as well, and somehow he had to kill all three of them without Lisa knowing. And to top it all off, he was unarmed and Izzy had been captured.

And there was more. He had the worst headache he'd ever experienced in his life, and he still felt half-dazed from the blow.

But at least he had determination.

Ms. Krunk was waiting faithfully for him, and he didn't want to let her down. He hoped his dumb brother hadn't let it slip who the killer really was, but if so, there was always a possibility Lisa would understand. And she'd forgive him if necessary.

He was looking forward to the end result, but first he had to get someplace safe and do some serious thinking.

As he dashed along the rear of the industrial units, he wished his head would stop hurting long enough to get through this mess.

He spun to his right and dove behind a rusting car that had been abandoned long ago. He stayed low, then slunk back and peered around the car. Jake Lincoln was rounding the corner of the unit now, Annie behind him. Jake ran to the door of the first building and checked the door. It was locked.

Carter rolled backwards out of sight and crouched between the front of the vehicle and the wooden barrier bordering the property. He looked up. The fence was six feet high, but he could make it over.

Pleasant thoughts of Lisa allowed him to disregard the throbbing in his head as he climbed onto the hood of the car. He crouched low, watching through the windshield until Jake's back was turned.

Now.

He stood, faced the fence, and leaped silently upwards, balancing his weight on the top rail a moment before tumbling to the ground on the other side.

He came to a crouch, then turned and looked through a crack between the boards. The Lincolns were fifty feet away now, checking all the doors and windows of the unit. And they hadn't seen him.

He wasn't sure where Detective Corning was. The cop must've gone around to the front of the building. He was pretty sure if they didn't find him before long, they would assume he'd gotten away, and they would return to where Izzy was being held.

At least, he hoped it would be the case. He was counting on it.

But he had to hurry. Other cops might be on their way.

He looked around him. There were more industrial units on this side of the fence. Some of them looked like they might be in use, so he'd have to be careful he wasn't seen.

He turned and scrambled along the fence, always aware of his surroundings, until he was adjacent to the unit where Izzy was.

Scaling the fence, he dropped to the asphalt and glanced around. No one was in sight, so he crossed to the building and peered in the back door.

His brother sat against the wall, his hands in his lap, his head down as though sleeping. Ms. Krunk stood a few feet from him, holding the pistol aimed at his head.

Carter walked boldly inside. Lisa turned her head toward him as he approached her, a pleasant smile on his face.

"The police are here," he said, stopping to face her. "Jake and Annie are out in the front talking to them. They should be right in."

Lisa breathed a sigh of relief. "It's about time."

Carter reached out a hand. "You might as well give me the gun. I'll take over until they get here."

Lisa hesitated, then handed him the pistol. "I'll sit down for a while." She turned and walked toward the front of the room.

Carter stared after her. "Ms. Krunk, you can go home if you want."

"I'll wait."

That wasn't at all what he was hoping for. He preferred Lisa not be around when he cleaned up the mess, and now he'd have to come up with a new plan.

He aimed the pistol toward his brother and spoke in a sharp voice. "Stand up."

Izzy raised his eyes in surprise, then rose to his feet and glared at him with a sullen expression.

Carter glanced over his shoulder. Lisa was twenty feet away, resting on one of the wooden crates. He turned back to his brother.

"Izzy," he whispered. "You have to do as I say."

Izzy's eyes widened.

"There's only one way out of this," Carter said, keeping his voice low. "Attack me and I'll let you take the gun. Wait for the Lincolns to come back, then shoot them and run."

Izzy shook his head. "I ... I can't."

"You must, Izzy. It's our only chance." He paused. "You can do it. Think of your mother. How much you hated her."

Izzy narrowed his eyes, deep in thought. Then he shook away the memories and nodded. "I think I can do it," he said.

"I can protect you," Carter said. "Things will be just like before."

"Why ... why can't you do it instead of me?"

"Because of Ms. Krunk. She's ... special to me, and I can't let her know I killed those girls."

Izzy cocked his head. "What about me?"

"They already think you're guilty. Let them continue to think it, and I'll be able to protect you."

Izzy nodded.

"You ready?" Carter asked.

Another nod, a pause, then Izzy leaped toward his brother, retrieved the gun, and spun toward Lisa as Carter fell to the floor.

Lisa gasped and stood.

Izzy pointed the weapon toward her. "Don't say a word. Sit down."

"Carter, what happened?" she said, taking a step closer as he climbed to his feet.

"He attacked me and grabbed the gun. I wasn't expecting it." Carter moved over, stood beside Lisa, and dropped his arm around her shoulder. "We'd better do as he says. The police'll take care of it."

Lisa sat back down onto the crate and frowned at Izzy. Carter crouched beside her, observing her out of the corner of his eye. She didn't look so great with her hair shaved off like that, but it would grow back. In the meantime, he'd make sure she got a wig to fix up her appearance.

He liked her better when she was strong and feisty, and it bothered him that she appeared frightened again. He didn't like to see her that way, and he'd hoped she'd leave and not have to witness the final showdown. He touched her arm and whispered, "I won't let him hurt you. Relax, and everything'll be all right."

He followed Lisa's gaze, watching as Izzy crouched by the back door, the pistol ready and waiting. He sure hoped his brother didn't screw this up. Their whole future might depend on it.

There was a minor problem with this hastily assembled

plan. Carter expected the cop would keep searching for him outside, but in the off chance the detective came back before the Lincolns, or even at the same time, things could get a little complicated. He doubted his brother could ever get the best of a cop in a shootout.

Izzy could end up dead.

He didn't like the idea of being forced to sacrifice his brother, but what will be will be. And if that was the way it played out, when everything was said and done, the cops had no real proof he'd killed those women. And when he'd shot the cop at Izzy's house, he'd worn a mask.

He shouldn't have said anything to Jake, but in the end, it was hearsay evidence and wouldn't be admissible in court.

And what did the cop know? Nothing. Detective Corning had only witnessed Jake holding a rifle on him.

Carter couldn't help but smile at the thought.

That was why he'd run. Jake threatened to kill him.

Either way, he was pretty sure he and Ms. Krunk would come out of this whole thing all right in the end.

CHAPTER 44

Friday, 11:58 a.m.

ANNIE TURNED HER HEAD as the faint whine of police sirens sounded off in the distance. Backup would soon arrive, and armed officers would take over the hunt for the fugitive. Before long, the entire area, extending for many blocks in all directions, would be sealed off and systematically searched.

Jake was peering through the driver-side window of a parked car. He returned to where Annie was standing. "The guy's completely disappeared." He shrugged. "He could be anywhere. Maybe even hopped the fence and took off the other way. We might as well go check on Lisa and let the cops roust him out."

Annie called Hank's cell and notified the cop where they would be. Hank was at the front of the property, several units away, and he hadn't seen any sign of the fugitive. "I've called for more officers, and I'll brief them when they arrive, and then I'll join you," Hank said. "I want to take Izzy into custody ASAP. I'll worry about Carter later. He can't get far."

"We'll meet you there," Annie said.

"Oh, and tell Jake not to shoot anyone if he can help it. We don't need any more of a mess."

Annie chuckled. "I'll tell him."

They hurried back to the unit where Lisa was waiting. Jake had lagged behind to peer over the fence, and Annie reached the building first and stepped inside.

She stopped short, and her eyes popped at the sight of Lisa sitting on a wooden crate, Carter crouched beside her.

Something was terribly wrong.

A strong arm wrapped itself around her chest and a voice hissed in her ear, "Don't move." She felt the muzzle of a pistol digging into her temple and she froze.

Carter sprang to his feet. "Don't do it, Izzy."

Annie stared in confusion. The brothers were in cahoots, but why was Carter now buddying up with Lisa? Something didn't make sense.

Izzy kept the pistol firmly to Annie's head and dragged her away from the doorway. "Don't say a word," he whispered.

Carter dashed toward them, stopping ten feet away, a wild look in his eyes. "Do it, Izzy," he said in a hushed voice.

The truth hit Annie. Carter wanted her and Jake dead, and he was using his brother to take the blame for everything. And it seemed like he wanted to keep his involvement a secret from Lisa. That meant he had no intention to harm the newswoman. He had a thing for her, and that was why he'd been so eager to make sure she was safe earlier.

Jake stepped inside the building and took in the scene

immediately. He raised the rifle toward Carter, then stepped aside and swung it toward Izzy. "Let her go."

"What're you gonna do, shoot me?" Izzy said in a scoffing voice. "You'll end up killing your own wife." He gave a mock laugh. "And if you miss, then I'll kill you both."

"Then let her go and take me," Jake said.

"No way," the gunman said. "I'm gonna kill you both, starting with you." He gritted his teeth. "Now, drop the rifle or I'll kill your wife first."

Jake hesitated a moment and glared at Izzy, then looked into Annie's eyes and let the rifle clatter to the floor.

Izzy turned the pistol toward Jake and tightened his finger on the trigger. Jake took a quick step sideways. A bullet whistled past his ear and smacked into the concrete wall behind him.

"Stay still," Izzy shouted.

Lisa jumped to her feet and dashed forward, stopping beside Carter. She raised her chin. "If you kill them, then you'll have to kill me too."

Izzy turned the rifle toward Lisa. "If that's what you want."

"No, Izzy," Carter said. He took a step and put his arm around Lisa's shoulder.

Izzy breathed heavily in Annie's ear, then spoke in a shrill voice. "I have to kill them all." With a trembling hand, he moved the pistol toward Jake, then back at Lisa.

"Not Lisa," Carter yelled, tightening his grip on her shoulder and drawing her closer.

"She's evil. Evil. Evil."

Carter released his grip on Lisa's shoulder and stepped in front of her, reaching a hand toward his brother. "Izzy, calm down."

Izzy's extended gun hand shook along with his voice. "Kill her, Carter. Kill her," he screamed.

"No."

"It's your job, Carter. It's your job."

Carter held out his other hand in pleading and spoke in a calm voice. "No, Izzy." He ran over toward Jake and picked up the rifle, then moved a safe distance away and aimed it at his brother.

"Are you gonna shoot me, Carter?" Izzy's voice was manic. His gun hand twitched and jerked, his other arm tightening around Annie's chest, almost cutting off her air.

Carter held the rifle steady. "I'm not gonna shoot you if you do what I told you to do."

Annie watched the scene in horror. She was caught between two gunmen, and Jake stood by helpless.

Izzy emitted a screech, then spoke in an ear-piercing voice. "You always tell me what to do. No more. No more. You killed Mother and those girls."

"Shut up, Izzy." Carter took a step closer, now five feet away. "You don't know what you're saying."

"You wanna blame it all on me," Izzy screeched. "But no more." The pistol exploded, once, twice, three times, and Carter sank to the floor. "No more."

Annie looked in horror at Carter as a pool of blood formed underneath his prone body. He'd taken three shots to the chest. No one could survive that.

Izzy gasped for air and expelled it, taking short, rapid breaths, in and out, in and out, his arm around Annie in a smothering embrace.

"Drop the gun." Hank stepped in the back door and took up a firing stance ten feet away, his weapon aimed at the killer. "Drop it now."

Izzy turned to face him and moved his weapon back to Annie's temple. "Never," he screamed. "Never."

Jake retreated and edged over toward Lisa, and the two of them watched helplessly.

"I won't miss," Hank warned. "If you wanna live, drop the gun and let her go."

Izzy said nothing, his breath rasping in Annie's ear.

Hank moved in a few inches and spoke in a soothing voice. "We know you didn't kill those girls. Drop the gun and we can sort this out."

"No." Izzy's voice was hoarse now. "No."

Hank moved in a few more inches. Annie knew he was an expert shot, but he wouldn't take a chance and fire with her almost completely blocking the killer's body. And Izzy was determined.

But she had an idea.

Her arms were trapped by Izzy's grip, but she could bend them at the elbow. She raised her right hand, her fingers extended, and spoke. "Five seconds."

"What're you talking about?" Izzy asked. "I want you to shut up."

"Nothing. I'm nervous."

Hank looked at Annie's hand, then upward to her eyes, and gave a slow nod.

294

Annie braced her feet and tensed her muscles, then closed her fingers, one at a time. As her hand tightened into a fist, she pushed with her legs, spun her body, and leaned forward as much as possible.

Hank's gun fired and Annie felt Izzy's grasp loosen as he tumbled to the floor. His gun hit the concrete, and Annie spun around as Hank moved in, keeping his weapon trained on the killer.

Izzy lay on the floor, blood flowing from a wound in the side of his head. His face was twisted in pain, and he glared at Hank with hatred in his eyes.

"Don't move," Hank said. "The next shot'll be through your forehead."

Jake dashed forward and put his arms around his trembling wife, holding her close as they gazed at the killer on the floor.

The shot had knocked the madman down, but unlike his brother, he was going to live.

EPILOGUE

Friday, 12:46 p.m.

JAKE STOOD BACK AND watched two ambulances pull away. One carried the body of a vicious killer, zipped up securely in a body bag, while the other vehicle conveyed a madman who'd killed but one person—his own brother.

He found it hard to have sympathy for the elder brother. Carter had been nothing more than a conniving psychopath. Strangely enough, Jake felt an odd compassion for Izzy. The man was not a cold-blooded killer like his brother. He was sick and needed help, but his sociopathic brother had manipulated him, and had partially contributed to the man's crazed obsession.

He glanced over at Lisa. She'd found a red-and-green scarf somewhere and had wrapped it around her head like a Christmas bonnet. The newswoman almost looked like her

296

old self again. She and Annie stood shoulder to shoulder not far away, watching the proceedings. Jake wondered how long their newfound camaraderie would last. He suspected Lisa would soon be up to her devious tricks, always in search of that one elusive story.

In fact, Jake had overhead a terse conversation she'd had with her cameraman, insisting he get here ASAP. She had a story to tell, and it couldn't wait.

When Hank came over toward Jake a minute later, Annie joined him, leaving Lisa waiting for Don.

"King's not gonna be too happy he missed this," the detective said, a crooked grin splitting his face. "He was a little late for work today, and I had to go on an errand without him."

"It might straighten him up," Jake said.

Hank chuckled. "I doubt that." He turned and looked at Annie. "I hope you realize, that was one of the hardest shots I've ever had to take. Not because of who I was aiming at, but because of who was standing beside him."

"You can chalk it up to all your time in the range," Jake said. "But you might need more practice. You only nicked him."

Hank shrugged. "That's what I was aiming for. The furthest point away from Annie. I didn't want to hit her, and I didn't want to kill Izzy. We're gonna need him to fill in some of the blanks."

"If he talks," Jake said.

"He will," Hank said. "According to his doctor's report, Izzy had been taking medication for years. His serious mental illness was rekindled when he stopped taking it. He's gonna have to be locked up for good, but once they get him back on his meds, he should be all right."

Annie changed the subject. "Have you talked to Amelia lately?"

Hank laughed. "Is that a loaded question? There's gonna be a ton of paperwork to do, but once I get this all wrapped up, I plan on spending some quality time with her."

"And?"

Hank paused. "And ... we'll see how it goes."

Typical guy, Jake thought. *He can't share his feelings.* But Jake could tell by the look in the cop's eyes, he was going to ask Amelia to marry him before long. But then, Annie knew it too. Hank was the only one who seemed to have no idea what his future held.

Jake winked at Annie and she returned a knowing smile, then turned back to the crime scene.

The Channel 7 Action News van had pulled up, and Don was climbing from the driver seat.

"I'm not in the mood for an interview right now," Annie said. "How about we sneak out the back way and disappear?"

Jake grinned. "Sounds good." He turned to Hank. "We'll drop by and give our statements later." He grabbed Annie's hand, calling over his shoulder as they walked away, "Have fun with Lisa."

They ducked down the alley between two buildings. Jake stopped and pulled Annie toward him, holding her in his arms. He stroked her hair, gazing down into her eyes.

"I could've lost you back there," he said with a faint

frown. "Seeing you in such danger reminded me how much I love you."

She tugged his head down and kissed his frown away. "It worked out okay."

"Yes, it did. And you were the hero once again." He gave her a teasing look. "You're making me look bad."

Annie looked up into her husband's eyes. "You're still my hero," she said. "And you'll always be my hero."

###

Made in the USA
Columbia, SC
26 September 2017